ANN JACOBS

Home Field Advantage
Gridiron Lovers

Ellora's Cave
Romantica Publishing

Naked Bootleg

When Bobby Anthony, rookie quarterback, signs a multi-million dollar contract with the Memphis Maulers, hot passes aren't the only thing on his immediate horizon. In a world where money is no object and women—young and old—are looking to score, easy sex fills the air and the lives of the superstar ball players. Bobby's not interested, because for him, one woman stands out from the rest.

Hot cheerleader Marly Ragusa has always been a Maulers fan but never a football groupie until she meets Bobby and falls hard for the hot young signal-caller. Marly fires his blood and captures his heart. Trying to quench the sexual attraction that initially brought them together, they spend long, hot nights in Bobby's bed, learning each other's bodies...each other's hearts.

When an ex-girlfriend comes to town, an old heartache that has left Marly with issues of trust comes to the surface—until Bobby proves he has eyes only for her.

Forward Pass

Keith Connors, widowed All-Pro quarterback, has never been one for the groupies or casual sex after a big game, unlike some of his teammates. And the last thing he's looking for is a woman to replace his dead wife. Until gentle Tina Black walks into his life and captivates his baby son's heart.

Still feeling the pain and shame of an attack by her perverted, dead-beat stepfather, Tina is looking for a fresh start. When Keith offers her a job as a nanny for his boy, it's a sanctuary, a place to heal that she can't resist.

From a tremulous relationship founded first on friendship, Keith grows to love the innocent, softly sexy woman inside Tina who turns him on like no other, while Tina sees behind the handsome quarterback façade to the loving family man, and together they decide to take a second chance on life—and love.

An Ellora's Cave Romantica Publication

www.ellorascave.com

Home Field Advantage

ISBN 9781419961717
ALL RIGHTS RESERVED.
Naked Bootleg Copyright © 2009 Ann Jacobs
Forward Pass Copyright © 2009 Ann Jacobs
Cover art by Syneca.

Trade paperback publication 2010

With the exception of quotes used in reviews, this book may not be reproduced or used in whole or in part by any means existing without written permission from the publisher, Ellora's Cave Publishing, Inc.® 1056 Home Avenue, Akron OH 44310-3502.

Warning: The unauthorized reproduction or distribution of this copyrighted work is illegal. Criminal copyright infringement, including infringement without monetary gain, is investigated by the FBI and is punishable by up to 5 years in federal prison and a fine of $250,000.
(http://www.fbi.gov/ipr/)

This book is a work of fiction and any resemblance to persons, living or dead, or places, events or locales is purely coincidental. The characters are productions of the author's imagination and used fictitiously.

HOME FIELD ADVANTAGE

NAKED BOOTLEG
~9~

FORWARD PASS
~151~

NAKED BOOTLEG
ဢ

Trademarks Acknowledgement
※

The author acknowledges the trademarked status and trademark owners of the following wordmarks mentioned in this work of fiction:

Chevy: General Motors Corporation

Commercial Appeal: The E.W. Scripps Co.

Escalade: General Motors Corporation

espn.com: ESPN, Inc.

Gatorade: Stokely-Van Camp Corporation, Inc.

Jacuzzi: Jacuzzi, Inc.

Jenn-Air: Maytag Corporation

Lexus: Toyota Jidosha Kabushiki Kaisha TA Toyota Motor Corporation

NFL, NFL Network: NFL Enterprises LLC

Ringling Bros.: Ringling Bros.-Barnum & Bailey Combined Shows, Inc.

Tiffany's: Tiffany and Co.

Author's Notes and Glossary

I'm a rabid football fan, or rather a rabid fan of several generations of quarterbacks I've watched play on TV and in person. This fandom caused me to come up with an idea for the Gridiron Lovers, a series of erotic romances about four star quarterbacks who just happened to have grown up in the same small west Texas town and who went on to fame and fortune as professionals. All of these guys and their teams are fictional, and any resemblance to an actual NFL player or team past or present is purely coincidental.

The four books' titles apparently need some explanation for readers who haven't been watching games every fall since...well, for quite a few years. Suffice it to say, I've watched every Super Bowl since number three, when Broadway Joe Namath came through on his guarantee of a win for the New York Jets. I was just a baby then (wink-wink).

So here we go. Mind you, these definitions may not all be technically correct, since they're based on my personal observations and comments I've digested from the media personalities who call the games on TV every Sunday from August through December and early January. Take a minute and read these pages first, or as my Aussie editor says, you may become totally confused.

Naked Bootleg. This is a play where the quarterback takes the snap, fakes a handoff to a running back but keeps the ball. He runs the opposite direction from the runner without a lineman protecting him—this makes the bootleg "naked"—and either passes to a receiver downfield or runs downfield himself. I thought it was a great play for Bobby Anthony to make during his first NFL appearance, as well as a sexy-sounding title for the first Gridiron Lovers book.

Forward Pass. The quarterback drops back from the line of scrimmage and throws the ball forward to an eligible receiver downfield. Eligible receivers, I think, are the backs, tight ends and wide receivers. Keith Connors is a master of the forward pass on the field, but he's pretty hot in the bedroom, as well.

Clutch, as in *Hot in the Clutch*. A player, usually a quarterback, who's especially good at coming through with points when the team needs them most. Dave Delaney's career is almost over, but he can still be counted on for a great play in the clutch, whether it's on the field or in a woman's bed.

Coach, as in *Coach Me*. The masterminds of the game, often former players great or average. Each team has several coaches, with the "head coach" in charge of it all. Colin Zanardi's playing days are over, but he's still in the game, not only with his team but also with the hottest of the local ladies.

Now for the glossary, which I'm putting in alphabetical order so you can refer to it as needed while you read:

Athletic waivers: a certain number of exceptions a college coach can use to recruit top athletes who don't meet minimum academic standards for the institution, which are determined by a combination of high school grades and standardized test scores.

Audible: when the quarterback calls out a change of the play at the line of scrimmage.

Block: what linemen do to keep defensive players away from the quarterback, as in "throw a block" or "miss a block".

Center: the player on the offensive line who snaps the ball to the quarterback when he's "under center" or "in the shotgun".

Clipboard: the object that all backup quarterbacks almost always have in their hands while standing on the sidelines; a backup quarterback's assignment, as in "carry the clipboard".

Depth chart: a chart that shows each player's status at his position—starter, second string, third string, etc.

Double coverage: two defensive players are covering (chasing) one potential receiver for the offense at the same time.

Field position: the spot on the hundred-yard field where the ball is spotted — the closer to the defense's goal, the better the field position is for the offense.

First down: when the offense starts a series or moves ten yards down the field toward the opponent's goal — can be a longer or shorter distance if penalties are involved — and is then given four more tries to make another ten yards or a touchdown, or kick the ball away.

Fumble: when the football gets loose from whatever player had it in his hands and is fair game for any player, either offensive or defensive, to pick up and claim — called a fumble recovery.

Groupie: a woman who's obsessed with professional athletes and wants any athlete, but preferably a star, for a day or night's fun and games.

Handoff: when the quarterback takes the snap from the center and immediately hands it to a running back.

Huddle: a gathering of the entire offense around the quarterback, who gives them the play the coach has sent from the sideline or via a speaker in the quarterback's helmet.

Interception: when an opposing player catches a pass, thereby causing the defense to get the ball.

Linebackers: defensive players who often break through the offensive line and go after the quarterback (there are three of them in some defenses, four in others); they also break up pass plays down field by stopping the receivers who are trying to catch passes and/or get additional yards after catching the ball.

Line of scrimmage: the point on the football field where the ball is placed.

Nose tackle: a defensive player who lines up in front of the center, usually a huge beast of a man who opens up holes in the offense so other defensive players can get to the quarterback (Note: this assumes the defense is what's called a three-four where the nose tackle and two defensive ends line up in front, with four linebackers behind them—the setup is different, although I can't explain how, if the defense is a so-called four-three with two tackles and two defensive ends in front and three linebackers behind them).

Penalty: a misdeed on the part of an offensive or defensive player that causes the team to be penalized from five to fifteen yards, and sometimes—in the case of a penalty on the defense—to create an automatic first down for the offense. Some of the reasons penalties are imposed are for holding, roughing the passer, unnecessary roughness, illegal motion before the ball is snapped, extra man on the field, or illegal formation.

Pick-six: an interception that the defensive player runs back for a touchdown.

Punt: kick on fourth down, so the opposing team will get the ball as far as possible downfield; *punter:* the player who kicks punts.

Receiver, or wide receiver: an offensive player whose main function is to catch passes from the quarterback.

Running back: offensive player who takes handoffs from quarterback and runs the ball, or who catches short passes "out of the backfield" and then runs for yardage.

Sack: when a defensive player gets to the quarterback before he passes the ball and throws him to the ground.

Scout team: a team of non-starting players who study and then try to duplicate the plays of an opposing team while the first team practices against them during the week before the actual game (the backup quarterback usually runs the scout team, although sometimes that job goes to the third string guy).

Shotgun: a formation where the quarterback stands a good distance back from the center to take the snap.

Snap: the movement of the ball from the center to the quarterback.

Taking a knee: when the quarterback takes the snap and goes down on one knee instead of initiating a play as the time is winding down to zero at halftime or at the end of a game.

Three-and-out: an expression that describes an offensive series where the offense goes three snaps without getting a first down.

Tight end: offensive players who generally line up at the ends of the offensive line (if there are two of them in for the play) and who block as well as catch passes.

Turnover: the offense gives the ball to the other team because of a fumble or interception rather than after three-and-out or a touchdown.

I hope you all enjoy this series as much as I've loved putting it together. *Naked Bootleg* starts it all, and it's the only book that takes place during football season—so you won't see a lot of actual playing—at least on the field—in the stories that follow. Kick back now and enjoy the story of the rookie and the hot cheerleader who tames him!

Ann Jacobs

Ann Jacobs

Prologue
The Rookie
ಐ

He was a fucking millionaire. Twenty-two-year-old Bobby Anthony stared down at the check, counting the zeroes again to be sure there were still six of them following the significant number nine, before the dot and the pennies he'd never have to pinch again.

Settling onto an old-fashioned wooden porch chair, he looked out over the arid west Texas landscape around tiny Hedgecock, Texas. Dust, oil wells and buildings that had seen better days partly blocked the view of Hedgecock County High School that could now boast it had produced four pro quarterbacks in the last thirty years.

Folks around here said it must have been the water that did it.

Bobby doubted that. After all, there were other positions in the game, but his alma mater had never sent anybody but quarterbacks to the pros, as far as he knew. He imagined it had been a need to escape from this one-horse town that drove the most competitive kids to the high-profile position. The need to become more than just high-school stars kept them working harder than anybody else. At least that was what had motivated Bobby to do what three others had done before him and move on toward a dream of fame and fortune.

That and old Coach Williams, who'd retired this year after nearly forty years. He had a real knack for picking and developing passers.

Bobby could hardly wait to get on with the next stage of his life. Not that he wouldn't always have fond memories of home. He'd always be thankful to his mom for keeping them together after his dad left. Glancing at the check to be sure one or two of those zeroes hadn't suddenly disappeared, he decided he'd use a chunk of his signing bonus to make Mom's life easier.

Opening the refrigerator door, he grabbed a gallon milk jug and some chili Mom had put away for his lunch. The first thing he'd do was get Mom all new appliances, and buy a new air conditioner for her bedroom to replace the one that had conked out a few years back. She wouldn't have to roast alive during another miserably hot west Texas summer. Hell, he'd have the whole damn house rewired and put in central air. That was the very least he could do.

After wolfing down his lunch, he headed to the bank, set up new accounts and deposited the check, taking bank president Caleb Tate's advice and spreading the money among several Texas financial institutions—ones that hadn't needed to take the stimulus money offered by the Feds.

Then he started up his mom's pickup and went to wait for her at the Burger Den across the street from the high school. At least the high-school hangout was air conditioned, which the pickup wasn't. It was damn hot for the first of May.

* * * * *

"Hey, Bobby."

He'd have recognized that voice anywhere. Tina Black. After all, they'd been friends since grade school, occasional lovers their last two years in high school. "Hi, Tina, what have you been up to?" He took a seat across from her in a worn wooden booth. He hated seeing her like this, all ragged out, not at all like the pert blonde he remembered. Even her sky blue eyes looked dull, as if she wasn't getting enough rest.

"Just working in the elementary-school lunchroom and taking care of Mom." She sounded tired, probably was. The stress of living in the same house with her slimeball of a stepfather had to have worn her down. "How about you?"

Somehow it didn't seem right to mention that he'd just become a millionaire. "I signed with the Maulers. I'll be heading to Memphis pretty soon for rookie camp."

Tina smiled, but still her eyes looked sad. "I've missed you. Welcome back for whatever time you'll be here."

Bobby had missed Tina too. Not that he had any interest in resuming their long-ago affair. What he wanted now was a woman who would represent his future, not his past. When he pictured that woman, he saw her as a lush beauty who'd keep his cock at attention. But he also wanted a woman who loved football almost as much as he did and who would capture his heart in a way Tina never had. He knew his college teammates mostly relished the idea of all the groupies who gave out head like candy, and he couldn't say he was immune to a woman throwing herself at him. But what he imagined beyond that was…more. Maybe it was Mom's fault he had the embarrassing romantic streak. He just liked the idea of finding a woman to love and protect, one who'd stand by him through the ins and outs of his career, have his babies and make him as proud of her as she'd be of him.

Still he considered Tina his best female friend. He worried about her, about her sick, narcissistic mother and the pervert she'd married a few years ago. "What's going on at your house?" They'd spoken on the phone after his graduation last December, and her silence about the strange household she lived in had concerned him. When she didn't answer right away, he asked, "Is your mom doing better?"

"Worse." Tina looked away, stared at the menu as if she were starving.

Bobby took her hand. "Worse how?" Since she'd had an accident that left her paralyzed a few months after marrying Edgar Garcia, Tina's mom had been fragile. Not to mention bitter and emotionally needy.

"She doesn't leave her room anymore. Her heart's not right, and she won't let anybody but me take care of her. Not even Edgar. Of course he's not upset about his newly found freedom."

The bastard. If he was still making Tina's life miserable, Bobby intended to have a chat with him. He clenched his fists, anticipating them colliding with Garcia's fat, obnoxious belly. "He's not bothering you, is he? Look at me, Tina, and tell me the truth."

"No. Not the way you mean. Edgar's got a new girlfriend at that strip club across the county line."

Better he hit on some hooker than Tina. Still, the creep's cheating had to be making her mother even whinier and more demanding than usual. "I wish I could help you, hon. Get you away from all this."

"I've got to stay. I can't leave my mother to die with no one but Edgar to take care of her." From the look in her eyes, Bobby guessed she'd welcome a white knight to rescue her from the hell her life must have become.

Too bad he wasn't that white knight, though for a minute there he wondered if he should try to be. "I know. Look, it's after four, so I have to go drag my mom out of the school office, or she'll keep working until dark. If you ever need to get away, just call me."

Tina smiled and squeezed his hand. "I will."

But he was pretty sure she wouldn't call. Tina had her pride, and she'd always been as stubborn as any woman could be. "You do that, honey. Remember, friends take care of one another." He bent and brushed his lips over hers then made his getaway.

Today he wanted to celebrate, not worry about Tina. After all, he told himself, there was nothing he could do to help her out of her situation at home as long as she wasn't willing to leave.

* * * * *

Walking through the school's entryway, Bobby spared a glance at the newest batch of football trophies behind locked glass doors of the same case that had been there ever since he could remember. He ran into several teachers he'd had, ones who'd been around since long before his time and would probably still be teaching until they died. After all, this was Hedgecock, and jobs other than working in the oil fields had always been hard to come by. When he opened the door and stepped up to the counter in front of his mom's desk, he cleared his throat. "May I have a tardy pass?" he asked the way he'd asked four years ago when he'd still been a student.

"Bobby, you scared me half to death. Did you get your business taken care of?"

He nodded. "Yeah. I'm glad you sent me to Mr. Tate. He helped me set up accounts so my signing bonus will be safe and earn a few bucks until I can get an investment manager to take it over. Come on, you've been working long enough. Let's go eat. My treat for once."

"Aw, you should be taking Tina. Or do you have a new girlfriend you're waiting to tell me about?" Bobby loved the way his mother smiled. She was forty-one, but she could have passed for thirty. Somehow the harsh environment hadn't scarred her or made her grow old before her time, the way it had a lot of the local women.

"No girlfriend at the moment. The ones I dated at Tulane were a little too rich for my blood. Besides, they all seemed to like dating the school's star quarterback a lot more than they liked me for me. When I find my dream girl, you'll be the first to know. Meanwhile, grab your purse and come with me. We're going to have steaks and share a pitcher of beer. Maybe we'll even sing some. I hear they've got karaoke down at the café now."

"Yes, they do. I'm not sure I'm up to singing but I'll help you celebrate becoming a very rich young man. I'm awfully proud of you, did I ever tell you?"

"All the time, Mom. While we're celebrating, I'm going to lay out what I want to do for you. And what you can do for me." Bobby thought of Tina, figured that if he asked his mother to keep an ear open for any problems that might crop up with her mother or Garcia, she'd do it. After all, she'd done all the right things for him when he was growing up. "Let's go."

* * * * *

The next day he took a bus to Pecos and bought his first car, a shiny red Escalade truck the soon-to-be-defunct GM dealer had special-ordered for some oilman who'd decided he didn't want it after all when the economy suddenly went belly-up. Bobby also bought his mom a tricked-out Chevy SUV, to be delivered as a birthday gift next month, when he'd be at rookie camp. That ought to surprise her big-time. And she wouldn't turn it down, it being from him for her birthday.

A week later, after watching the installers hook up the new appliances and drag away the old ones, Bobby left home and Hedgecock, Texas, headed for a new, exciting life, new challenges. He also hoped he'd find a woman who cared more about him than the position he played.

Chapter One
ൕ

After he'd gotten to camp and spent a few minutes thumbing through the biggest playbook he'd ever seen, Bobby decided the women would have to wait. He'd have to spend most of his waking hours studying, not checking out the incredibly hot young women who were on one corner of the second football field, trying out for the Maulers cheerleading squad. He noticed one, though. A gorgeous girl with a hot body, creamy skin, big brown eyes and long black hair that looked so soft he wanted to run his fingers through it. And he couldn't resist making a point of running into her on the training center parking lot.

"Hey there!" he called out, and she turned and shot him a thousand-watt smile.

"Hello to you, too." She stepped over closer, close enough that the sweet smell of her perfume wafted into his nostrils. "Good luck making the team, rookie." Her gaze slid slowly up his body, and it was all he could do to resist pulling her close and seeing if he could rest his chin on top of her head.

"Thanks. I'm Bobby Anthony. And you are?"

"Marly Ragusa. Maulers fan forever." She paused for a minute, her pretty mouth gaping open. "Omigod, you're the new quarterback the Maulers took in the first round."

"Yeah. That's me." Another woman with a love affair for passers, he imagined. But that was okay. He didn't have to find his dream woman right away, and at the moment he sort of liked the idea of latching onto this gorgeous QB groupie. When they talked, he found he liked her sassy smile and big brown eyes. What really turned him on was her frank interest in him, along with the whole package of slender but curvy babe. If only he didn't have to hit this book tonight...

"My dad and brothers have been shaking their heads ever since the Maulers picked you. Surely you don't think you'll knock Keith Connors off the top of the depth chart."

"I'm gonna try." They'd told him Keith wanted to keep his personal life out of the news, so Bobby couldn't explain to shocked teammates and fans why he'd been brought in, an elite prospect to back up the league MVP. "I'm also thinking about having some fun, but if I'm going to have a shot at doing more than carrying the clipboard for Keith this season, I'm going to have to get up close and personal with this playbook." He showed her the fat book then tucked it back under one arm. "Maybe you'd like to help me find a place to live once the preseason is over?"

"Sure. I've lived in Memphis all my life. I'd love to show you around."

Bobby would have liked to show Marly around his bedroom, but now was hardly the time, confined as he was to the practice field and a two-bedroom hotel suite he was sharing with three other rookies. "It's a date then. After the first home game. Here's my cell phone number."

She loaded it into her phone, grinned and gave him her number, too. "Call me when you get a chance. You go on now. Study. I want you sticking around at least for this season." With that she stood on tiptoe and gave him a hug. "Welcome to Memphis. You're gonna like it here."

He had to touch her, hold her, tilt her head back and give her what he'd meant as a casual peck. But it was more. When she traced her tongue along the seam of his lips he gave up, deepened the kiss, held her so close that her heart pounded hard against his chest. "I think I'm gonna like it—and you—a lot," he told her when he finally came to his senses and let her go.

* * * * *

Although he'd much rather have spent the night getting to know Marly, Bobby managed to shove his fantasies into the nether reaches of his brain and concentrated on memorizing the Maulers' incredibly complex playbook, breaking only for dinner in his room—a large pizza with salad that he washed down with a carbo supplement drink. Nobody could accuse him of ignoring the trainers' suggestions that he pack on five or ten more pounds.

It was eleven o'clock. Lights-out time. Bobby picked up a funny card Tina had sent him and tucked it into the playbook to hold his place. Sighing, he stripped to his boxers and crawled into bed. Lying in the dark listening to his roommate snoring on the other side of their hotel room while the air conditioner hummed in the background, Bobby closed his eyes.

And let the hot cheerleader with the big smile and soft, sexy drawl invade his mind. He imagined her silky hair draped across his chest, her legs tangled with his. Her breath would tickle him, turn him on as he explored the velvety smooth expanse of her back and perfectly rounded ass. Pleasantly aroused, he wrapped his arms around the extra pillow and drifted off to sleep.

It wasn't a pillow but a slender, curvy woman whose hard little nipples burrowed into his chest while her legs opened enough to let his cock between them. Her arm felt warm around his midsection, her fingers gentle as they kneaded his butt. Marly.

"Fuck me, please," she murmured against his throat, the arousing feel of her warm, damp breath punctuating the request he wasn't about to deny.

"Like this, Marly baby?" He pulled her close, dragged her over his body, guided his sex to hers and sank inside the hottest, tightest pussy he'd ever had.

"Mmmm. You feel so good. I love it." The way she moved on him was his steamiest fantasy come true. Her long hair fell over them like a silk curtain, creating erotic sensations when strands brushed

his chest and throat every time she sank down on him, taking him, squeezing him as if she wanted to keep him inside her cunt forever.

He grabbed her hands, drew them to his chest. "Fuck me harder, sweetheart. Oh yeah, that's right. Keep squeezing my cock like that." God, but he wanted to come so much. Yet he wanted this to go on and on, the dizzying sensations and slapping sounds of sex. The sense of closeness he'd never felt before with Tina or any of his college groupie lovers.

"Oh yes. You feel so good inside me." She squeezed him harder then leaned down to sip the sweat from his brow. "I love the way you fuck me."

Because he couldn't take the delicious torture much longer, he rolled her over onto her back, raised her legs over his hips and claimed her. Hard, fast, he pounded into her, barely cognizant now of anything but her hot, wet cunt surrounding him, grasping his cock. And the sounds of wet flesh on flesh, the musky smells of sex, the feel of her firm breasts beneath his chest. Her nails dug into his shoulders as if she was desperate to hold on, enjoy the sensations as long as she could before letting herself come.

"Go ahead, Marly, come for me." His control was gone, the humanity in him losing out to pure animal lust. Gathering her in his arms, he gave in, coming in hot, short bursts as his climax triggered her own.

Bobby woke suddenly when he heard himself bellowing out his satisfaction. Fuck. He'd forgotten to put on a condom. "Marly, I'm so damn sorry," he whispered, gathering her close, not realizing for long, terrifying moments that the delectable woman he'd just fucked had morphed into a standard, hotel-issued bed pillow.

Embarrassed, he looked over toward his roommate's bed, relieved to see the guy still snoring away, seemingly unaware of the noisy fantasy Bobby had just enjoyed. Good thing he slept like a rock!

What a dream! As Bobby used a towel to clean the mess he'd made, he shook his head. Damn it, he intended to make this dream come true—and to find out if the real thing was as mind-blowing as his wet dream.

* * * * *

Time flew when you were having fun. By the time the regular season began, Bobby had gotten to where he could almost come just listening to Marly's voice. All summer they'd talked on the phone nearly every night. About football. About things to do in Memphis. About their very different college experiences. About each other and the immediate chemistry that seemed to be mutual. He'd have initiated phone sex but he didn't want to take a ribbing from his new roommate who slept much less soundly than the first one, who'd gone along with the other players who hadn't made the final team roster.

Although his body ached every day after practice sessions that were twice as hard as he'd been used to at Tulane and ten times what Coach Williams had put him through back in Hedgecock, Bobby always looked forward to calling Marly before lights-out. Every time they spoke, he got more and more certain that she might be the perfect match for him.

Today the first regular season game had been easier than a practice, since all he'd done was stand on the sideline and try to look busy as he held the clipboard for Keith Connors. He arranged the pillows on his bed, waited until his new roommate started snoring, and grabbed his cell phone.

"Marly?"

"You looked good out there today. I watched the game on TV. When are you coming back to Memphis?" She sounded so sexy he had no trouble imagining her stretched out in bed, holding out her arms to him. Blood slammed into his cock so fast he damn near lost his train of thought.

"In the morning. I'll grab the key to this condo the team found for me to rent and go over there after the team meeting. We're off from practice Tuesday, so if you like we could do something." *Like check out my bed for a few hours.*

"Wish I could," Marly said, her tone heavy with disappointment. "I have cheerleader practice in the afternoon and I promised to babysit for my brother and his wife tomorrow morning so they can shop for new living room furniture."

Evenings were out. He had to get full nights' sleep before practice. After all, he had to run the scout team. He also had to hit the weights, watch game film, attend meetings and get ready to play in case something happened to Keith. "Hate to say it, but we'll have to put off our first date until after the game on Sunday. We can go out, eat and get to know each other up close and personal. Don't know about you, but our phone conversations just make me want to be with you."

"Me too." Her voice sounded husky. Sexy as hell yet sweet too, like the honey his mom used to pour over his pancakes when he was a kid.

"You sound like you're sleepy," In his head, he pictured her cuddled up under a comforter, her black hair spread across a snowy pillowcase. If only he were there with her…

She laughed. "I was, sort of. I was lying in bed, waiting for your call."

"Were you?" The idea that she was home, waiting up to hear from him, made Bobby feel ten feet tall. "Wish you were here, sleeping with me."

"Bad boy." She didn't say anything else for a minute. "Guess I'm bad, too, though, because I wish you were right here with me, too."

"If I were, what would we be doing?" His cock twitched when he imagined having her in bed, breathing in her scent, touching her soft skin. "Would I be running my fingers through that beautiful long hair of yours? Or tasting your lush red lips?" *And other more interesting body parts?*

"Maybe. Or maybe I'd be running my hands over your hot, muscular body, seeing how hard you are."

"Oh I'm hard, all right. All over. I can hardly wait to show you." She blew his mind and had him fully aroused and ready for action. "We'd better stop this talk or I'll never get to sleep." He wouldn't anyhow, not until he jerked off imagining Marly's hands and mouth on him.

"You're right. Sweet dreams to you, too. I'll be counting the days." With that Marly said good night and ended the call. Was it Bobby's imagination or had she really said she wanted to get as physical as he did?

Yeah, he wanted her to want him. For the first time since high school, he thought a woman might actually want him for himself and not the position he played. There were some benefits to being a backup. If Marly wanted to score with just any quarterback she'd obviously have set her sights for Keith now that he was widowed and back on the groupie fantasy market.

* * * * *

Time had gone quickly since that day in June when she'd run into Bobby Anthony. The regular season had begun. Marly looked around the stadium, found it looked the same, even though her own excitement was off the charts. It was the prospect of seeing Bobby again, the anticipation of their date following the game.

They'd talked nearly every night since then, sometimes for hours, other times for just a few minutes. She felt like she knew him, deep inside, even though they'd only met in person for a few stolen moments. Tonight...

Tonight would take care of itself. Meanwhile she had some cheering to do.

Already the crowd was making plenty of noise and the players hadn't even come on the field for warm-ups. A brisk wind had pennants dancing around on top of the stadium. Small planes towed ads for various businesses, and a giant helium-filled balloon bounced on its tether on the wall above the south end zone. Larger-than-life images of Maulers players past and present flashed in unison on two jumbotrons.

Marly loved it. The excitement. The beginning of another thrilling season, this one where she could yell not just for the team as a unit but for Bobby. Even if he did nothing but pace the sidelines carrying a clipboard.

The day couldn't have been better. Not a hint of rain on the horizon, and that was good. So was the fact it was a comfortable seventy-three-degree day in mid-September. Coming home after a successful season opener on the road, the team was certain to be fired up for their old nemesis, the Milwaukee Marlins. Bobby had mentioned when they talked last night that the team was out for revenge since the Marlins had blown out the Maulers the last game of the previous season.

Liz Grady, a fellow cheerleader, joined Marly in the formation at the end of the tunnel where the players would emerge. "Who're you trying to catch the attention of today?" she asked.

"You can pick from the rest of them. I want Bobby Anthony." Marly and Liz watched the players come out of the tunnel as they waved pompoms along with the rest of the Maulers' Molls who had formed a double line for the players to go through. "He's so hot. Tall, dark and sexy. We're going out after the game."

What was Marly saying? What was she thinking? Here she was, drooling about getting involved with a player even though she'd had no intention of becoming a football groupie. She guessed Bobby had changed all that.

Liz kept her pompoms dancing, but she shot Marly an incredulous look. "How'd you manage that?"

"We ran into each other — almost literally — when he was here for rookie camp during cheerleader tryouts. We've been talking on the phone ever since." Liz didn't need to know those calls had been fodder for her fantasies, or that Marly was a lot more involved than she'd planned to be with the rookie signal-caller. "He's..."

"I know, I know, he's got you creaming your panties just thinking about him. Just keep in mind how many other women are doing the same." Liz paused for a minute, watched Keith Connors warming up his arm with one of the receivers. "Did you hear, Keith lost his wife during the offseason, right after their baby was born? His mom's staying with him, taking care of the baby until they find a permanent nanny. I wonder if he's getting lonesome yet. I sure wouldn't mind fucking him until he can't see straight. Bet he's horny by now." Liz glanced toward the stands where a lot of the players' wives and girlfriends were sitting. "I don't see his mother over there."

Was Liz thinking... No, she couldn't be. "She could be in one of the luxury boxes," Marly pointed out.

"Yeah, or she could be home with the kid."

"If I were you I'd stay far away from Connors. I heard one of the cheerleaders went groupie on him last year, and she was tossed off the squad. Management doesn't take well to cheerleaders chasing their married players."

"Yeah, I know. Still, a girl can always dream. Besides, Connors isn't married anymore."

For the next few minutes, while they waited for the National Anthem and coin toss, Marly stared at the number four on Bobby's jersey. The legendary Brett Favre wore that number, too. The Maulers had probably given the number to Bobby because he'd worn it at Tulane and it hadn't already been issued to a Maulers veteran, not because it also happened to belong to one of the greatest quarterbacks of all time. But Marly saw the coincidence as a sign that good things were going to happen for the rookie.

Dark-brown hair, a little on the long side as if he'd been too busy to find a barber shop, made Bobby look adorable, and awfully young. Or maybe he looked young because he *was* young. Straight out of college, he looked the part of the golden rookie, chomping at the bit to get his chance. He could make it with her right now. Let Liz lust after team captain Keith Connors.

Just looking at Bobby made Marly start to salivate. His long, lean, muscular body tempted her to explore...to taste...to drive him so crazy he'd take her like the alpha jock she was sure he'd be when they got between the sheets. Not that his baby face didn't turn her on, because it did. Big time.

She couldn't have lusted after Bobby any more if she'd made up an order for her dream lover and had the Maulers general manager fill it for her on draft day. Smooth, tanned skin with no more than a hint of a dark beard she was sure would thicken as he got older framed deep-set brown eyes—not hazel but clear, coffee-colored eyes that had held her gaze for more than a second as he passed by her on the sideline, clipboard in hand. Damn, but his smile was to die for. She could hardly wait to taste those inviting, firmly chiseled lips that framed gleaming teeth. Again, she amended, recalling that one mind-blowing kiss one sweltering day in June.

Marly sighed when the Milwaukee team went three-and-out and the Maulers took over on their own twenty-yard line. Keith Connors trotted onto the field, his attitude as sure and cocky as befitted a seven-time All-Pro. He always liked to come out passing, and this time was no exception. Lined up in the shotgun, he took the snap, looked out to find his receiver...

Omigod! That hurt, just watching Connors get blindsided and knocked flat on his back. The tackler then came down on top of him and the ball popped loose. Luckily it was recovered by one of the Maulers offensive linemen, probably the same one who had missed the block on the Marlins All-Pro linebacker who leveled Keith. Marly took a deep breath. Like everybody else in the stadium, she hoped Keith wasn't badly hurt.

When he didn't get up right away, the team's medical people swarmed onto the field. The crowd went silent. They knew as well as Marly did that if Connors was out, Bobby was in for a quick and probably terrifying baptism of fire. It looked as if that would probably be the case when one of the EMT people drove a cart out onto the field. She looked along the sideline, trying to find Bobby among the other players.

There he was, talking with the quarterback coach and offensive coordinator. He stood by the stretcher for a minute and shared a few words with Keith. Then, with a resolute look on his face, Bobby put on the helmet he'd been holding. Shoulders squared, he trotted onto the field and into the huddle. Marly stood, her gaze locked on the guy she considered her very own rookie quarterback as he lined up under center and took the snap.

He handed off to wiry running back Dan Morales then ran the opposite direction, or at least that was what it looked like at first. But no, Bobby still had the ball, and no protection from a lineman on the bootleg play. Bobby looked downfield and found his receivers covered before tucking the football and running. Twenty-six yards later, a Marlins player finally shoved him out of bounds.

Less than a minute went by before the Maulers scored. Bobby had completed three of four passes, the last one for a touchdown. That wasn't bad at all for a rookie's first series as a pro.

Marly made sure she was in his line of vision as he trotted off the field before shooting him her sexiest smile along with a thumbs-up. Before the players went to the locker room at halftime she handed Bobby a note. Liz gaped at her, obviously surprised that Marly would be so blatant. "All it says is that I'll meet him outside the players' exit after the game."

She knew Liz must have thought she was a QB groupie. Her friends had teased her about that since she first told them she was going to try out for the cheerleading squad. Despite the fact their date had been in the works for months, she guessed she must be a groupie, something she'd been vehemently denying to her friends who'd teased her for going out for the Maulers cheerleading squad last spring. But Marly loved the game. She loved the Maulers, and she was proud to be a cheerleader.

She didn't mind the teasing, because she knew why she'd done it. However, she hoped Bobby Anthony didn't think she was a typical groupie. If that was the only reason he was going out with her...

She felt a spear of hurt the thought provoked, but quickly pushed it away. She liked Bobby, and if she was a groupie, it was for one specific guy. She wouldn't care if he was the number one quarterback or the water boy, though she certainly didn't mind looking at his big, toned body. Not that the body was all she was interested in. From the late-night conversations they'd shared, she'd learned she liked his attitude, his sense of humor, his open affection for his mom...just about everything she'd learned about him. And she wasn't about to let Liz's or anybody else's opinion spoil her excitement about their upcoming date.

* * * * *

"What's that, Anthony?" Third-string quarterback Ellis Tripp gestured toward the folded scrap of paper Bobby was looking at.

"A note." Ninety percent of his mind was on what Coach Lyle had just said about what they had to do to hold their lead. The rest focused on Marly, who looked even hotter today than she had the day they first met. "From one of the cheerleaders," he added when Ellis looked confused.

"If all it takes is to play a few downs to get hot babes crawling all over you, then I'd better start working harder in practice so I can get a shot at some of them." Ellis grinned, his sun-roughened cheeks crinkling like paper when he curved his lips. At thirty-eight, the journeyman quarterback was past the stage of jockeying for position since he'd gone from sometimes-starter to third-string hanger-on pretty smoothly over the sixteen years he'd been in the league with various teams.

Bobby hoped his own star would rise, not hit a downward spiral the way Ellis' had. "Come on now, you know your wife would kill you if you started fucking around with the groupies."

"Guess so. You gonna take her out?" He gestured toward the paper in Bobby's hand.

"Yeah. Where's a good place to go after the game?" After the last preseason game he'd gone straight home instead of taking his teammates up on what had sounded like it might become a wild celebration of their victory. Ellis scratched his head. "Probably the Fifth Quarter over on the river. That way a lot of her buddies will see her with the hero of the day. That ought to make her happy. Come on, it's time to go finish this game."

"Yeah." He'd managed pretty well so far. Bobby gave himself a pep talk as he trotted back onto the field. Thirty minutes more of playing and his NFL debut would be a success, assuming he didn't panic and the defense managed to stop the Marlins' Brand Carendon from tossing any more seventy-yard touchdown passes the way he'd done just before halftime. While the receiving team was on the field, Bobby found Marly near the bench and said, "I'll meet you outside the players' exit. It may be a while though, because I'll have to do a postgame interview."

Marly grinned, her eyes sparkling. She looked cute in her uniform with its short skirt and boots and bare middle. "You sound like you're more worried about that interview than you were about playing your first series in the pros," she said, clearly teasing him.

"Maybe I am. I've played football lots of times, a whole lot more than I've given interviews in front of a bunch of TV cameras."

"You'll do fine. You know, I like you all wound up and glistening with sweat the way you are right now. Now go win this game for us." With that she stood on tiptoe and brushed her lips across his cheek.

* * * * *

When the game was over, Bobby figured he'd played all right. The Maulers won the game by three, and he'd thrown for two touchdowns and only one interception. But he wasn't at all sure he'd aced the postgame interview. Hell, he'd never before faced what seemed like hundreds of microphones or gotten spots in front of his eyes from staring into harsh lights that had shone directly at him. Doing interviews wasn't something he'd practiced, since the only time he'd had to talk with reporters in college had been after his one bowl game appearance.

Back at his locker, he wondered for a minute if he ought to change out of the suit he'd put on to appear in front of the network cameras.

The hell with it. He'd lived through the torture of trying to come up with honest but tactful answers to stupid and leading questions. Answers that didn't make him sound like an asshole or an idiot. Questions about the game, the likelihood of Keith's absence for a few games or more, even about how he felt about the Maulers and his teammates. Bobby figured Marly would probably like him to look like the Maulers quarterback, not the green rookie he was. Hanging the T-shirt and jeans he'd just grabbed back in his locker, he loosened his tie and left his shirt open at the collar so it wouldn't keep choking him. Sooner or later he was going to have to get used to dressing up, he supposed. Besides, he wanted to be with Marly now and it would take time to change.

He'd better get going. It wasn't in him to make a woman wait longer than he had to. As he made his way out of the dressing room, he had to restrain himself from sprinting. After all, he told himself, if she was a proper groupie she should be the one panting after him, not the other way around.

Chapter Two
෨

Bobby had looked good enough to eat in his red and black home game uniform. But in the gray pinstriped suit he had on now, he looked every bit the successful young executive. Only his hair, still damp and curling above the collar of a pale-blue shirt, gave a hint he might have recently come off the football field and out of the interview room. "I loved watching you play," she told him when he stopped in front of her and took her gear bag out of her hand. "You're damn good for a rookie."

His grin warmed her heart and her body. "Thanks, baby. I'm counting on playing some more later today, with you. Shall we go over to the Fifth Quarter?"

No shy guy here. Marly liked her men self-confident to the point of egotistical, and she'd never met a quarterback who wasn't, except maybe Ellis. But he didn't count since he was married and about ready to hang up the pads. "Let's." She didn't mind being Bobby's arm candy, not at all. As a matter of fact it pleased her that he wanted to show her off to the big contingent of players and fans the rustic sports bar and restaurant always attracted after a Maulers win. "Where's your car?"

"In the lot over there. What about yours?"

"I came with one of the other cheerleaders. I figured you'd be taking me home."

"Your home or mine?" His dark eyes twinkled, as though he might be teasing her. When she'd asked about taking him apartment shopping after the preseason was over, he'd told her about the place he'd lucked into—a condo on the riverfront that belonged to a former Maulers scout.

She really wanted to see the place he'd described as too big for just him, but she didn't want to sound too eager. "We'll see. You know you look almost as good in a suit as you did in your uniform." Marly crooked her arm through his and noticed how he slowed his pace to accommodate her shorter legs. "You're too good to be true—hot as all get-out, and polite, too."

When they reached his shiny red Escalade pickup truck, Bobby set their bags on the backseat then opened the passenger door. "My mom taught me to treat the ladies right."

Marly watched him circle in front of the truck to get to the driver's side. She liked the way he moved, with purpose, comfortable in his body like so many athletes were not when taken out of their work environment. When he slid behind the wheel, he leaned over and took her hand.

"I'd really like to kiss you hello." His deep drawl poured over her, soaked in like butter melted and sunk into hot buttermilk biscuits.

Her pussy clenched. This was definitely the man of her late-night dreams. "I can hardly wait for you to kiss me." *For starters.*

"Good." His breath smelled sweet, like toothpaste and mouthwash. As he lowered his head, she got a glimpse of his long, dark lashes, his strong brow.

And then he kissed her. But it wasn't just any old peck. It was the real thing, a tongue-tangling, mind-boggling locking of his firm, mobile lips with hers. He framed her face between his big, calloused hands, pressing the back of her head against the cool, beige leather upholstery.

She had to regain her self-control or she'd be taking one of those big hands and drawing it to her breasts, her damp pussy. When he broke the kiss and turned to take the wheel, she still wanted more. Now. She wanted Bobby to take control over her the way he'd overwhelmed the Marlins' acclaimed defense.

"Hold that thought. Right now I'm hungry for something hot and spicy. Not that you're not both." He shot her a sexy smile that got her even hotter.

"I am?" she asked, her tone as innocent as she could make it, wanting him the way she did.

"Yeah. If you weren't, I wouldn't be almost ready to pass on food for a long, hot roll in the hay—or rather in the king-size bed at my place. We'll pass the building on the way to Fifth Quarter." Bobby backed up and headed for the gate. He frowned at the dark-green Lexus, one of the few cars left in the lot. "Keith's car's still here. Guess they must have taken him to the hospital in an ambulance. I hope he's going to be okay."

For a minute, Marly doubted that last statement. Most backup players she knew would be thrilled that the guy in front of them was out of commission. But then she figured Bobby might really be concerned for Keith's well-being. After all, from what he'd told her during one of their long phone conversations, the two men had grown up in the same west Texas town that had produced not only them but also the Rebels' Dave Delaney and his coach, Colin Zanardi. "Did you know Keith back home?"

He glanced her way as he made the turn onto Riverside. "Not really. I saw him play in high school, but he wasn't especially interested in messing around with annoying grade school kids. Of course I can't blame him. I didn't much like being followed around by the younger boys when I was playing high-school ball either."

Still, that connection had to have meant something to both men. "How did it make you feel when you saw him go down today?"

Bobby didn't answer right away. When he did, his tone was sober. "Scared. The guy was my idol for a long time. I never expected the Maulers to draft me, or that I'd be playing behind him. Keith is too young for the front office to think about him retiring, not to mention way too good. I guess the main thought running through my mind was whether or not I was about to go on the field and make a huge fool of myself. But I was hoping there wasn't anything serious wrong with Keith."

"Is there?" It wasn't curiosity, or even wishful thinking. Marly didn't wish Keith ill. Not at all. He'd brought a lot of good things to Memphis, besides keeping the Maulers in contention almost every year since he'd arrived nine years ago. Too many bad things had happened to him lately.

"They took him to the hospital for an MRI on his throwing shoulder. Could be it's nothing but a strained muscle and he'll be back next week. I hope so."

The way Bobby said it, Marly believed he wished the other quarterback well, even though the longer he was out, the longer Bobby would have to show his stuff. "I hope so, too." She laid her hand on Bobby's knee then continued. "Even though I love seeing you play."

He grinned, guiding her hand up his thigh until it rested on his very impressive package, already hot and throbbing beneath the lightweight fabric of his pants. "You ain't seen nothing yet. Not until you and I've done some playing on a different field. See how you've already got me paying attention?" he asked as he pulled in Fifth Quarter's packed parking lot and skillfully squeezed his truck into a parking space that must have been meant for a compact car.

"Oh yeah. I see." There was nothing like a quarterback for cool self-confidence to match a healthy, well-fed ego. She loved it, and the more time she spent with him she was learning she liked Bobby beyond his obvious potential as a hot sex partner. Their phone conversations had let her guess, but seeing him in the flesh solidified her first impressions.

"I'm not exactly ready to go inside yet. How'd you get interested in cheerleading?" He turned off the truck and moved her hand from his now-throbbing erection, his grin a little one-sided as if he'd embarrassed himself but didn't want to say so.

"I like dancing and gymnastics, and I love football. Being a cheerleader for the Maulers lets me indulge all three loves. Besides, after I finished college I didn't find any jobs here where I could use my education and make money. And I didn't like the idea of leaving my family and going someplace where I didn't know a soul."

"That was hard for me, too, at first, leaving everything familiar for a new, uncertain job even though I've wanted to play pro football since high school. Guess I've been lucky, because the Maulers front office people made sure I found a place to live and some new friends, so I'm okay now — especially now that I have a beautiful woman like you to show off to all my teammates." Still a little red-faced, he shifted on the seat and readjusted his pants. "Sorry, Marly. I don't like giving you the impression all I'm out for is a piece of ass. I'll behave — at least for a little while."

She hoped for more than that, of course, but she'd take all of Bobby that he was willing to give. "You didn't make me think that. Ready to go inside?" If they didn't, she didn't know if she could keep her hands to herself — and for the first time in her adult life of fantasizing about hot young studs, she really didn't want this very real one to think of her as just another football groupie lusting after the latest tasty acquisition by her hometown team. "I find myself wanting to dance with you. And getting to know a little bit more about you than I've read in the *Commercial Appeal* and at ESPN.com."

"I think I'm okay for now. You probably don't want to dance with me, though. I'm strictly a Texas two-step kind of guy."

Oh yeah, Marly wanted to dance with him. Vertically, horizontally and every way from Sunday. The more he talked, the more she thought this one might be a keeper, if only she could successfully fight off all the other groupies who'd kill for a night with the Maulers second-string quarterback. She'd win because she'd be fighting for Bobby, not just his undeniable prowess on a football field—or, if her guess was on target, in bed.

* * * * *

Bobby tried to tell himself as he stretched one large draft beer to wash down barbecued ribs and potato skins that he'd better not get too attached to Marly. She liked him now, but he wasn't too sure about how she'd feel if he bombed next week in his very first start. But she was making it damn difficult for him to keep his feelings in check. As if she was hot for him, not *any* Marlins player, she stuck at his side, ignoring the other guys who were making thinly veiled passes. He was finding it hard to keep from thinking about her as way more than a one-season distraction.

"Dance?" A slow country ballad had just started, one he thought he might be able to manage without stomping all over Marly's feet. He hated dancing just like most unusually tall guys he knew, but he wanted to hold her, feel her heart beating against his. Dancing was the only socially acceptable way he could think of doing that in a public place with people all around. When she stood, he got up and led her out on the small dance floor. She stretched to put her arms around his neck, and her firm, ripe breasts rubbed hard against his chest. His pulse raced as he tried to keep his mind on the four-beat box step he thought he'd mastered back in middle school physical ed classes.

No luck. What he wanted to do, he couldn't, not now when half the team was looking on, most likely laughing their asses off at his feeble attempt to dance. He rested his chin on top of her head, inhaling the sweet smell of the wavy black strands that cascaded down her back, tickling the arms he was holding firmly around her waist. He managed to restrain himself from sliding those hands lower, cupping her rounded butt cheeks and pulling her tight against his raging hard-on.

After talking with her about the game while they were eating, Bobby realized that Marly was a football player's dream. She obviously loved the sport and knew a good bit about it. Not too many women would have recognized his first professional play as a naked bootleg, but she'd mentioned the term first instead of picking up on it from someone else's comments.

And she had a knack for making him feel powerful...in control. He'd never felt that way around a woman before. Not Tina and not any of the girls at Tulane who'd wanted to be seen on campus with a football star. Bobby held Marly closer, bent and brushed his lips against her earlobe.

"I should've worn high heels." Marly stood on tiptoe, nuzzled at his throat.

And I should have kept my jockstrap on. Good thing he still had on his suit jacket, because she was getting him so hot that no one could possibly fail to notice the bulge in his crotch. "If you've had enough socializing, we can take a walk along the river, or go to my place. It's not far."

"I say there's no place like home. Especially when the mosquitoes are still nibbling on people who're brave enough to walk along the riverbank."

Chapter Three

"Be it ever so humble…" Bobby opened the door for her then followed Marly into the entry foyer of his sixteenth-floor condo.

"Humble? This is gorgeous." She made a beeline for the floor-to-ceiling window overlooking the Mississippi River and sighed. "Hardly humble." To her the soaring ceiling and opulent contemporary furnishings seemed incongruous with her impression of who Bobby was. "I was disappointed that you didn't need me to help you hunt for apartments."

"I was looking forward to that, too. But one of the front office people found this place for me. It came furnished, and comparatively cheap. I'm house-sitting for a former team scout and his wife. They didn't want to try to sell now, with the housing market so depressed." He came up behind her, wrapped his arms around her, blew lightly on her ear then drew her closer. "Sometimes I like to sit by that window and watch the boats go up and down the river. It's different—a lot different—from Hedgecock County, Texas. A lot more soothing to look at from a distance."

"And how about up close?" she asked, imagining the small-town boy might have been a little intimidated by big-city life.

"I like being up close to you." His hard cock probed against her ass cheeks, its message unmistakable.

He picked her up as though she weighed no more than the beer stein he'd nursed while they were at the bar, and carried her to a beige leather lounge chair where he sat and held her on his lap. Having him gather her in his arms and hold her as though she was precious to him made her heart beat double time. He aroused her, certainly, but she felt his affection, too. "I meant, how've you adjusted to the city, up close?"

"Fine. I went to college in New Orleans. Memphis isn't that much different, just a little quieter and less rowdy. It's even on the same river."

"I bet you were a rowdy one." Marly imagined him in the French Quarter, living it up with teammates and a devoted bunch of hot sorority girls.

He laughed. "Not really. I had to work pretty hard to stay in football shape year-round and handle a full load of academic courses."

She'd heard he'd won a scholar-athlete award of some sort last year. "I find it hard to believe you never found time to play on Bourbon Street."

Bending down, Bobby caught her hair and laid it over her shoulder then blew on her neck. The warm, damp burst of air sent shivers all the way to her toes. "I didn't say I never got to play. I just didn't do it very often. No time and not a lot of spending money."

"So they didn't find you a cushy job where you could study and make money? My college's basketball team got suspended from postseason play for a long time because most of the starters had jobs working for companies a rabid team supporter owned. Only they didn't actually work."

"Nope. I had a full scholarship but no jobs, real or fake. Tulane's more academic than sports-orientated, although they have made some good runs at football championships over the years. I never heard of any player there getting money without working for it."

"Oh." She should have figured that. Unlike the state university she attended, Tulane was well-known for being one of the most prestigious schools in the South. She'd have loved to go to Tulane, but they'd never have let her in with her very average high-school grades.

"I got what I wanted from my four years there — a good education I can use once football runs its course, and a chance to start all four years and get drafted into the pros." He traced the length of her arm, stopping to stroke the sensitive flesh in the crook of her elbow. "How about you?"

She snuggled against his muscular chest, enjoyed the heat and the slow, steady beat of his heart. "Daddy footed the bill for my higher education. I wasn't the world's best student, but I got a liberal arts degree a year ago and came back home. Someday I'd love to do work helping disabled people, but nothing has come up so far except for some volunteer fundraising I do for Angels Unaware. I work part-time in the family restaurant, and pretty much full-time at being a Maulers cheerleader, at least during the season."

"Do you still live at home? I don't believe that's ever come up during any of our conversations."

She hoped he didn't mind. "Yes. If you want to keep seeing me, you'll have to meet the parents eventually. They're great, but they have a tendency to push their kids at whoever they happen to be dating. Speaking of which, are we? Dating, that is."

"Yeah. We're dating. Have we been dating long enough for you to join me in my new king-size bed?" He nibbled on her earlobe, and that sent what felt like a lightning bolt coursing through her.

"If I were the nice girl my folks brought me up to be, I'd have to say no. But since I'm not, and since you turn me every way but loose —"

"We could wait, you know. It might kill me, but there's something about you — about us — that's about more than getting naked and fucking like minks."

Marly could hardly believe her ears. Bobby's words proved he was much more than a hot jock, hinted that he might be as emotionally invested as she was. "Really?"

"Yeah, there is." Bobby reached around and laced his long fingers together over her belly, using his thumbs to massage the lower swell of her breasts. His hands stilled, and when he spoke it was little more than a husky, provocative whisper. "Or we could do what we both want and call it getting to know each other better."

That sounded good. Instead of saying yes or no, Marly twisted around and began unbuttoning Bobby's shirt. She couldn't resist running her hand along the muscular expanse of his lightly furred chest. "Don't you think we both have on too many clothes?"

"Yeah. You're right. What say we check out the bedroom?" Not waiting for a reply, he stood and carried her where he wanted them to be. There was something thrilling about having a lover strong enough to carry her around like he might a small child, something exciting, a little intimidating about knowing he had the physical ability to command her to his will. He set her down in a large room dominated by a massive bed, and she immediately missed the close contact.

Unlike some guys she knew, including her brothers, Bobby kept a tidy bedroom. The bed was even made, its beige and red woven coverlet neatly pulled over what she imagined would be sheets that had a hint of the outdoorsy scent he was wearing. He probably had a housekeeper, but for some reason Marly got the idea he was just naturally neat. Before she had a chance to ask him, he scooped her up again and set her on the side of the bed. Then he took a knee.

"What, are you proposing? Or do you have a foot fetish?" The careful way he untied and removed her cross-trainers, and his sensual touch as he rubbed her feet through the short socks before pulling them off, too, made her think he just might.

"No, I'm not proposing. And you've got a lot of body parts that turn me on more than your pretty feet." He paused, massaging the balls of her feet with his strong fingers for a long, delicious minute before stopping and looking up at her.

His expression was taut, his eyes almost black. "Stand up now and unfasten your shorts. I'll take care of the rest."

She had no doubt he would. In his own time. It was obvious he'd grabbed the reins, taken control. She loved it. At that moment she realized she could very easily love him. Right now this burning lust would have to do for both of them. Standing, she lowered the zipper on her shorts then unfastened the belt and snap. The sturdy denim slid down her legs, the abrasion slight but ever so arousing. Maybe that was because Bobby was watching every inch of their slow descent, his breathing ragged.

As if crawling in that bed and getting it on were the least of his concerns, he picked up her shorts, folded them and put them on a club chair that was within arm's reach of where they stood. It was obvious that he was trying to go slow. Doing a damn good job of it, too. Instead of going for her thong panties, he lifted off her knit polo shirt and loosened her bra, all in a continuous, practiced motion. How many other women had he taken in this bed? In other beds in other places? Before she could clamp her mouth shut, she blurted out the question she had no right to ask. "How many women have you brought here? Omigod, I'm sorry. It's not my business."

He cupped her chin, tilted her head back until she could look him in the eye. "It's okay, Marly. You're the first woman I've brought here. The first I've been in a bedroom with since I've been in Memphis, actually. Tell the truth, I've always been pretty selective about my sex partners, and I haven't had that many. You may find I'm not all that unforgettable in the sack. But baby, you're inspiring me."

Ever so gently he bent and stripped off her thong to find her sweet pussy bare except for a thin line of neatly trimmed black curls on her mound. "What?"

"It's a Brazilian. Naked except for that little landing strip. I can't stand black hairs creeping out of the legs of my bikini bottoms." She sounded nervous, as though she thought he might object.

Object, hell. He loved the feel of a naked cunt, had regretted that the coed who'd introduced him to hers had had nothing on her mind—other than fucking him every chance she got—but showing him off to her sorority sisters the way he might show off a trophy. "I like it. A lot." Then, before she could get too nervous, he blew on her bellybutton as he straightened up.

"One of us has too many clothes on." When she looked pointedly at him, he realized he was still fully dressed while she was bare-butt naked. "May I help fix that?"

"Oh yeah." While he toed off his loafers, she slid his shirt off and pulled up his undershirt.

"Bend over please." She moved around him so she could pull the undershirt off. "I can't reach up high enough to get this shirt over your head, big guy. What are you, six five or six?" Whatever, he was close to a foot taller than she was.

"Six five and a half." He bent over so she could pull the offending garment off. "Two hundred forty pounds soaking wet, or at least I was before the game. I probably sweated off a couple of pounds." He unfastened his pants and let them pool at his feet. "I'll let you get the rest."

She draped his pants over a chair then turned back to him. "Omigod, you're even more gorgeous than I imagined. I can tell you spend a lot of time in the weight room."

"Nowhere near as much time as linemen do. The last thing quarterbacks need is to be muscle-bound." When she raked his body with a burning-hot gaze, his cock rose to full attention. Her eyes widened when she noticed it tenting his underwear, before her gaze slid back up his chest.

"You're hurt." Her hand went out, and she very gently touched one of a colorful collection of bruises that dotted his left shoulder and rib cage, and the long vertical bandage that started just below his ribs and disappeared inside plain white boxer shorts.

The injuries weren't serious, just the expected results of a hard-fought game. "I'm okay. The bumps and bruises are side effects of the job. I'm used to getting them. If you think I look bad, you should see some of the other guys. Don't worry, I won't break."

She didn't look all that reassured. In fact she looked downright disbelieving.

He grasped her chin, making her look him in the eye. "You haven't messed around with a lot of football players, have you?" She couldn't have, not and still be shocked over seeing a few dents and dings after games, whether they were high school, college or pro.

"No. But I don't want you to hurt yourself anymore. You probably should be in a whirlpool or something." When she laid her hand over the bandage on his side, he grabbed it and brought it to his lips.

It made him feel good, suspecting that his hot, gorgeous groupie hadn't been handing herself out to every player she came across. He was pretty sure now that what he felt for Marly wasn't just a matter of scratching a mutual itch. It was more. He didn't know how much more, but he was eager to find out. "Honest. It's nothing. I've gotten hurt worse in practice." That wasn't exactly true since quarterbacks wore distinctive colored shirts in scrimmages that made them off-limits to potential tacklers, but if it made her feel better...

"Under the bandage there's an ugly-looking cleat cut where I got stepped on during that sack in the fourth quarter. But it's not serious. The trainer said it didn't need stitches and that he expected it to heal in a few days. Come on, baby, you're killing me." Not waiting for her to answer or finish undressing him, he hooked his thumbs inside the waistband of his boxers and slid them down his legs. Her sharply indrawn breath made him smile as he sat on the bed and peeled off his socks. "See something you like?"

"You—you're huge. I'm not sure you'll fit."

Apparently the sight of his erection had cleared her mind of worries about him being hurt. "Trust me. We'll fit together just fine. Come here."

When she did, he pulled her close. She felt good, all silky skin and curves just where a woman should have them. Slowly, as gently as he could manage, he ran his hands along her back, clasped her sweet, rounded ass and brought her so close he could inhale her flowery scent, smell her arousal. When she wrapped her arms around his waist and held him tight, he felt her ragged breathing against his nipples. Her heart beat in synch with his own, strong and fast.

The smells of sex surrounded them, fired his need to fuck her now, with no more preliminaries. "Lie down on the bed, baby. I've got to get some condoms." Why hadn't he thought of putting some in a drawer of one of the nightstands by the bed? Fat lot of good they'd do stuck in the bathroom linen closet, unless…

Maybe they'd have some leisurely sex in the hot tub after they took the edge off this lust. He had the feeling that with Marly, he could go all night and still not get enough. Bobby tore open the box and grabbed a handful of protection, tossing all but one onto the nightstand closest to him as he looked down at Marly.

She'd turned down the coverlet and top sheet, and she lay in the middle of his bed, gloriously naked, her legs slightly apart. He figured she must like sunning herself, because while the rest of her was deeply tanned, there were triangular patches of pale, creamy skin on her breasts. The outline of relatively modest bikini bottoms drew his eye, but only for a moment before his gaze moved lower, to her pussy.

Her clit poked out between satiny outer lips, and he had to taste her. Bending over her, he lapped at the little button, felt it go hard beneath his tongue.

"Yes, please. Don't stop." She sounded breathless, as hot as she looked. When she caught his hair and pulled him closer, he knew she liked this. A lot. "Turn around and let me taste you, too."

Bobby raised his head, looked up at Marly. "Next time, you hot little bitch. Sixty-nine's damn near impossible when you're such a tiny little thing. If you want, though, you can tease me with your hands." He shifted so she could reach him.

Omigod. The way she gripped his cock, squeezed him, was almost enough to make him come. And when she cupped his sac, rolled his balls against her small, soft hand... "Stop, or it's going to be all over."

"Fuck me then. I'm so hot for you. Don't want to wait." Her words came out harsh, fast. The way she stroked his thighs and belly had nearly the same effect on him as when she'd been playing directly with his balls.

"Not yet, baby. I want you so damn hot and wet that you'll enjoy the main act. And I want to taste you some more, too." Not too much more because he wasn't at all sure he could hold out for very long. He lowered his head again, licked along her wet, swollen slit. He found her cunt, stabbed it over and over with his tongue while he tried to ignore what she was doing with her hands on his throbbing cock and balls.

Maybe he should let her take the edge off. But he wanted inside her almost more than he wanted to take his next breath. She was wet enough now. They'd take it slower next time. Taking one last nibble on her clit, he sat and reached for a condom.

He handed it to her, trying to keep his hand from shaking. "Put it on me. I want you so damn much." Even her touch as she rolled the condom over his cock had him practically jumping out of his skin. Never before—

God but she was everything he'd ever dreamed of in a woman—gorgeous, smart and sexy as hell. And she seemed to want him, not just the jock image but all of him. "Hurry, baby. I can't wait much longer."

"There. All done." Marly lay back, every nerve in her body humming as she spread her legs and raised her knees to give Bobby room. He was so fucking hot, so everything she'd dreamed of in lonely late-night fantasies. When he came over her, his expression taut as though he was barely in control, she held out her arms, welcomed his heat and hardness, the feel of his weight on her, his soft chest hair tickling her. Arousing her more than she'd thought possible.

"Put your legs around my waist," he whispered in her ear, his breath hot and sweet, reminding her that his huge, rigid sex stood poised to impale her. "I'll be careful. Don't want to hurt you."

That was the least of her worries now, when she was beneath him, loving the way his hard, perfectly sculpted body controlled her, the pulsating heat of his cock outside the opening to her pussy. She wanted him. Longed for him to take her, stretch her. She wanted him to claim her as his own.

She raked his back with her nails, softly, the tips of her fingers exploring the smooth, warm skin, the taut muscles beneath. Then she felt it. The bandage. And she imagined how much pain he'd endured to finish the game after being stomped on with a cleat attached to a lineman's beefy foot and leg. "Are you really okay?"

"I will be as soon as you let me inside your sweet, wet pussy." When she spread her legs farther apart and draped them over his tight ass, he pressed the blunt head of his cock inside her, slowly, gently as if he was afraid he might hurt her. "Omigod. You're tight. So hot and wet I don't know how long I can last."

It hurt. But it also felt delicious, him stretching her almost beyond what she could take. "Yes, honey. Fuck me. I love having you inside me this way."

When he propped his upper body up on his extended arms, his whole body trembled. Sweat beaded on his brow. From his clenched teeth and bulging biceps she guessed he was having trouble going slowly, imagined he longed to sink all the way inside and fuck her hard. "It's okay. I won't break."

"No it's not. I want you to enjoy this as much as I am." His breath was hot and incredibly arousing against her throat when he lowered his head and licked the upper curve of her breast. "You're so wet. So fuckin' tight. Relax, baby, let me in."

She framed his face between her hands, looked into his lust-glazed eyes. "Just do it. Please." She didn't think she could stand another minute in sexual limbo, wanting him to claim her fully as she hovered on the cusp of an orgasm she somehow knew would be the best she'd ever experienced. "Really, I won't break."

On his knees now, he grasped her hips, withdrawing a little then coming back, deeper with every careful stroke. The delicious fullness expanded as he fucked her, still slowly but deeper, their bodies making the erotic slapping sounds of sex. She turned her head and closed her eyes, concentrating on the wetness, the heat, the heady smells of him and her mingling around them, joining them as close as a man and woman could get.

His balls were tight, pressing against her slit when he finally pushed inside her all the way. She felt the pressure of his cock head deep inside her, the throbbing of his hot shaft against her vaginal walls. Omigod, she was going to come and there was nothing she could do to hold back.

"Oh yes. Please don't stop."

"I won't, baby." He moved faster now, his balls slapping noisily against her wet, hot flesh. He grew harder, bigger with every stroke. She wanted him to drive her higher, higher than she'd ever been. And he obliged her. Every cell in her body felt as though it would explode, and waves of fulfillment poured over her, shattered her control. Nothing mattered but Bobby. And how he was making her feel.

His big body trembled then tightened. His muscles bulged. Impossibly, he grew even bigger inside her. His teeth clenched, he held back his own climax as she flew higher with each hard, fast thrust. "God, baby, I'm coming," he said, gasping. He was buried inside her all the way, so deep the force of his climax set off another wave of pleasure that flowed through her like molten fire.

She trembled in his arms, panting, gasping out words that sounded a lot like "I love you" and "Oh God yes", words she'd never have uttered if she'd had control of her mind. She heard her own ragged breathing as she clasped him with her legs and dug her nails in his shoulders.

"Oh yeah, baby, you make me feel like you can't get enough. Fuck, you make me want to be everything my beautiful lover ever wanted."

"God yes. I'm coming again." She clutched his shoulders, hung onto him like a lifeline.

"It's okay, baby. I've got you. Won't let anything happen to you."

"I know." As if the last bubble of her climax finally had burst, leaving her limp and satiated, she loosened her grip on his flesh, stroked where her nails had bitten in. "That was good. So, so good."

"Oh yeah. And that was just the beginning."

He rolled to his side and took her with him, holding her as if he'd never let her go. Sweat mingled on their bodies, slick and warm as they explored each other not with fevered passion like before, but in the rosy aftermath of the best sex she'd ever had. From the possessive way he ran his hands along the curves of her neck and back, she thought he'd liked it, too.

She hoped he liked her and wanted, as he'd said, to explore feelings that had erupted like wildfire even before—

"Marly?"

His breath was warm, sweet. It ruffled her hair, had her heart fluttering again. Certainly he couldn't want more. Not so soon. "Bobby?"

"I'd like to meet your folks. And I'd like to see where this goes. This may have been our first time together, but I feel like I've known you forever. Guess those long late-night calls meant a lot more than just helping me pass the lonely nights."

"To me, too." They might not have learned so many of the really important things about each other if they'd started dating right away, because she figured the chemistry would have overwhelmed them both and they'd have been between the sheets while still being virtual strangers.

He ran his hand down her spine, parked it casually on her bottom. "It's not just the sex, it's a feeling I have that we're gonna click in other ways, too." He stretched out, his long body taking up a big chunk of the bed as he lifted her and set her on his belly. "I'm hoping you feel the same."

"I do." She'd never felt so complete, and though she'd never before believed in love at first sight, she thought, just maybe, it could happen. That it had happened that afternoon in the training center parking lot. "I'd love to take you home to Mom and Dad. Do you like Italian food?"

He cupped both breasts, brushed her nipples with his thumbs. "Spaghetti and meatballs. They've been favorites since I was a kid. I even learned to like some real Italian food at a little neighborhood restaurant not far from the Tulane campus. Chicken cacciatore and lasagna and such. I can't imagine liking anything more than increasing my knowledge of Italian cookery with you. Along with other things. I've got the feeling I'm going to enjoy doing many things with you."

Could he possibly have meant that he wanted this to be more than a brief fuckfest? It certainly sounded like he did. His words echoed in Marly's ears, so full of promise yet so frightening.

But were they, really? He hadn't sworn his love or declared any forever intentions. If he had at this point, he'd have set off warning bells in her head and triggered memories of the college boyfriend who'd told her he loved her flat-out then dumped her. No, Bobby's words seemed honest, trustworthy, devoid of empty promises to be broken. *I can't imagine liking anything more* echoed in her ears.

She could accept those words, cherish them, even hope a little bit that the day would come that he'd say he loved her…and she'd dare to believe him and love him back.

Meanwhile she'd try not to think of all the other women who'd be chasing Bobby, and to concentrate on him.

Chapter Four

But Marly wasn't very successful at keeping the competition out of sight or out of mind. With every Maulers victory, Bobby's star was rising. Number four jerseys were showing up at home games in larger numbers each week he started in place of Keith Connors. Gorgeous women stalked him even when they were out together. Why not? The man was the ultimate groupie magnet. It didn't matter that he was only twenty-two and on the second rung of the Maulers depth chart. He was playing every week while Keith's stretched biceps tendon healed, and the groupies were zeroing in.

She couldn't help noticing the way they looked at him. Every time she saw a woman staring at him, practically salivating, her own insecurities would rear their ugly heads. She'd think about the college boy who'd sworn he loved her days before going home for a weekend and bringing back a brand-new bride. He'd been a hot one, but Bobby was so much hotter, not to mention he'd just been named on Memphis' most-eligible-bachelor list. Even with Marly's long-time friends and family, he drew hot looks and subtle flirting from women from eight to eighty.

When she'd taken Bobby to her dad's restaurant after the third game, even the waitresses there who'd been her friends since she was a kid fawned over him. And total strangers came up to them and asked for his autograph when they went to the mall. Marly would have been flattered if only she'd been positive she wasn't just the rookie passer's flavor of the month.

But she wasn't at all sure. The self-confidence she'd reconstructed piece by piece after her college boyfriend dumped her for his high-school sweetheart started to flag under the weight of the adulation Bobby was getting. She'd convinced herself she was strong enough to reach for the moon if it struck her fancy, that she could fight off anyone who might want Bobby for herself. But now she was staying up nights, wondering when the bubble of her fantasies was going to burst. She imagined how she'd hurt if he dumped her for somebody hotter, smarter or with family connections that could further his career. She pictured the willowy blonde who'd practically attacked Bobby after the Monday night game. The shameless hussy just happened to be a niece of one of the team owners.

Stop it, Marly. Bobby treats you great. He doesn't pay much attention to the other women who want a piece of him. She listened to her inner voice and got out of the chair by her bedroom window, where she'd been indulging in a pity party for one and watching leaves swirl around the backyard the way they been doing every fall that she could remember.

* * * * *

"What's the matter, baby?" Bobby asked when he picked her up after practice the next day.

So it showed? Marly tried to put on a happy face. "Nothing, I was just missing you." No need to feed his ego by letting him know how insecure she was feeling.

"How about going over to my place?" He helped her with her jacket then draped his arm around her as they walked out to his truck.

"Mmmm. What do you have in mind?" A hot roll in the hay would do a bunch toward bolstering her shaky ego, but another voice—her evil twin—whispered in her head that he might have had another woman there last night, when he'd begged off coming over, saying he was too tired to move.

"That, too, honey, but I want to talk with you first."

Talk. Good talk or bad talk? Marly tensed. It couldn't be too bad if he was planning on some bedroom action afterward. She simply had to get over this nagging anxiety or she would lose Bobby for sure. "Okay. Want to give me a hint about what we need to talk about?"

"Living arrangements. Yours, mine and ours."

* * * * *

His twice-a-week housekeeper had done it up right. Bobby glanced around the living area, saw the catered dinner set out on the glass-topped dining table he'd never used before. She'd even dragged out his landlord's good dishes and put some candles in the middle of the table. "Want to eat?"

"Sure." Marly looked a little puzzled when she looked at the table. "How'd you manage this?"

"My housekeeper. I'll have to slip her a few extra bucks. I'd never have thought about doing all this—I just asked her to stay and arrange the stuff I ordered from the caterer. Sit down."

He could bark out orders to ten guys, most of whom outweighed him by sixty pounds or more. He had no trouble calling audibles at the line of scrimmage. Why was it, Bobby wondered as he buttered a roll, that he was having trouble deciding how to ask Marly to come live with him?

Maybe it was his upbringing. People in Hedgecock didn't generally move their girlfriends in unless they married them, and when they did, the people in question became the major subjects for local gossip. *Why don't you just ask her to marry you?* Bobby heard his mom's voice in his head, even though he hadn't discussed the subject with her.

Hell. This wasn't Hedgecock and Marly wasn't a semi-innocent former virgin he'd deflowered then banged every time he got a chance until the worst had happened and they'd gotten caught. He had no reason to hesitate.

He looked across the table, loved the way the candlelight flickered over her face, put highlights in her hair. She ate quietly, as if she was in her own world wondering what was going on. Sort of like he was. "Marly?"

Her smile warmed his insides. "Yes?"

"I've never done this before, so bear with me." He hoped he didn't sound too fucking stupid. "I want you to come live with me."

"Why?" She looked even more confused than she had when she first saw the table all gussied up.

Why, indeed? He wanted to sleep with her, have her there so he could wake up and make love whenever the need arose, but somehow that didn't sound like a reason a woman would want to hear. He wanted to let her know she was his only woman, and that the women who chased after him meant nothing to him. He also wanted to be with her whenever he could, just because he needed her, wanted her nearby. And he didn't want to sneak around her house like a horny teenager, waiting until her folks left before fucking her in that frilly bedroom of hers.

Before speaking, he chose his words carefully. "Because I want you with me. Because I want to wake up looking at your beautiful face. Damn it, Marly, I want you to live with me because I love you."

She dropped her fork onto her plate, as if it had suddenly gotten too heavy to handle. "You love me?"

"I just said I do." He'd done everything short of saying the words pretty damn regularly over the past weeks. So why did his coming out and saying it now have her all flustered? "Well, will you move in?"

"My parents..."

"Your parents know you're a grown woman. I'm fairly sure they've guessed that we don't spend all our time together watching DVDs or playing cards."

She frowned. "They still won't like it. They're pretty old-fashioned. But I'll do it. It's not like I'm an eighteen- or nineteen-year-old innocent. If you want me around 24/7, then I'll be here."

"I do, baby. And I'll take good care of you."

Her eyes glistened with tears. "I know. And Bobby, I love you, too."

But she should have looked happier. It bothered Bobby that Marly still had that half-scared look in her eyes. "Let's go tell your folks now." Maybe if they got that over with, she'd revert to the Marly he'd fallen in love with, and they could do the physical celebrating without the nagging doubts she'd exhibited the past couple of weeks.

* * * * *

Their lovemaking had been hot, almost desperate, after Marly's parents had both expressed stern disapproval of their plans to live together. Now Bobby was gone, off for a road game in Los Angeles. His condo seemed cold without him, too big and too contemporary, like a furniture showroom at a fancy decorator's salon.

Funny, she'd never gotten this uneasy feeling when he was here with her. Her mind drifted back to his bed, where he'd made her feel completely at home, as though they belonged together. He'd explored her body all over, made her feel content as well as tingly with anticipation, taken his time before letting go the reins on his passion and fucking her like there was no tomorrow. His hard thrusts, the slap of his balls against her wet slit, the squeezing of his hands on her breasts stayed in her mind now, even though he'd rolled out of bed at five a.m. to catch the team plane to LA.

Why couldn't she quite believe him when he said he loved her? He'd given her no reason to doubt. She didn't feel like this when he was with her, but now she didn't feel like she belonged here when he was gone.

She still was moving in with him, just as soon as he got home. She loved him, damn it. She'd rather have what time she could with him, even if it meant hurting her mom and dad. Even though she knew she'd be risking hurt that would be much worse if he dumped her than it had been when her college romance had ground to a heartbreaking end.

She'd go home and pack up some of her clothes. She'd stay there and watch the game with Dad on TV. And she'd count the hours until Bobby got back on Monday morning.

* * * * *

Today's practice at the Rangers' complex following a red-eye flight from Memphis had been a bitch, with Coach Lyle snapping at everybody and swearing under his breath because the team's two bad boys hadn't shown up. Every muscle in Bobby's body ached as he bent to grab his dirty workout clothes and stuff them in a laundry bag. But that was the least of his worries. The talk he'd had last night with Marly's dad hadn't gone well. Not that he'd expected it would. He'd realized even before bringing up the idea of Marly moving in with him how conventional and old-fashioned Marly's parents were.

His own mom hadn't been too happy, either, when he'd told her he was thinking about asking Marly to move in with him, although she'd wished him well. Like Dom Ragusa, Mom had pointed out that in her day most couples waited to live together until after they got married. She'd also mentioned Tina, whom she loved like a daughter now that Bobby's former girlfriend had come to stay in his old room after her mom's death.

Damn it, he should have known his mom was hoping Tina and he would get together. And he hated disappointing her. After all, she'd sacrificed a lot to see him get as far as he'd come. But Tina wasn't happening for him. Not now or ever. Yeah, he loved her, but as a good friend. He had no desire to fuck her again, couldn't imagine enjoying the staid life she'd insist upon. He doubted Tina was still remembering those few nights under the Hedgecock County High bleachers with anything resembling longing, either. He'd been damn green—a virgin, even—when they'd laid a blanket under the bleachers and had their first sexual experience. When he looked back on it, he wondered why Tina had agreed to keep on doing it. Amazing what a guy could learn about sex in six years.

Bobby liked living the life of a successful jock with Marly beside him. He loved the way she set his libido on fire, and that she enthusiastically embraced everything about him, bruises and unruly testosterone and all. He especially liked the way they clicked, not only in bed but whenever they spent time together.

He'd never felt that way about anybody else he'd ever dated, especially Tina. If they hadn't been curious kids, Bobby was pretty sure she wouldn't have let him fuck her at all. And he was almost as sure the hots he'd had for her were purely the result of teenage boy hormones. He sure as hell had never wanted her the way he wanted Marly now.

If he were certain Marly loved him, and would even if he weren't a successful pro athlete, he'd marry her tomorrow. But he wasn't, and he sensed she wasn't quite sure of his commitment, either. Still he wanted to go to sleep feeling her soft, warm skin against him and wake up every morning sharing sleepy sex and the great companionship they'd shared from their first date.

He wished he'd had time to move Marly into his apartment before coming out here, so she'd be waiting in his bed when he got back. The last thing Bobby wanted was for her to slip through his fingers. She was everything he wanted in a woman, and not just because she was the best fuck he'd ever had. Yeah, she'd agreed to move in with him, but she was fretting about her parents' disapproval and he worried she might change her mind.

"I don't blame her dad for not wanting her to move in with me," he told Ellis, who had the visitors' locker next to his.

"Times have changed," Ellis responded. "But I don't blame you either, wanting to go slow on the marriage thing. Maybe it would smooth things out with her folks if you got engaged."

To Bobby, that meant as much of a commitment as standing in front of a preacher and saying the words. Still… "Maybe I will." He loved Marly all right, he just wasn't sure she'd love him as much when Keith came back to practice next week and he was standing on the sidelines again. More important, he wasn't at all certain she'd be willing to leave her close-knit family and go with him when he was traded away from Memphis. His agent was positive a trade would happen, maybe almost as soon as Connors took over the reins again. That shouldn't be long now. Maybe in the next week or two, certainly before Thanksgiving.

Bobby wasn't used to being indecisive about anything. But then he'd never wanted anything the way he wanted Marly with him day and night. He even wanted her more than he'd wanted to play pro football before last spring's draft. Damn it, he'd follow Ellis' suggestion. It wouldn't be deceiving Marly or her folks to put a ring on her finger, because he did want to marry her someday if things worked out.

He turned to Ellis. "You know, I think you're right. Want to go help me pick a ring out before we have to go back to the hotel for dinner?"

"Sure. Where shall we go?"

Bobby grinned. "How about Beverly Hills? I've always wanted to go shopping on Rodeo Drive."

"It's your money, bonus baby." Ellis sat on a bench and tied his cross-trainers.

Though Bobby wasn't into wasting money needlessly, he wanted to get something Marly would always treasure, the way his mom still occasionally teared up when she glanced down at the narrow gold band she'd still been wearing last time he was home. Recalling her mentioning that she was spending time with Mr. Tate when they'd talked on the phone this morning, Bobby wondered if she'd finally taken off that ring. He hoped so, because it was about time for her to get a life of her own.

"I'm not gonna go crazy, but I want Marly to know how much she means to me. Thanks to the media, everybody knows I got that signing bonus."

"That makes sense. Come on, we only have a couple of hours until we've got a team meeting at the hotel."

* * * * *

Tiffany's on Rodeo Drive was a hell of a lot fancier than the only other jewelry store Bobby had ever been inside. Dazzling diamonds practically blinded him as he let the saleswoman point out details on an array of pre-made rings. He finally chose a two-and-a-half carat round stone set in the jeweler's signature platinum setting, and escaped without being talked into adding an obscenely expensive tennis bracelet to go with the ring. The distinctive-looking ring box now rested inside his jeans pocket. He figured he'd stash it inside his equipment bag once they got back to the hotel for the team meeting.

* * * * *

When he and Ellis walked into Coach Lyle's suite five minutes late, Bobby thought everybody was awfully quiet. Even Coach seemed subdued as he preached about how the Maulers defense would have to play their best to get a win against the Rangers. "You can never count Casey Weldon out. He may be old, but he's still got an arm and the kind of football smarts you don't often see." Next to Dave Delaney, another of the Hedgecock, Texas, quarterbacks, Casey had been one of Bobby's childhood heroes. Getting the chance to see Weldon play was almost as exciting as it was going to be to go up against him. Bobby told himself he'd just have to see that he made no mistakes, that his throws would be on target whenever he got on the field.

Coach Lyle moved away from the bar, paced among the players. Bobby watched his hands clench into fists, as if he wanted to lay into somebody. Bobby hoped it wasn't him and Ellis for having arrived five minutes into the meeting.

It seemed the coach's ire was meant for the entire team, which was a relief. "Okay. You guys keep your noses clean. No partying tonight. It's going to be bad enough answering questions about what got Mort and Willis locked up last night without having anybody else run afoul of the law." Coach scowled, and the collective silence could have deafened them all. "No doubt about it, no matter what it does to our chances of winning, I'll suspend anybody who breaks curfew. And curfew is now."

"What's that all about?" Bobby asked Dan Morales as they waited for an elevator in the hotel lobby.

"Your head must be up your ass, rookie, if you didn't know our two resident idiots sneaked out of the hotel and went out to a club right after we arrived. They got drunk and roughed up a couple of strippers bad enough that they had to get admitted to the hospital. Both of our teammates are locked up, at least until court opens on Monday."

"No shit?" Bobby didn't know either of the so-called idiots well, but it did register in his mind that one of them, Willis, was his number two wide receiver. Mort was a second-string defensive player who'd roughed his receivers up unnecessarily a couple of times during practice. "So we play without them tomorrow." He let out a sigh. "Willis is pretty damn good."

"On the field. Off it he's downright poison. So is Mort. It wouldn't surprise me if Coach cut one or both of them this time. Those boys need a good whomping by their mamas. Or a few months' free stay courtesy of the penal system. Maybe both."

Bobby nodded. "You're right about that." Just because somebody came from a dirt-poor background didn't excuse him for being a thug, but too damn many players kept proving you could take the boy out of the 'hood, but no amount of money was guaranteed to take the 'hood out of the boy. "See you in the morning," he said as he got out of the elevator on the eighteenth floor and stepped into the suite he and Ellis were sharing.

Not for the first time, Bobby felt small-town. He guessed he'd been sheltered, not only as a kid but at Tulane, where the athletic director hadn't put up with players doing stupid things and ending up on the wrong side of the law. He hadn't gotten many bad apples either, because he'd insisted that every player they recruited met the school's rigorous academic standards. He hadn't ever used athletic waivers, a policy Bobby thought every college coach would have been wise to follow.

Sighing, Bobby opened a bottle of Gatorade and took it over to the couch. When he was just about to take the first sip, his cell phone rang. "Hey, Mom," he said after glancing at the caller ID. Taking the ring box out of his pocket and setting it on the table, he sat and stretched his legs out beside the box.

"Son, I heard about your teammates getting in trouble. It was on the six o'clock news. I'm so sorry."

"Me too. It's not good for the sport. But you don't need to worry about me hanging out with the two clowns who got arrested."

"I know. That's not why I called. Tina's stepdad has been stalking her, even since she moved over here. The other day he attacked her when she went back to the house to get some clothes, and she's been getting more terrified of him every day. She hasn't said so, but I'm afraid he's raped her, or that he's come close enough to make her afraid of even going to work. She has to get away, out of the man's reach, so Cal Tate and I decided the best thing would be for us to send her to you so she'll be safe."

Shit. What was Bobby going to do with Tina while he was moving Marly into his place? Still, Tina was his friend and he wanted to help keep her safe. "I'm in Los Angeles, Mom.

Won't be home until Monday morning. Besides, weren't you the one who told me just a few days ago that you didn't think it was a good idea for me to move Marly in?"

"Well, this is different. Getting Tina away from here could be a life-or-death matter. Having your girlfriend move in when she has a perfectly good place to live with her parents doesn't seem anywhere near as urgent." Mom had the good grace to sound a little apologetic.

"You're not trying to get Tina and me together, are you? It's not going to do any good if you are, because I just bought Marly an engagement ring and I plan to propose to her as soon as I get home." Bobby tried to sound stern, strong—not like the little boy who usually tried to keep his mom's approval.

"Oh no. I'm so sorry, Bobby. Not about Marly, I'm sure she's a wonderful girl and that you've made a good choice. It's Tina I'm sorry about sending to you now, when you're getting engaged and all."

"Can't you send her someplace else?" A guy could always hope.

"I wish I could. Cal and I dropped her off in San Antonio earlier today, and she'll be flying to Memphis tomorrow morning. I gave her the extra key to your apartment, the one you sent to me, so she can settle in a bit while you're away. Maybe you could get Marly to come over and make her feel at home. Tina's a basket case, between burying her mama and dealing with that pervert, Edgar Garcia. The man belongs in jail as much as any of the drunk roughnecks who're already there."

"Okay, Mom." Bobby couldn't say no. After all, he was the one who'd asked his mother to take care of Tina, only he'd never imagined her doing it this way. He should have. "But…"

"No buts. Tina's practically family, and she's hurting. You need to take care of her, help her settle down and find a job that will pay her a little something and keep her mind off Edgar and her poor mom. Folks are saying Edgar may have done something to hurry along Linda Ray's death, rest her soul."

Okay. Bobby's mind spun. He hated surprises like this, almost as much as he hated opposing linebackers who got through his offensive line and blindsided him. He rewound his mother's conversation. What the fuck? "You and Mr. Tate took her all the way to San Antonio?"

"We were going here anyhow, for a weekend getaway. I told you we've been seeing each other." Mom sounded a little embarrassed, as if she thought she didn't have the right to have a life other than taking care of him and going to work. "It's getting pretty serious between us. Do you mind?"

"Mind? No, you need somebody, now that I'm all grown up. I'm glad you've finally accepted that Dad is never coming back."

She sighed. "It's taken a long time, but I think I'm there. Now, tell me I haven't messed up your plans by sending Tina to you."

Mom had always been able to read between the lines, at least when it came to Bobby. "Some. I'd been hoping to do something private and romantic with Marly, and then give her the ring."

"Why not fly her out to see you play? You could take her out afterward and give it to her."

"No, I couldn't. I've got to stay with the team." Especially since Willis and Mort fucked up so royally. The situation had Coach breathing fire.

"You couldn't get special permission, bring her back with you on the team plane? Seems to me that if there's a will, there's got to be a way."

Bobby sighed. "If I were Brett Favre or maybe Keith Connors, there would be a way. But I'm not. I'm just a rookie backup, close to low man on the totem pole." He wouldn't dare ask Coach Lyle now, considering the mood the man was in. And no matter how he explained to Marly why they'd be having his old girlfriend staying in his spare bedroom, he had a sneaking feeling it wasn't going to go over well. Not at all.

"You could always ask." When Mom got an idea in her head, she hated to let go.

"Thanks anyway, Mom, but I'll have to do this my way. I just hope I don't lose Marly in the process."

"If she loves you, you won't lose her. Maybe she'll even think better of you for not turning your back on an old friend."

If she loves me. She said she did, but he hadn't tested her yet, and it seemed that test was coming a lot quicker than he'd thought. "I'd better call her now and let her know. Love you, Mom." With that he ended the call and started to dial Marly's number.

No, he'd call Coach first. It was no crime to ask, and all he could do was get his ass chewed out six ways from Sunday. "It's Bobby Anthony," he said when Coach Lyle picked up the phone. "Would you mind if I flew my girlfriend out and proposed to her after the game?"

"You can propose to the whole cheerleading squad if you win this game for us without Willis, that fucking moron. Mort's no big loss on the field. We can even fly Marly back on the team plane if you think she'd like that, since we'll have two extra, empty seats."

Bobby couldn't have been more shocked if he'd been casually given permission to skip two days of practice next week. Coach must have been more worried about the defense being able to stop Weldon and his two all-pro receivers than he'd let on in the meeting earlier. "Thanks, Coach. The whole cheerleading squad sounds interesting, but just Marly will do."

"Then get her out here if you can. You may be filling in for Keith the rest of the season if he can't find a reliable live-in nanny for his kid. His mother had to go home this week, and he can't keep on bringing the baby to work for the office women to take care of."

"Okay. I'll get Marly a ticket out here and arrange for a limo to bring her to the stadium. Then I'll call and let her know." Bobby thought he might have an answer for Connors' babysitter problem as well as a solution for his own dilemma, but he'd wait to mention it until after he ran the idea by Tina.

* * * * *

Marly didn't know quite what to think, other than that Bobby had to have lost his mind. Significant others didn't join players on road trips very often, and when they did, the women were usually wives and the reason for their presence was compelling. Still, she was glad to be going, even if it meant being here at Memphis International Airport at six a.m. waiting for the first nonstop flight to LAX. Glancing at her boarding pass as the flight was called, she noticed Bobby had sprung for a first-class seat.

He'd been uncharacteristically quiet when they talked last night. After telling her he had a surprise for her, he'd mentioned something about an old friend from his hometown coming to Memphis for a visit, and hung up rather abruptly. She thought he hadn't sounded any too pleased about this upcoming visit.

Oh well, she'd find out soon enough about his surprise and his guest. Meanwhile she didn't know how she was going to last through the four-hour flight, a cab ride to the Rangers' stadium and two hours of football game without curiosity killing her. Flipping open a copy of *Forbidden Fantasies* that she'd found on a rack in the front of the airport bookstore, she tried to decide which of the erotic stories she wanted to read first.

I can always use some ideas to try out on Bobby. She grinned at the thought of driving him crazy as she settled in to read the first story, written by one of her favorite authors. When she put the book away before getting out of a sleek silver limousine and heading into the stadium, she'd just finished the last titillating, steamy story.

She could barely wait to blow Bobby's mind. Would he like the idea of a ménage? Or would fucking where they might be seen turn him on? Marly's favorite fantasy scenario was one where the lovers were into light bondage and discipline. Maybe that was why she loved the sense of helplessness that came over her when her big, powerful man gripped her wrists, held her steady as he claimed her.

Would the sex be even better if he sometimes tied or cuffed her while they fucked? Her pussy contracted and her panties felt damp when she pictured Bobby claiming her every possible way, the way the two heroes took their woman in that vampire ménage. She imagined Bobby would like that sort of a scene, minus the bloodletting.

That thought made her laugh, even as she felt her pussy contract. Bobby was pretty damn possessive, and as far as she could tell in the short time they'd been together, his tastes ran to one woman at a time. Right now she was that woman, and she was glad. Finding her seat, she settled down and watched the Rangers cheerleaders go through their routine.

Chapter Five

೫

"She's up there, kid." Ellis used the clipboard to point up to the second row of seats along the fifty-yard line. "Show her what you've got."

Bobby waved and grinned at Marly then trotted onto the field for the coin toss. The Rangers called heads and won, so Bobby had to stand on the sideline and watch Weldon throw the ball almost the full length of the field for a quick touchdown. The Maulers had some catching up to do. The return team at least gave them decent field position at the thirty-yard line.

On the first play the left guard lost out to a Rangers defensive end, and Bobby got sacked by a linebacker who burst through the resulting hole. Marly finally let her breath out when the pile of players broke up and Bobby got up, seemingly unharmed. He got a drive going with a thirty-yard pass down the left sideline then stalled again until he handed off to Morales on third down and the running back broke loose and took the ball to the Rangers' three. First and goal. Marly stood, a lonely Maulers fan in a sea of Rangers jerseys.

Wish I'd worn Bobby's jersey. No, she didn't. If she had, the Rangers fans surrounding her probably would have devoured her for lunch.

She clenched her fists so hard her knuckles turned white when she saw Bobby line up in the shotgun. He took the snap then handed off to Morales, the tailback. No, he still had the ball and was rolling left, looking downfield for his wide receiver in the end zone. Was he going to throw into double coverage? No. Tucking the ball, he ran, a play just like his first one for the Maulers. A naked bootleg. He straight-armed a defender then turned in and scored as another Ranger laid a vicious hit on him. She shuddered when she pictured the array of bumps and bruises he was going to have tonight.

She was bad luck for him. Marly sensed it as she watched Bobby limp off the field, accepting congratulations from his teammates. Unlike the first Rangers drive, this one was unfolding slowly, with incomplete passes and short runs into coverage, several measurements to see if they'd managed first downs. Marly hoped it would give Bobby time to recover as she watched a trainer tape his left knee. But his expression was pained, and she couldn't help worrying.

The rest of the first half went uneventfully, with both sides moving by inches and kicking field goals or having to punt the ball away. When the Maulers went into the locker room, the Rangers were up by three. Bobby had looked a little off since taking that hit. Marly prayed he'd be all right.

The Maulers fan in her hoped Bobby would be back. The lover prayed they'd pull him and play Ellis instead. But she knew that wasn't likely to happen as long as Bobby was conscious, upright and moving. Apparently admitting weakness wasn't something any quarterback ever wanted to do—at least the best of them. Favre had once played almost a whole season with a broken thumb on his throwing hand. The Rangers' certain future Hall of Famer quarterback, Casey Weldon, was playing now with his left forearm in a cast. The best of them just wouldn't give in to anything short of a torn-up knee or a messed-up shoulder like the one that had Keith sidelined.

Marly was confident Bobby would be one of the best, like Keith Connors and the other great ones who'd come before him. But he was her man, and she hated to think about him playing hurt. She distracted herself for a few minutes, watching the Rangers cheerleaders do their thing, until the second half was starting with the Maulers getting the ball.

Bobby was moving better, she thought as he went onto the field and into the huddle. He led the Maulers on a determined drive that ended with a field goal, but when they kicked off, the Rangers return man raced down the sideline for a touchdown. The Rangers were ahead by seven.

Marly said a prayer as the Maulers got the ball. Bobby was under center just a foot or so away from a three-hundred-fifty-pound nose tackle with only his center to keep the monster out of his face. It seemed like hours before the handoff, centuries as Bobby dodged a tackle and threw downfield to his tight end who'd run a pattern up the middle.

She cheered as the receiver leaped, wrestled the ball out of the hands of a Ranger defender and cut downfield. Touchdown! Bobby had just thrown a seventy-yard touchdown pass, his longest as a pro. Marly stood and screamed, oblivious to the incredulous looks of the Rangers fans around her. Her man had come through in the clutch, but now he lay on the ground holding his knee. Not for long, but long enough to make Marly's heart practically stop beating until he got back up and limped to the huddle.

"Thank God!"

They went for a two-point conversion, made it on a pass from Bobby to the same man who'd caught the touchdown pass. The Maulers were ahead by one, but there were still nearly nine minutes left in the third quarter, plus the whole fourth quarter to go. The next Rangers possession ate nearly seven minutes, mostly with short ground gains. Weldon wasn't passing as much now, and Marly wondered if he was getting tired. After all, he was thirty-eight or thirty-nine years old.

He was also one of the all-time best. He showed that on the next play by throwing a perfect pass for another touchdown. Now the Rangers were up by six points and there was a minute left in the quarter.

When the Maulers took the field again, Marly held her breath. But nothing happened. The Maulers went three and out as the third quarter ended. Both teams seemed to be off a little as they ate up the clock for twelve more minutes without scoring.

When there were just three minutes to go, Bobby came out throwing. In only three plays, the Maulers had a one-point lead again. But the Rangers still had thirty seconds. The game wasn't won yet. Marly's heart nearly stopped when Weldon took them to the ten-yard line with three seconds to play when he called the last time-out.

She couldn't bear to look. The Rangers kicker was deadly accurate from this close, and the Maulers hadn't blocked a field goal all year. Eyes closed, she prayed for the guy to miss, or for the Maulers to get a hand on the ball. When moans and curses surrounded her, she opened her eyes. The Maulers had blocked what would have been a sure three-pointer, and they'd held on and won against an incredibly tough foe.

Standing, tears running down her cheeks, Marly hurried to the gate, flashed the press pass he'd sent along with her ticket and moved onto the field, just in time to catch Bobby and give him a huge, wet-mouthed kiss.

"Great game, honey." She stroked his sweaty face. "Is your knee okay?"

"It is, now that you're here. Thanks for coming."

"Love you, big guy," she murmured as he turned to go to the locker room.

* * * * *

"Wish I didn't have to send you out there." Coach Lyle's usual booming voice was at about half-strength, and he looked pale when he came out of the interview room and stopped in front of Bobby. "Those reporters are out for blood. Apparently one of the women the idiots mauled has started bleeding internally and may end up dying. Just keep your cool. I don't want the entire damn world thinking all the Maulers literally live up to the name."

Now Bobby's head ached to match his sore, taped knee. "I'll try." These interviews hadn't gotten to be fun, but Bobby had managed to control his nerves a little better with each trip before the press corps. At least he thought he had. He doubted his dripping forehead had much to do with his damp hair, and he tugged nervously at the knot in his tie. "What the hell do I say when they ask me about Willis and Mort?"

"As little as possible. Platitudes about innocent until proven guilty, maybe a comment about how much you missed Willis on the field today. You can even say you've been told not to comment further when they start going for your throat. Good luck."

Good luck indeed. Bobby would not only be facing a hostile bunch of reporters, he'd be looking at Marly while he sweated blood, because he'd already glanced inside and spotted her in the second row of reporters. Why the fuck had he sent her a press pass along with her game ticket?

He recalled her teasing him about being nervous before his first interview. Well, he was more nervous now.

Damn it, doing interviews was part of his job. Most folks would say it was less dangerous than staring over his center's back at nose tackles big enough to kill him without putting forth much effort. Bobby doubted the reporters would literally knock him down and stomp on him the way defenses wanted to do so badly, but they had the power to make being trampled seem to be a better option. "I'll be okay, Coach." *If I don't lose my voice or say something I'll regret.* He squared his shoulders, stepped into the interview room and strode to the microphone, making an effort not to limp and bring on more questions.

This wouldn't take long, he hoped, because he wanted to get Marly alone. He tightened a fist around the ring box in his pants pocket. Hers was the only smiling face in the room. Glad she was there for him, he shot her a heartfelt grin.

"So what do you think of your teammates now, Rookie?"

"What does it feel like to throw passes to a thug who assaults women?"

Marly wanted to turn around and whack the reporter behind her who'd just bellowed the question. She hoped Bobby didn't feel he had to answer. It had been bad enough, watching Coach's face turn red then deathly pale as he fielded questions. Now she focused on Bobby's face, tried to lend him the support he wasn't likely to get from the LA reporters.

Bobby cleared his throat, took the mike off its stand. "Okay. I know and believe that professional athletes should set good examples. From what I've heard, two of our players exercised poor judgment yesterday, and I apologize for that. But I'm just a player. I'm not a team spokesman, so I won't be talking about what happened or what I may think about it. If you want to ask me about the game, I'll be happy to answer your questions."

Then he smiled straight at Marly. "Marly, come up here. Guys, Marly's one of the Maulers cheerleaders. She flew out today to see the game. She's also the woman I love. You want a piece of news, try this on for size…"

He wasn't, was he? She was going to kill him as soon as she got him to herself. As Marly made her way onto the platform, inwardly seething, she hoped she wasn't shaking so much that everybody would notice. Did her hair look okay after getting whipped around in the wind? She'd kill Bobby. The big lug should have asked her first if it was okay for him to call her up there in front of all these people.

But he'd just told the world he loved her, at least those few million folks who were tuned in to ESPN or the NFL Network postgame interview. Oh God, that would include her dad and brothers, wouldn't it? Taking a calming breath, she told herself this would be okay. After all, she was no shrinking violet. She loved performing in front of a crowd and Bobby knew it.

She gave the assembled reporters her brightest smile, and when she got to Bobby, she dragged his head down and gave him an enthusiastic kiss and hug. "Show-off," he whispered before wrapping one arm around her and turning her so they both were facing the reporters. Then he looked straight into her eyes.

"Marly Ragusa, will you marry me?" There was no mistaking the words, recorded as they were for everybody to replay.

Her eyes blurred from tears that had started rolling down her cheeks. She really was going to kill him now. No, she was going to hug him tighter than the Rangers linebackers had been doing most of the afternoon. "What? Omigod, Bobby."

"Will you marry me?" This time his words were soft, husky, meant for her alone. His hand tightened at her waist and he pulled her even closer. "Please?"

There'd be no mistaking her reply. She spoke out, so even the vultures in the back of the room could hear. "Yes, I'll marry you, Bobby Anthony." Her heart pounded when he set a small box on the dais, opened it, and held a ring up to catch the light from the strobes. And the reporters stared, apparently distracted for the moment from their line of vicious questioning.

Marly gulped. She could hardly believe Bobby had actually gone out and bought this gorgeous engagement ring, so his proposal must not have been just a spur-of-the-moment impulse intended to take the reporters' attention away from what had happened. Unless...

Apparently he guessed what she'd been thinking. "I bought this for you yesterday after practice. I'm hoping you'll wear it." The look he gave her held a little apology, but she couldn't be too mad when he slipped the sparkling diamond solitaire onto her ring finger then brought her hand to his lips. "I'd intended to take you out for dinner and give this to you over dessert, but then I thought why not do it here, so your folks and my mom can watch us on TV."

Marly felt tears sliding down her cheeks. She couldn't help it. And she could barely wait to show Bobby just how much she loved him...wanted him. Anytime, any place. She could hardly wait to be in the quiet intimacy of their bed, wrapped around each other, him buried deep inside her, a physical reflection of the promise he'd just made to be connected to her forever. "Better let your guests ask you a few questions, hadn't you?" she asked instead, and the reporters cheered. "I've got something for you, too, but later when we're alone."

For the life of her, Marly couldn't remember a word Bobby said after he turned back to the microphones and tackled the reporters' shouted questions. She was glad when he cut off the questions quickly and herded her off the platform and out the door.

"I'll take that kiss now, for real." Stopping in a hallway, Bobby lifted her off the floor, backed her against the wall and took her mouth. "Welcome to LA, Ms. Marly. How about we go find the nearest horizontal surface and celebrate our win."

She'd drink to that.

* * * * *

"Nice room. Nice view, too." When they finally got to his room after dinner for two at one of the hotel's four-star restaurants, Marly looked out the window at a tropical courtyard. A lagoon-shaped pool glowed with reflected light from torches set around a tiki bar and in each of the lush plantings. Yesterday she wouldn't have believed she'd be here with Bobby. She still was having a hard time digesting the fact he'd asked her to marry him on national TV.

She barely managed to avoid pinching herself. Bobby loved her and she adored him, too. The nagging doubts wouldn't quite go away—she knew he'd be tempted and wasn't a hundred percent positive he wouldn't succumb—but she shoved those fears firmly to the back of her mind.

He came up behind her and nibbled at her earlobe. "One thing I've learned this season is that all hotel rooms are pretty much alike. The view from this one is pretty spectacular though, but nowhere near as gorgeous as you. Come here, my brand-new fiancée."

When she turned and settled in his arms, she started to kiss him then pulled away just a little. Enough, though, that he felt her withdrawal. It stunned him until she asked, "Where's Ellis?"

Was that what had her suddenly reluctant to get up close and personal? "He moved over to the room Willis and Mort vacated when they got slapped into jail cells. Coach thought you and I might like some privacy, but if you want Ellis to join us, I'll give him a call." Unlike some of Bobby's teammates who occasionally bragged about their nights of debauchery with groupies in the plural, Ellis wasn't likely to accept an invitation to join a *ménage a trois*. The man was squeaky clean and still wild about his wife after more than ten years together.

He wished he were as certain Marly wouldn't take him up on the offer. The idea of sharing her made him want to hit something, which surprised him because he'd never before felt so possessive of a lover. As a matter of fact he and one of his college roommates had once gotten it on with one very kinky coed and he'd thoroughly enjoyed the action. But now he found he wanted to keep Marly strictly for himself. "Well, baby, do you want to take on two of us?"

She reached up and stroked his cheek, and when she did her smile lit up the whole room and made him feel warm inside, too. "Not really. I know from experience that you don't need any help. You've never failed to satisfy me and you know it. Now, before your head swells so big it won't fit through doors, where's that horizontal surface you were telling me about before we left the stadium?"

"Right through that door, the one next to the mini-bar. Are you ready?"

"Sure. I'm fine, but the plane ride left me a little stiff."

Bobby laughed. "Just being around you keeps me stiff."

"You're so bad." Marly stood on tiptoe and placed a wet kiss on his neck just below his earlobe. The warm, smooth caress of her tongue sent shivers all the way to his toes. Not to mention that it coaxed his cock to full attention.

Feeling her warm body flush against him had him determined to ignore the knee throbbing behind a tight elastic wrap. There was nothing wrong with the rest of him, and he figured the knee would forgive him. Saying nothing, he scooped her up in his arms and strode through the bedroom door, determined not to limp. He was intent not to do anything that would slow down the progress toward getting them naked and letting him warm his cock in her sweet cunt.

"Bet I can get undressed before you can." He shed his jacket, shirt and tie before she managed to get off her loose-fitting sweater. "Slowpoke."

She shot him a sexy smile as she unfastened her jeans and toed off her shoes. "No fair, you got a head start."

"I did, didn't I? How about if I watch while you catch up?" He stared at her body now clad only in a lacy red bra and thong. His ring sparkled in the lamplight, reminding him that he'd staked his claim. God but she was beautiful, not just outside but inside, too. "You're so fucking hot. And you belong to me now."

"That's right, I do. Does this mean you belong to me, too?" She wiggled her finger, looked down at the ring before sliding that sexy thong down and off. "Like what you see?"

"Oh yeah. I'm yours to do with however you want. But then you already know that. Get rid of that bra and come here, I can't wait to taste you."

And he did. Tossing away the blanket and coverlet, Bobby laid her down on the bed and knelt beside her. More like, he took a knee the way he sometimes did on the field the final play of a game the team had already won, because he balanced on his right knee while keeping the left one bent but off the bed. As if she were the most precious thing in the world, he stroked her. His warm breath tickled her belly. Apparently he felt that putting a ring on her finger had settled all the questions about their relationship, and now he seemed satisfied to go slow, pay homage to every inch of her.

She loved it, loved her man who could laugh one minute, become deadly serious the next. But in the sensually charged space that surrounded them, her own hormones kicked into gear, made her restless under his seeking hands. When she shifted and brought her knees up, he reached down and massaged her feet. "You've got pretty feet. Pretty everything."

"Glad you think so, honey." Marly had never thought having her feet rubbed could be such a turn-on, but it was. The firm brush of Bobby's thumb across her instep sent staccato jolts of electricity up her leg, straight to her wet, swollen pussy. She wanted to grab his massive shoulders, drag him up her body, feel the weight and heat of him all over.

But he seemed content to touch her, almost innocently, as if they were youngsters just discovering all the sensual ways they could give each other pleasure. She'd never felt so cherished or so in love as well as in lust with anybody. Ever. "That feels so good," she murmured when he slid huge hands up her lower legs then stopped to tickle behind her knees. "Don't stop."

"I won't, baby. Not ever." Bending, he took her lips, a slow, sweet claiming that made her want to scream for more. She didn't though. Instead she raised a hand to his cheek, traced the high cheekbones, felt the slight rasp of his light evening stubble against her palm. When he ran the tip of his tongue against her lips, she opened to let him in.

His rigid cock throbbed against her side, its heat a reminder that he was as ready as she, yet apparently determined to hold out until she screamed for release. She felt her pussy weeping, squirmed when the hot liquid made its way to her butt. Her nipples ached for his hands, his wet mouth. "You're torturing me," she said, gasping for breath when he broke the kiss.

"All you have to do is tell me what you want." When he met her gaze, she saw barely masked lust in his expression.

She dragged his hands to her breasts, gasped when he rolled the swollen nipples between his thumbs and forefingers. "Oh yes, that hurts so good." It was as though by pinching that rigid nub of flesh, he shocked her into full, screaming need. "Don't make me wait any longer. Just fuck me. Fuck me hard."

"Thought you'd never ask, baby." Rising onto both knees, he swung a leg over hers, flinching just enough for her to notice as he settled between her legs.

His knee. He'd favored it before. It had to be hurting him now to bend and rest his weight on it. But she was too needy to stop now, and she could tell from the heat in his expression that he was, too. Trembling, she took the condom he handed her and smoothed it over his shaft.

When he shifted and took her in one hard thrust, she moaned. Wet, arousing sounds of sex filled her ears. Her climax was coming fast. The heat. The sense of surrender…the feeling of acceptance, of sharing. Pressure built as he fucked her deeper, harder. Her clit throbbed at the contact he made with every inward thrust, each grinding motion of his hips.

Pressure built inside her, demanding release. She dug her fingers into his muscular upper arms. Needing. Wanting. Loving. Sensations bombarded her. The mingled smells of sex with his cologne and hers. The lusty look in his eyes that reflected her own. The heat of his pulsing cock pressing against her vaginal wall, the sounds of their labored breathing.

"Come for me, baby. I can't hold out much longer."

The bubble inside her shattered at his command. Suddenly all the sensations inside her came together, made her pussy contract and spasm as Bobby thrust deep one more time and bellowed with his own release. Then he rolled over, taking her with him and cradling her in his arms. "Love you, baby. Gotta rest the knee, though. The doc says it's just a stretched ligament but it hurts like hell."

"I'm sorry."

He held her a little tighter. "Not half as sorry as I am. I'd planned to make love with you all night long then sleep on the plane ride back to Memphis. Didn't count on banging up my knee during the game."

Snuggling closer, Marly laid one hand over his side. "Rest now. You should have told me you were hurting. There are ways to make love that wouldn't have put stress on your knee. We'll have plenty of time to play when we get home."

But they wouldn't, at least not right away. How the fuck was he going to tell her the guest he was expecting would be staying at his condo? He was pretty damn sure Marly was going to throw a fit because Tina was a girl.

Bobby swore softly. There was no way to do this graciously, so he might as well get it over with now.

No, he'd get rid of the condom first. "Be right back."

As he rinsed himself and watched water bubbling over the washcloth, he told himself what a fucking coward he was. Determined not to be a wimp any longer, he limped back to bed and stretched out beside Marly.

He propped his head up on one hand, looked down at the silky cascade of her hair on the white pillow. "I told you about us having company, didn't I?"

"Uh-huh." Marly stretched and yawned. "When's he coming?"

He? Bobby only wished it were a guy. It took a lot of effort but he managed to look her in the eye. "*She* may be there before we get home."

Her look reminded him of thunderclouds gathering before a gullywasher back home. "Don't tell me you've got a girlfriend coming for a visit. Not right after you asked me to marry you." As though she wanted to be anywhere but close to him, she sat up and scooted up to the head of the bed, dragging the coverlet over her.

"Not a girlfriend, babe. An old friend who happens to be a girl. She's been staying with Mom since her mother died. Her stepfather's a real asshole. The bastard has been stalking her ever since her mom died, and she's afraid of him."

Marly looked him in the eye. "Did you sleep with this girl?"

"If you mean did I fuck her, yes, a few times back when we were both in high school. I'll never lie to you, baby." He moved closer, laid a hand on her cheek. "But I never slept with her. Or asked her to marry me. Don't you know you're the only woman I want?"

When Marly finally met his gaze, he thought she really wanted to believe him—but that she still had her doubts. "I want to believe that, but it's damn hard. Why haven't you told me about this old girlfriend before? Especially since you say she's been staying with your mom?"

"Because what Tina's doing and where she's living isn't that important to me. Besides, you've never asked about the other women I've laid, not since our first night together." Fuck it. Marly hadn't been a virgin, either. Why did she seem to believe he should have been? "I haven't asked about your old lovers, either. I assumed they didn't matter anymore."

"Well, I thought that too, until you come telling me, out of the blue, that this Tina's coming to live with you. With us. Well, put that out of your head, because it's not happening. I'm staying at home as long as she's living with you."

Oh hell. Why had Mom dumped Tina on him? Why hadn't the sheriff locked up her pervert stepfather a long time ago and thrown away the key? "Please, Marly. I know this is a little awkward—well, a lot awkward—but it doesn't have to be. You're my fiancée, you belong in my bed. Together we can find Tina a job and a place to stay."

"You're insane if you think I'm going to share you with her, even for a little while. I may have to share you with the fantasies of a lot of lascivious groupies, but I sure as hell don't have to step aside and make a place for your down-and-out ex-girlfriend. You make enough money. If you feel you owe her, rent her an apartment of her own. I...am...not, repeat not, sharing space with her, and if you want me, you won't be having her live in your place, either." With that, Marly got up and wrapped the sheet around her. "I'm sleeping on the couch."

Bobby wasn't surprised at her reaction. He was all too aware of her insecurities. But at least she didn't throw her ring back in his face. For a long time he lay there, his head throbbing almost enough to make him forget about his sore knee, trying to decide if he should let her cool down or follow her and fuck her until she saw reason. Women!

He balled up a pillow and buried his head in it. He'd get no sleep tonight, no rest on the trip home. But it would all work out. Marly would see Tina and realize right away that she had no competition.

Meanwhile he wanted Marly in his arms. Getting up and moving gingerly on his aching leg, Bobby went to the couch. "You belong with me," he growled, scooping her up and taking her back to bed. "Get it in your head, I don't want Tina or any other woman, I want you. Not just now but always."

"Beast. You've got no business walking on that knee, much less carrying me around like I'm a stuffed toy or something." She still sounded pissed, but not as much as she had when he first told her about Tina. "Come over here, warm my back. You need to rest that knee."

He figured they'd work this out, just as they'd work out a lot of disagreements over the coming years. Rolling onto his side, he lay down, tucked her tush against his groin and enjoyed the closeness he wasn't about to give up on.

Chapter Six

Tina set her luggage down in what she figured was the guest bedroom, sighed. What she really would have liked to do was rest, but she imagined Bobby would be home in a few hours, and the least she could do was feed him. After all, he'd opened up his place to her.

She felt awkward, here in this elegant condo that outshone any house she'd ever seen yet didn't remind her at all of Bobby. Maybe if she kept busy…

Not even the beef stew and peach cobbler she put together from the sparse supply of comfort food in the sparkling kitchen took Tina's mind off why she'd left Hedgecock and come to live for a little while on Bobby's charity. Her skin still crawled when she remembered her last encounter with Edgar Garcia. The stench of cheap beer and even cheaper perfume had almost choked her as he held her down and raped her in the back room of the school cafeteria where she'd been tidying up after the lunch crowd left.

She'd scrubbed and scrubbed and scrubbed, but still she felt the humiliation, the filth…the terrible fear that had driven her here, to safety. No matter what, she'd never go back, never risk encountering her bastard of a stepfather again—unless she had the protection of a strong man.

That man wouldn't be Bobby. She'd known for years that he thought of her as a good pal, not a potential bride. Besides, she heard on the evening news yesterday that he'd asked one of the Maulers cheerleaders to marry him. Marly Ragusa. A dark-haired beauty with a brilliant smile, she'd seemed fully comfortable up on that podium when Bobby had introduced her to a crowd of reporters.

Tina would have sunk into the floor if she were ever put in that position. But then she wouldn't be. Men didn't flaunt girls like her, and she was glad. She'd find a job, a little apartment she could afford and maybe, someday, a man who'd love her the way she'd dreamed of all her life. A simple man with simple needs, not a superstar athlete like her first teenage lover.

* * * * *

"You'll like Tina. Everybody does." Bobby spoke over the low purr of the engine as he drove himself and Marly out of the Maulers practice field parking lot where the team bus had dropped them off. "Let's go by your folks' place first, though, and pick up a few of your things."

"No." Who did Bobby think he was, to expect her to merrily accept the presence of his old—probably his first—girlfriend? "I said I'd meet her. I didn't say I'd live with you when she's staying there."

"Looks to me like you'd want to be there to make sure I'm not fucking her, which I won't be." He ground out the words, as though he'd taken just about all her petulance he was going to endure. "Tina is my friend. I'm going to help her get settled here, and if you love me like you say you do, you're going to help."

Marly wished she could shake the feeling that there had to be more than friendship that made him so damned determined to help this Tina out. But she couldn't imagine any of her brothers having gone out of their way to help old girlfriends. "Are you sure you want me to?"

"Yes. I want you and Tina to be friends. How many times do I have to tell you it's you I love? You I want to sleep with every night, and someday to have my kids?" Bobby was gripping the steering wheel so hard that his knuckles were turning white.

She twisted her new ring around, stared at the beautiful diamond, recalled the college boyfriend who'd dumped her their sophomore year for a high-school lover he'd gotten pregnant over Christmas break. Maybe she should tell Bobby about Wes. But no. Even four years later, the humiliation still stung her deep inside, and the last thing she wanted was Bobby's pity. "I'll try. It's just that every woman on Earth seems to want what's in your pants."

Bobby's laugh sounded forced. "I doubt that, and you're the only one I want to want me that way. Come on, smile for me."

Marly tried, but she still wasn't convinced. After all, he was a rising star, and according to the gossip columns, a lot of the studs on the football field scored more often in groupies' beds than in the games. Even some of the married ones weren't averse to playing around. A few of them were even wide-open about their cheating. Longtime star Dave Delaney was almost as famous for his bedroom heroics as he was for having tossed some huge number of touchdown passes in his many years in the league. "Do you know Dave Delaney?" she blurted, recalling that the aging quarterback hailed from Bobby's hometown. Bobby seemed different, but...

"No. He graduated from high school when I was maybe a year old. As far as I know, Dave never came back to Hedgecock once he left for college. I guess we'll meet later on this year though, since his team's scheduled to play the Maulers. What does Dave have to do with us?"

"He's supposedly one of the biggest womanizers around the league."

Bobby reached over and pinched her thigh. "So you think there might be something in the Hedgecock water that turns guys into satyrs? Think about Keith, baby. He didn't play around while his wife was alive. Doesn't now, so far as I know. He kind of shoots that theory down."

"I guess you're right." Marly figured she'd give in. After all, at least part of her worry stemmed from a putdown that was ancient history. It had nothing to do with Bobby. When he pulled into his parking spot at the condo, she leaned across the console and gave him a kiss. "It's just that I love you so much, big guy."

"Love you, too. Remember that." He slid out of the truck and strode around to her side. "Let's go meet Tina."

* * * * *

Even before they stepped off the elevator and opened the door to Bobby's condo, Marly smelled something savory. Something delicious that she bet Tina had spent all morning cooking to draw Bobby in.

The bitch. Sure, the woman was just Bobby's friend. Well, as far as Marly was concerned, it was clear she wanted to be much more. Trying to keep a pleasant expression on her face, Marly stepped inside ahead of Bobby and looked around for signs of the other woman in the entry foyer.

Nothing. No suitcases. Just that damn enticing smell of home-cooked food.

"Tina?" Bobby sounded a little bit too pleased at the prospect of seeing his guest, at least it sounded that way to Marly.

"Bobby? I was hoping you'd be home in time for lunch." Tina stepped out from the guest bedroom and ran toward the sound of Bobby's voice.

"It sure smells good." Bobby stepped forward to hug a slender—almost skinny, Marly thought uncharitably—dishwater blonde who looked like Texas cowgirls she'd seen on TV in her tight jeans and a leather vest over a nondescript long-sleeved shirt.

Cowboy boots? Yeah, Tina had those on, too. Marly tried to hold onto her temper when the hug went on much longer than she thought it should. Damn it, Tina was nuzzling at his neck. Friend, hell.

Focusing on Bobby's declaration of love a few minutes earlier, and the warm feel of his ring on her left ring finger, Marly managed to stay quiet, let the disturbing scene play out.

"Tina, this is Marly Ragusa. My fiancée." Bobby finally stepped away and pulled Marly to his side. "Marly, Tina Black."

Tina gave Marly the once-over, at least that's the way Marly considered the long, hard look. "Hello. I'm sorry, I didn't mean to be impolite. It just surprises me that you're…"

"Marly's Italian-American, not Mexican like your stepfather," Bobby interjected, drawing her closer. "Not that it would make any difference to me. You two are gonna get along just fine. Is whatever you've been cooking ready to eat, Tina?"

Tina's face brightened. Marly conceded that she was pretty when she smiled. "Yes, it's ready. I thought we'd just eat at the kitchen table."

Cozy. Real cozy. It pissed Marly off that this woman had cooked a meal in Bobby's kitchen before she'd had a chance to show off her own cooking. The only eating she'd done here was carry-out from her dad's restaurant—and they'd nibbled it at the bar while looking down at the river and counting the boats. "Whatever you're cooking smells awfully good," she said, remembering her manners even as she watched Tina set an extra plate and silverware on the table.

She hadn't planned on me coming with Bobby. Marly bit her tongue to keep from laying into the cowgirl. She just hoped the woman hadn't dared to stash her belongings in Bobby's bedroom.

By the time they finished off dessert, Bobby felt like a bone being fought over by two pit bulls. Marly was barely being civil, and Tina? Tina seemed determined in her quiet way to repeatedly point out their shared past to Marly. "This was good," he told Tina. "I'm tired, though. Make yourself at home. Marly and I are going to go over to her parents' and get some of her things. Tomorrow we'll try to figure out what kind of work you'd like to do." *And get you set up somewhere else before the tension here drives me crazy.*

Why had his mom done this to him? Hell, he knew. He'd have to have been an ogre to resent Tina being here when he knew some of what had been going on with her stepdad back in Hedgecock. "Come on, baby, let's grab your things."

* * * * *

Tension reverberated through the truck cab. This wasn't the way a girl should feel when taking her brand-new fiancé home to show her ring off to her parents. Marly took in the tight set of Bobby's jaw, the way his knuckles turned white when he gripped the steering wheel. Even the usually seductive purr of the Escalade's powerful engine took on an eerie tone.

Why wouldn't he say something?

Why wouldn't she say something? Anything, even getting his ass chewed out, would have been better than the heavy silence that had set in the minute they got in the truck. Bobby's knee throbbed, but it was the pregnant silence ringing in his ears that really bothered him. "Marly?"

"Yes."

"What's wrong, baby?"

"Nothing." He watched Marly toss an unruly curl behind her left ear. "Oh fuck it. Everything's wrong. Maybe I'm dead wrong, but I feel like Tina's out to get you. Not like an old high-school-girlfriend-turned-buddy, but like a woman who wants to get back with a guy she never got over."

Bobby swore as he got in the left turn lane and pulled in at a scenic overlook above the river. "You hit it on the head, baby. You are dead wrong." He got out of the car and limped around to her side. "We're going to have a nice, long talk, and we're not going anywhere until you believe I meant it when I said 'I love you'. Come on, there's a bench over by the river."

He thought she moved too slowly, as if she were less than anxious to sit with him and watch leaves fall from the big water oak next to the bench where they were headed. Maybe it wasn't the leaves, but him that she didn't want coming so close. "Slowpoke." He made sure his tone was light, hoping she'd respond to the gentle tease.

"Don't patronize me. I'm coming with you. I'm probably going to let you persuade me my instincts are off-base." Marly paused then let Bobby take her hand and bring her close enough that he couldn't help smelling her cologne. She settled her gaze on the dark shadow of a beard on his chin. "Why don't you shave every day like most guys do?"

"Scruff makes me look a little older. And a little meaner, for the benefit of the defenses we play against. I would have shaved after lunch, though, if you hadn't dragged me out as soon as we polished off that peach cobbler Tina made… 'Cause I don't want to tear apart your pretty skin."

"I don't mind. It feels pretty good. I just wondered. Thought maybe you were imitating another number four." Brushing off leaves from the bench, she sat down.

"Nope. I'm not trying to be a Brett Favre clone, even though I idolize him for the way he plays, like he thoroughly loves what he's doing on the field." Bobby figured Marly was trying to avoid talking about what had made her draw a curtain of silence around her.

That wasn't going to work. But what could he say? He'd already told her he loved her, wanted to marry her and for her to have his kids someday. Bobby had trouble understanding that his gorgeous Marly might be jealous of a woman he hadn't fucked for more than five years. "Got a mirror in your purse?"

"Yes. Why?"

"Because I want you to take it out and look at yourself. Tell me honestly, why in hell would you think I want Tina when I can wake up looking at you?" What he felt for Marly wasn't just because of her looks, but that was a start.

"Looks aren't everything." Marly put the mirror back in her purse and zipped it up. "Is that the only reason you noticed me?"

Oh shit. What had he done now? "Of course not. Not that I mind that you're the most beautiful woman I ever saw, or that you're fun to be with, in bed and out of it."

"Tell me about you and Tina. And don't leave out anything." She stared down at the river, at a paddlewheeler that was making its way from St. Louis to New Orleans.

Bobby was getting madder by the minute. "I already told you, baby, Tina and I fucked under the high school bleachers after some of the football games my junior year. We went to the local movies together maybe half a dozen times, and we occasionally had a hamburger and fries at the restaurant across from the school." He took in a deep breath. "I had more intimate relationships with a dozen or so girls at college, but they don't mean anything to me now either, at least not in a sexual way."

"That's what Wes said, before he went home on spring break and married his pregnant high-school girlfriend."

A green monster he just realized he had bubbled up inside him, made him want to kill someone. "Who the fuck is Wes?"

Marly had her head bowed, and Bobby suspected she was hiding tears. "Someone I dated in college. Ancient history."

"Ancient history be damned. This bastard had to have hurt you bad to have made you feel you can't trust me now. Have I given you reason to believe I'd cheat on you with anybody, old high-school girlfriend or not?"

When she looked up at him, tears floated in her eyes, as if they were insisting on escape. "No. You haven't given me reason to think you would go out of your way to..."

"Fuck everything in skirts that sends out signals she's available?" Bobby was furious. Unlike a lot of athletes he knew, he'd always been pretty careful. Sure, he'd had sex for sex's sake. Who hadn't? But he'd had no desire to touch anybody but Marly since they'd started dating—even since they first met in the parking lot during rookie camp. "But you apparently believe I'll stray first time my eyes start to wander. I won't." He took her hand, held it on his thigh.

"How do you know that?"

Marly didn't protest when Bobby slid her hand higher, close enough that her fingers came in contact with his half-hard sex. "Because I've never been in love with a woman before. Never cared about anybody the way I care for you. And I've never before lived with a pretty constant hard-on because I was constantly thinking about getting into anybody else's pussy."

"I know. I just—"

"Put a little faith in me, baby. I won't let you down. Ever. Not even if there is a prettier woman on this earth and someday I find her, which I don't believe will ever happen. We're gonna be good together. Really good. I'm gonna be there when our babies are born and when they need a dad to cheer for them in high school and college. I know what it's like to grow up without my father, even though Mom did her best to make up for him not being there."

Marly sniffed. "I'll try. Shall we go to my house now so I can grab some things? Mom's dying to see this." She held up her left hand then reached around to give Bobby a quick kiss. "You know, I do love you. Really. I'm just so afraid of losing you."

Bobby knew that. He didn't care much for the unexpected lack of self-confidence he'd discovered in Marly, but he figured he could be careful, protect her from the mere idea that he might be on the prowl, even when he wasn't. "You won't, baby. I love you. Now let's go show off this rock to your folks, pick up your clothes and hurry back to our bedroom. It's been too damn long since I've been able to make love with you."

Chapter Seven

൩

Except for the shadow of her insecurity, it was the announcement Marly had always dreamed of making to her delighted parents. They'd loved Bobby from the first day they met him, anyhow. Her mom's eyes widened when she first saw the ring. "Oh my."

"You got her ring at Tiffany's, right?" Her dad lifted her hand so he could examine it more closely. "You've got good taste, son. Welcome to the family."

Bobby grinned. "Yes sir. I bought it Saturday at the store on Rodeo Drive. Thanks for the welcome."

Marly hadn't realized Dad knew so much about jewelry. All she knew was that the ring Bobby gave her was magnificent, much more than she'd ever imagined the man she loved would choose.

Yes, Bobby fit in with her family. In some ways he reminded Marly of her dad, who hadn't let success go to his head, either. They still lived in this old-fashioned brick house in a neighborhood that had gone way down before new owners started buying and fixing up the run-down properties. While Bobby lived in a posh condo, she sensed he'd pick comfort over chic when they bought a place of their own.

"That big old brownstone on the corner is up for sale. You might want to take a look. It should be a steal right now, the economy being as it is. Needs some renovation, but you might get a tax break because it probably qualifies as a historic preservation project. The man who built it back in the 1890s later became a congressman."

Oh no, Mom. "Bobby will probably be traded soon after Keith gets over his shoulder injury. Besides, we're not getting married right away."

"Of course not! It will take a year to plan your wedding." Mom turned to Bobby. "Are you Catholic?"

"Yes." Marly could tell Bobby was uncomfortable. As he'd told her after the first time he'd picked her up here, *there are Catholics...and then there are Catholics. I'm more of the Christmas and Easter sort of a Catholic.*

That was just one good reason she didn't think it would have been a good idea for them to buy a place within walking distance of her childhood home. Not that there weren't others. "Mom, we just got engaged. There's no reason to start planning our wedding. If you want the truth, we may just take a notion and do it one weekend, with you and Dad and Bobby's mom as witnesses."

"Dad and I will give you the kind of wedding you'll always remember," Mom said, apparently not willing to give up the idea of a huge blowout with half of Memphis in attendance.

"We'll see. Honestly, we haven't thought about weddings yet. We just got engaged yesterday." Bobby held Marly's hand, and its warmth snaked through her veins. "We'd better grab some of her stuff and get on back to my place. After all, we have a guest to entertain."

Obviously, he wanted to go as much as she did, but he was being diplomatic about it. Marly guessed it was better to use Tina as an excuse than to tell the parents to back off or that what they're looking for right now was a bed—any bed—as long as they both were in it.

"It's okay, kids. I've got to get to the restaurant before the chef decides to try another new entrée like the one that bombed last week." Dom stood, held out his hand to Bobby. "Congratulations. And welcome to the family."

"Thank you, sir."

"Mama, why don't you come on down to work with me? I'm sure the kids can handle packing without our help. Marly, be sure to lock the door when you leave." With that, Dad got up and smiled at her and Bobby. "You know, I've never trusted anybody else my daughter was dating with the keys to our house. But I like you, Bobby. And I trust you to take care of Marly."

"I'll take good care of her. We won't be here long, just enough to get Marly some clothes. We really do need to head on home."

* * * * *

The first thing Bobby noticed when they went into Marly's bedroom was the four-poster bed with sheer curtains and a ruffled floral canopy that matched the coverlet. Curtains that hung over the sheers over wide windows that overlooked a huge pine tree in the backyard. They'd made love here before, one afternoon when her parents had both been out.

It was definitely a girly room, yet irresistible. Bobby wanted to stake his claim, realize another of the midnight fantasies he enjoyed while on the road. "Come here, baby. The clothes can wait. I want to make love to you."

She turned away from the closet and shot him a knowing grin. "Here? Mom will have a fit." Then she laughed. "You know, besides my dad and brothers, you're the only man who has ever set foot in here."

"I'm glad. Now take off your clothes and crawl in bed." His heart pounded in his chest as he watched her peel off her sweater, and his hands trembled when he worked the buckle loose on his belt. "God, but you're hot." *And mine. All mine.* When his jeans hit the floor, he stepped out of them. His cock throbbed when she started to shimmy out of those tight jeans.

"So are you." The hungry look on her face sent blood rushing to his sex, made his pulse race. "We'd better turn back the covers or you'll be in a heap of trouble."

"Honey, it's you that Daddy would skin alive. But that's okay. I have the feeling he gave his blessing by leaving us all alone today." After Marly laid back the covers, she stretched out across the bed Bobby imagined she'd slept in ever since she graduated from her crib. "Come on, you talk a good act. Now it's time to deliver."

Bobby's cock told him it was past time. Retrieving a condom from his wallet, he let his jeans slide back to the floor. "I'm ready, baby," he told her, tossing the prophylactic next to her on the bed. Being careful not to put pressure on his sore knee, he crawled into her cozy cocoon and gathered her in his arms. "You're gonna have to help me here. The knee feels even worse today than it did last night."

"Oh. Maybe we should pretend we're kids, experimenting with sex for the first time. Worried that my folks are going to barge in, or worse, one of my brothers. They put the fear of God into some of my boyfriends when I was in high school."

"Did they?" The prospect made Bobby hornier than ever. Taking risks did that to him, had since he was a high-school stud gettin' it on under the bleachers after the lights went off. "I'm pretty sure I can handle an irate brother or two."

Marly leaned back, shot him a questioning look. "You don't know my brothers, honey. You haven't seen them mad."

"I have seen them, though, and I'm pretty sure I outweigh either of them by at least seventy-five pounds. Don't worry about my hide, it's tough. Remember I play football for a living."

"Braggart. Come on, show me how you're going to take care of me."

She ran a finger down his chest, circled his navel then closed a fist around his raging hard-on. He imitated her motion, ending up with two fingers in her wet, warm pussy and his thumb moving in circles around her swollen clit. "Like this?"

"God, yes."

Bobby liked the way she purred when he touched her, felt more a hero when they made love than he did after a perfect touchdown pass. Hating that she wasn't quite sure of him, he stroked every inch of her soft, smooth skin, inhaled her special aura of hot woman and some sort of heady cologne. Damn if it didn't smell a lot like the Confederate jasmine that grew up the sides of the Tulane dorm where he'd stayed until this spring. Tempted by her hardened pink nipples, he propped himself on an elbow and flailed first one and then the other with his tongue.

"I wonder what it would feel like to play with these if you had pierced nipples."

Marly drew his head down to her other breast, ran her fingers through his hair. "I imagine it would hurt, at least until they healed. Do you have a thing for body piercings?"

"Not really. I just wondered." Teasing now, he drew a nipple into his mouth and suckled until she squirmed and tried to pull him on top of her.

"Let's fuck now." She grabbed the condom, unwrapped it and rolled it over his cock.

This place, where she'd grown up among her loving family members, seemed more a sanctuary than Bobby would have liked, a place where fucking wasn't appropriate but gentle lovemaking was. "We're not fucking, baby, we're making love." He straddled her, cradling her head between his hands before swooping down and claiming her full, pink lips.

She tasted like the apple pie they'd eaten with her folks, as if being home had made her shelve the sassy cheerleader who had a thing for jocks. He imagined it was the room and all the memories she must have of it that lent an air of innocence, as if she were a teenage virgin eager to taste the pleasures a man could offer. Slowly, he slid his legs between hers, balancing himself as their kiss went on forever.

His cock ached. Her lubrication made it easy for him to find and fill her swollen pussy. He broke the kiss, met her heated gaze. "You're my woman. My only woman. Know that. Know I never felt about any woman the way I feel about you."

Tears came to her eyes, and she lifted her hands to his shoulders. "You're just so damn hot, I'm afraid I'll have to fight off a slew of panting women. If you weren't so irresistible I'd be looking for a guy who doesn't attract women the way picnics attract flies."

Slowly, he pulled almost out of her tight, hot cunt and slid back in, loving the heat and wetness and the way she wrapped her legs around his hips to take him deeper. "I'll help you beat the groupies away, I promise."

"We'll see. Meanwhile make love to me, fulfill the fantasies I spun alone in this bed before I met you."

"I will. I do." The tacit admission that he was the only man she'd brought to her bedroom pleased Bobby immeasurably. He didn't know why, but he knew it made him want to cherish her, protect her...love her even more than he had before. He started to move, slow and deep, holding back the urge to let himself go until he'd felt her contract around his cock and heard her little scream. "God, baby, I'm coming." Pressure built in his balls. His cock stiffened painfully then exploded, the bursts of his seed taking his breath away. He choked back his cry of release, as if it might be heard by anybody who happened to be downstairs.

They snuggled for a few minutes before Bobby got up. Usually he liked to cuddle after they made love, but not today. He felt a need to put on his clothes, grab whatever Marly wanted to take with her and leave. He was washing up at the vanity sink when Marly joined him, wrapping her arms around his waist. "You're awfully quiet."

He laughed. "I don't really feel comfortable being naked in your parents' place. I know they're not here, but..."

"Shy, are you?"

He'd never thought so. He'd fucked Tina and a couple of other high-school girls under the bleachers at the football field, had a few encounters in strange places when he was at Tulane. Like most athletes, he wasn't shy about wandering around locker rooms buck-naked, even if there were female reporters trying to get interviews. But now —

Now he didn't want his future in-laws to become aware he was in Marly's bedroom, making love instead of grabbing an armload of her clothes. Because she wasn't just any woman. He wished to hell he could drive away her doubts about that, make her believe she was all he'd ever wanted.

"I'm not exactly shy. Just careful. The picture of your dad pointing a shotgun at me isn't something I'd like to see in real time. And I'd hate for us to shock your mom. Come on, let's get the clothes you want for the next few days and get out of here."

"Okay." She followed him back to her room and began laying clothes out on the bed. "These ought to be enough for now, unless you see something else you particularly like," she told him as he was slipping his T-shirt over his head.

"I've never not liked anything you put on your hot little body. Do you have something to put this stuff in?"

"A suitcase. There are two or three in the closet." She shimmied into her jeans while he brought the suitcases in and opened them up on the bed.

They packed quickly and took the luggage to his car. As he opened the door for her, he thought about that sex toy store a few blocks away and wondered how she'd feel about experimenting a little. "You know that toy store we drive by on the way here?"

"Uh-huh. Mom had a fit when it moved in where her favorite bakery used to be. Have you tried any of the stuff they sell?"

"Nope. But I've always thought it might be fun to play."

She grinned. "It might be fun, at that. Are you offering to take me there?"

"I guess I am. Maybe we can kick our sex lives up a notch or two. We'll stop by there, then head on to Keith Connors' place. I need to talk to him in person."

* * * * *

Marly thought she'd gotten over blushing a long time ago, but she was wrong. When the adult store clerk recognized Bobby, he insisted on giving them a complete tour of the store—even the BDSM room with its scary-looking torture devices and all sorts of black leather. There were chaps that left the dummy's sex hanging out, women's bodysuits with holes cut so breasts, pussy and ass were readily touchable. When Bobby shook his head and told the clerk that wasn't exactly what he had in mind, she let out a sigh of relief. She thought. But she couldn't help imagining Bobby wearing those chaps and one of the full-face leather masks.

Laughing nervously, she helped select some milder toys, a big dildo and a set of butt plugs. "No, honey, you don't need that," she said when the clerk showed Bobby how a device called a penis enlarger would make him grow bigger and harder. When they left, they had a big bag of flavored oils, some battery-operated vibrators and the silicone plugs and dildo they'd selected first. And a blown-glass dildo Bobby threatened to fill with ice water to cool her off. "We should stop over at Keith's and get on home to entertain Tina."

"Yeah," Bobby said as he helped her climb into his truck. "Baby, I'm sorry she's here, I was looking for a lot of one-on-one time with my brand-new fiancée. You do know Keith, don't you?"

"I know who he is. I've never actually met him. Why are we stopping by there now?" At one time Marly would have drooled to actually get the chance to see the All-Pro's home, but now that she had her own quarterback, meeting Connors didn't seem all that exciting.

"I'm going to try to sell him on Tina as a live-in babysitter. Coach said the other day that if he couldn't find one, he might have to sit out the rest of the season. Apparently his mom had to go back home."

That would be good—that is, it would solve the Tina problem for Bobby. Marly wondered, though, why he was willing to move back to the bench just so he could get Tina out of his place. "Are you doing this for me?" She didn't want that.

"No. I'm doing it for me. And for Tina. She has no education past high school, and she needs a job and a safe place to live, far away from her bastard of a stepfather and with somebody strong enough to protect her from him if he should be so stupid as to follow her here. Besides, she's always liked little kids. She'll make a good nanny."

Marly couldn't imagine anybody really wanting to take on the responsibility for somebody else's children, but then Bobby had a point when he said Tina wasn't prepared for a job that required a lot of training. "Have you talked to her yet?"

"I thought I'd run it by Keith first. He may already have somebody lined up." He turned into a gated community north of the stadium and showed his ID to the guard. "Keith said he'd called down so we could go on in."

"Yes sir, he did that. You've been filling in for Mr. Connors real well so far. Would you mind signing this for me?" The guard held out a marker pen and a football that already had a lot of Maulers signatures. While Bobby signed it, he chatted easily with the stranger. Marly guessed his six weeks of filling in for Keith had lent a bit of polish she hadn't noticed when they first met.

"Here you go."

"Thanks, sir. Take the first right and drive around until you get to the first big white two-story house. That's where Mr. Connors lives."

The house was magnificent, almost like an antebellum plantation house with its carriage lights and a porch with white columns. Bobby whistled. "Well, Keith certainly didn't model this house by any back in Hedgecock. This must have been his late wife's choice."

"You're probably right. It's usually women who get the say about what style of home they want. After all, they spend more time in it than their husbands—especially if their husbands are star athletes."

"I guess so. Do you want to pick out our house when we settle down?"

"Probably. I guess we should go on in." She'd grown up comfortably well-off, but this place intimidated her. The idea that she might be expected to pick and live in a showplace like this one didn't set too well. "I hope you don't want a place this elegant."

Bobby got out of the car and opened her door to help her out. "I'm just a west Texas country boy at heart."

Marly grinned. "So is Keith."

"Yeah, but from all I've heard, he grew up wanting all the trappings of success, more than I did. His mom remarried and moved out of Hedgecock as soon as she found a rich oil man to latch onto, or anyhow that's what Mom has always said."

When they rang the doorbell, the door opened right away. An infant's cry resounded from the back of the house, and Keith Connors greeted them with a frustrated look on his face. "Sorry about my son. He doesn't seem to like me nearly as much as he does the women who work in the Maulers front office. But he doesn't like the housekeeper at all and the feeling's mutual, so he's all mine when I get him home. Come on in."

* * * * *

The room reminded Marly of the parlors in a downtown men's club, all dark wood paneling and burgundy leather upholstery on a huge sectional sofa. Barrel chairs surrounded a game table, and an ornate pool table with carved mahogany legs and a navy-blue felt top dominated one side of the room. As her feet sank into plush navy carpeting, a plaintive cry drew her to the playpen that looked incongruous in such a men-only setting. "May I see if I can calm him down?" she asked Keith who apparently was planning to ignore the baby and sprawl on one end of the sofa.

"Be my guest. I've fed him and played with him and even tried to walk him around the house, hoping something would put him to sleep. Nothing worked. Would you all like soda or beer?"

"Not me. I have a feeling this little bruiser will be a handful." Not having handled a lot of babies since she'd baby-sat for neighbors during high school, Marly bent and gingerly picked up the gorgeous little boy, who had an unmistakable ripe smell coming from his squishy butt that was encased in a bright-blue plush sleeper. "I think he needs a change, Daddy. And he might be too hot in this outfit."

"Would you? His stuff's over on the bar." Keith turned to Bobby. "This trying to take care of that little guy by myself is gonna kill me yet. Not that I'd give him up for anything."

Marly extricated a handful of her hair from the baby's fist and laid him onto a pad on the counter behind the wet bar. Two neat stacks, one of disposable diapers and the other of tiny clothes, flanked the pad, and cleaning stuff was lined up in front of the bar sink where she imagined they'd displaced bottles of cherries, bitters and other condiments for adult beverages. By then his cries had slowed down. Apparently he knew she was going to change him even before she started to unzip the sleeper. "What's your name, little fella?" It felt weird to be undressing somebody when she didn't know his name, baby or not.

"John Keith Connors, but I call him Jack. Do you have everything you need? He has a lot more stuff upstairs. I've found he gets clean enough when I hold his bottom under the faucet in the sink. There's some baby-smelling soap in that pink bottle."

"Oooh." Jack seemed to like getting clean, because his howls stopped and he broke out with a silly grin. "He seems to like water."

"Yeah. He doesn't like being dirty. I can't imagine me ever having been that particular, can you, Bobby?"

Bobby laughed. "It's hard to worry much about dirt when you make your living the way we do. I've dreamed about walking off the field someday without a bit of dirt on me or my uniform, but I don't think it will ever happen."

"Not unless they get a couple of beasts to fill out the offensive line." Keith laughed. "Are you okay over there?"

Marly diapered the wiggly Jack then kept him still with one hand on his belly while she found him a clean sleeper, this one a stretchy terry cloth that looked like it would keep him warm enough without being oppressively hot. "We're fine."

"Need a job? I'm looking for a live-in nanny for him so I can get back to work." Keith paused, shot a wicked grin toward Bobby before turning back to Marly. "No, I guess you wouldn't. I imagine you must be the only Maulers fan around who prefers seeing him taking snaps."

"Possibly. But Bobby may have a solution for you." Jack in hand, she came to the sofa and sat between the two guys. Boy, wouldn't Liz Grady turn green when she heard Marly had sat within touching distance of the great Keith Connors? She was already halfway jealous that Marly had caught Bobby's attention. "We have a guest from back in Hedgecock."

"And this might affect me how?" Keith reached over and took Jack, who laughed out loud when his dad lifted him over his head then brought him down to sprawl on his six-pack abs.

Bobby put an arm around Marly, as though he thought she needed the contact before he actually mentioned Tina. "Do you remember Tina Black?"

Keith's look of puzzlement morphed into one of recognition. "A kid about your age, always hung around with you and a bunch of boys. I remember you all pestering me to play with you my senior year in high school."

"Yeah. You know, back then I never really thought we were pestering you. I figured it out, though, when I was trying to avoid pesky little ones later on. Guess you deserve an apology, even though it's been a long time. Anyhow, Tina's here now, and she needs a job and somewhere to stay. Marly's understandably not very happy at having my old friend staying in our guest room."

Marly turned to Bobby. "Friend? You admitted you two had sex under the bleachers after games. Besides, it's not that I'm unhappy, it's that I want Tina to have a place to stay and something to keep her occupied."

"Sure." The men said it in unison, and little Jack let out a baby cackle, as if none of them believed Marly wasn't dead set on getting Tina out of Bobby's line of vision as quickly as possible. Bobby pulled her closer to him and blew in her ear. He sent delicious little sparks clear down to her toes when he did that—and he knew it. She hoped her glare let him know she was a little unhappy about him obviously not believing her.

Bobby turned to Keith. "Tina's dad died about the time my dad left, and when we were seniors in high school, her mom married again. The guy's a real bastard. According to Tina, he left her alone until they were in an accident and her mother was left paralyzed. By then I was off to college. Her mom died this summer, and she moved in with my mom to keep away from her stepfather. Apparently he started stalking Tina, and Mom thought the best way to deal with it was to get her out of the creep's reach."

Keith got up with little Jack and fished a bottle out from under the bar. When he came back and sat down, he opened the bottle and held it to the baby's mouth. "Sorry, when he starts getting restless, the only thing to do is feed him. Tina didn't have anybody there to chase this creep away?"

"No. Garcia's big enough and mean enough to intimidate most everybody left in Hedgecock. And he seems to stay one step ahead of the sheriff. So Tina's here, bunking in with us until she finds a job. I thought about her when I heard Coach Lyle mention that you had a real babysitting problem."

Shifting Jack on his lap, Keith shot a doubtful look at Bobby. "Most young women want a little better job than being a nanny. The few who've applied seem to be auditioning for a spot in my bed."

That made sense. Marly had no trouble imagining Liz Grady or a few hundred other rabid female fans angling to get a piece of Keith by way of babysitting his son. "That must be pretty tough to take," Bobby commented.

"Yeah, it is. I've got no interest now in women—Jackie's still very much a part of me, even though she's dead. A few nice young women have seemed to get along well with Jack, but even they seem as interested in a Marlins quarterback as in—" Keith shot an apologetic glance toward Marly. "Present company excepted."

"You're excused. You've gotta know that even before I fell for this big lug, I was a rabid football fan. After all, I decided to devote the better part of a year to being a Maulers cheerleader." She squeezed Bobby's muscular thigh then leaned back in the cushions while he continued.

"Tina doesn't have any education past high school. No money. She's always been quiet and I doubt she'd try to seduce you because her stepfather's undoubtedly done a good job of turning her against men in general. But she's smart, and I'm pretty sure she'd fall in love with little Jack." Bobby paused. "I can't imagine she'd be afraid of being in your house, either."

Keith looked down at Jack, who'd grabbed hold of his big hand on the bottle and was squeezing it as though that would make the milk come faster. He looked down on his son with a loving smile. "She'd be safe all right. I'd never let a bastard like her stepfather anywhere near Jack—or Tina, if she's his nanny.

I'd pay her well, of course. Taking care of this little guy is a big responsibility. I know."

Marly didn't doubt that. And she imagined Keith would be as good a protector as Bobby's old girlfriend was likely to find. Except for Bobby, she thought before slamming that thought to the back of her mind. "If you'd like, I could bring Tina down to the practice field with me and we could have lunch or something after you two finish practice."

"That would be good. Keith could collect Jack and we could go grab some takeout and bring it back here." Bobby stood and pulled Marly up from the sofa. "We've got to get going—not that you're not good company, but we've got a guest to entertain."

Keith got up, too, and walked them to the double door. "See you tomorrow then. I hope Tina will want the job. Congratulations, by the way, on your engagement. It made big news today in the Memphis papers."

"Yeah, I know." Bobby grinned and gave Marly a little hug. "You think your shoulder will be well enough for you to play this Sunday?"

Keith shrugged. "Probably. But I want it to be a hundred percent before I go rushing back out there. How's your knee?"

"I'll be okay to play on Sunday if I need to."

"You're doing a great job—for a raw rookie," Keith said.

"Thanks. See you in the morning then. We'll talk to Tina tonight so she won't be blindsided when you guys meet her tomorrow." With that Bobby steadied Marly as they walked down the stairs to the circular drive where he'd parked earlier. On the way home they sat in a comfortable silence Marly hadn't experienced with Bobby since he told her about his old hometown girlfriend's impending arrival into their lives.

Chapter Eight

Tina seemed surprised but not disturbed when Bobby told her about Keith and mentioned he needed a live-in nanny for his baby. Marly couldn't believe it! Tina might have been Bobby's girl when they were kids, but she didn't start breathing hard at the prospect of living in the same house with Keith Connors, the way most unattached women their age would.

Maybe she didn't know who Keith was. After all, he was eight or nine years older than Bobby. Marly herself didn't remember guys who'd grown up in her neighborhood but were that much older, but then none of her neighborhood guys had become household names. "Didn't you watch football when you were a kid?"

Tina smiled. "Of course. There isn't much else to do in Hedgecock during the football season. I didn't know Keith, though. He wasn't interested in snot-nose brats, the way I remember him calling us kids when Bobby and the other boys were trying to get him to play catch with us."

"He has a little boy now," Bobby said.

Marly figured Tina could use a little more information than that. "His wife died this spring when the baby was born. Little Jack's a cutie, but he's apparently too much of a handful for the housekeeper to handle. Keith said he needed a young, energetic woman who'd love Jack like her own and be there for him while he has to be away."

"He doesn't want this nanny to take care of him, too?" The idea seemed to disturb Tina, not thrill her the way it would excite most of the girls Marly knew.

"No. He told Marly and me he wasn't looking for that." Bobby's expression turned serious. "Tina, the man lost his wife less than eight months ago. Don't you think he needs some time to grieve?"

"I guess so." But she didn't sound certain.

Marly reached over and patted Tina's hand. "Keith's a decent man. He'd never force himself on any woman. Let me tell you, if he gets horny, there are hundreds of groupies who'd be thrilled to spend an hour in his arms and walk away. A dozen or more on the Maulers cheerleading squad would die to find out if he's as hot in bed as he is on the football field, but I've never heard any of them say anything about scoring with him."

"Oh. He must really have loved his wife."

When Bobby picked up Marly's hand and brought it to his lips, she bent and kissed his knuckles. "I wasn't around here when Jackie was alive, but from all the guys have said, he was one of the good ones, never taking groupies up on invitations for sex while on the road. He's probably one of the best-known athletes in the country, but from all I've heard, he was totally faithful to his wife."

"The baby's adorable. I think you'll like him a lot." Marly sensed that Tina needed love but didn't want it tied in with sex, not after the experiences with her stepfather that she'd confided when they first started their talk. Although she didn't come out and say it, Marly thought the filthy creep had probably raped her. "And I don't think you'll have anything to worry about with Keith."

"Well, I do need a job and a place to live. I guess this would take care of both. After all, it's not as if we're total strangers. I used to play sometimes with the girl who lived across the road from his mom's ranch. And I've talked with his sister several times when we'd run into each other at the grocery store." Tina looked around the condo. "He doesn't live in a place as fancy as this, does he?"

Bobby laughed. "Keith Connors is one of the biggest names in football. He lives in a huge place behind gates with burly guards. The man's last contract was for a hundred million dollars. His furniture is more traditional than this, but I'm pretty sure that unless his wife was an interior decorator, they had a professional lay out the place—and that it cost a bundle more than what I've got here. Right, Marly?"

"You're right. From the gossip columns I read before they got married, Jackie Connors was a socialite from up around Chicago. As far as I know she never worked at all, and I'd say just by looking that her house was put together by professionals." She wondered if Bobby would expect her to go all out in making their home a showplace, hoped not because she wanted a home that felt like home.

Tina smiled. "I think I might like this job. At least it would get me out of your hair so you can enjoy being engaged, doing whatever it is that engaged couples do."

"It's not that we're trying to get rid of you, Tina." Bobby's voice was hearty, but he didn't sound very sincere. Marly was sure he seemed less so when he laid a big, roughened hand on her thigh and gave it a squeeze.

"Yes you are, but that's okay. I tried to talk your mom out of sending me here, but she insisted. I don't know how she thought it was going to work, the three of us. And once I saw Marly and you together I knew you'd found the perfect match."

"Yeah, I found Marly. She's the only woman in the world for me. But I want you to be happy, too. If you'd rather, I'll send you to college so you can get a better job." He turned toward Marly, as if to gauge her reaction.

Tina didn't show any surprise when Bobby made that offer, but it set off alarms in Marly's head. "No need to waste your money. If I'd been a good student, I'd have found a way to do it myself. I find I like the idea of being a nanny."

Her response made Marly reluctantly start to like the woman and realize, just possibly, that the situation was exactly what Bobby had said it was. Tina just wasn't used to a decent guy, she guessed. They were old friends, and unlike a lot of players, Bobby apparently remembered his roots enough to offer a hand up to friends in need.

"As long as you're sure you'll be okay." Marly's antennae went up when Bobby seemed to press his offer, but she hadn't seen any indication that keeping Bobby away from Tina was likely to be a problem.

"I'll be fine as long as Edgar Garcia's hundreds of miles away." Tina paused for a minute. "Taking care of a baby whose father's still in love with his dead wife sounds like an ideal job, especially if he'll toss in tickets to home games so I can teach his son to love the game."

* * * * *

"See, baby, I told you that talking to Tina wouldn't end up being a disaster." Bobby slid off his jeans and laid them neatly on the chair beside the bed. "Wanna play?"

"I always want to play with you, big guy." Marly stretched out, naked, on the middle of the bed, reaching into the bag of toys she'd left in easy reach. "Lie down before your knee starts hurting again."

"It's already hurting, but not as bad as my cock. Ever since we were in that store, I've been thinking about using that big dildo to fill your sweet, hot pussy."

Marly laughed. "Then do it."

He'd never used toys and that scared him a little, but Bobby took the purple gel dildo. It seemed huge, bigger than his cock. "Give me that tube of lubricant. I've got the feeling this monster may hurt you."

"It's not as big as you, honey," she said as she handed him some cherry-flavored lube after sampling it and smacking her lips. "This stuff tastes good."

He took a little on his finger and brought it to his lips. Like Marly said, it tasted sweet and tart, sort of like cherry pie filling. Instead of spreading it on the dildo, he smeared some on her tight little nipples and bent to taste it for real. "I like your own taste better, but this is cool. Wanna taste some, too?"

Marly rolled on her side and grasped his erection. "Put some on here."

The red gel felt cool on his heated flesh, but then she took his cock head into her mouth and began to suck. "Yeah, baby, that feels great. Don't stop." The pressure had his balls tightening, but the heat of her mouth felt fantastic. Maybe he could contort himself enough so he could sample her, too.

There was no way, they'd tried it before. But he could make her feel good. Trying to maintain control and not come before he'd given her an orgasm, he smeared some of the gel on the dildo and lay back until he could see her pretty cunt. "Keep sucking me. I'm gonna give you some store-bought cock."

The dildo slid in easier than he'd imagined it would, and he absorbed the trembling that resounded against his own cock. Slowly, carefully, he moved in and out as she moved her lips up and down on him, sucking harder with each inward motion. It felt great. Different. "Feel good, baby?"

"Oh yes." The vibrations of her words against him got him even hotter.

"Then grab one of those plugs for me. Imagine I have three cocks and each one of them's inside you." When she found a plug and handed it to him, he lubed it before penetrating her tight anal sphincter with it until she cried out. "Does that hurt?"

She raised her head and looked up at him, tears in her eyes. "It hurts, but it feels good, too."

"Relax. This is all new to both of us. Go on sucking me but feel free to bite if it hurts more than it feels good." He wanted to see her come apart, lose every bit of control and come from the play alone. "God but I love you." Very gently he worked the plug up her ass until the flared end was flush with her body. "Okay?" He hoped so because she was sucking him as if she never wanted to quit, so hard that he was going to explode if she didn't let up.

"Oooh yes. Do you want to put this up my ass? You can if you want to." She punctuated the question by licking lubrication from the slit in his cock head. "Does the idea make you hot?"

"Yeah, it makes me damn hot. But then I'm about to explode anyhow, from what you've been doing to me. I think I'll get rid of the toys and we'll have a wild, old-fashioned fuckfest." Rolling out of Marly's reach, Bobby came on top of her, kneeling between her legs while he retrieved the dildo. "Maybe I'll leave the plug in." Stroking her wet, hot pussy, he jiggled the butt plug and made her squirm.

"Oh God. Leave it there and come inside me."

When she begged that way, he couldn't say no. Shifting, he found her cunt and plunged inside. "Baby, this feels so damn good."

"Oh yes. I love the way you feel inside me…and how the plug makes me feel like my whole body's stuffed full."

He moved on her, fast and deep, stretching out his legs to take pressure off his knee and lowering his body. "You've still got one more hole to fill," he growled before taking her mouth and devouring it, loving the taste and smell of his own body mingled with cherries and the musk that surrounded them.

Sensations bombarded him, the silky feel of her body beneath him, her warmth and wetness that caressed his flesh like a velvet glove, the knowledge that he was taking her, claiming her in every way he could envision. When she shuddered and he caught her scream of completion against his throat, he came as he'd never come before.

It was a hundred times the high of throwing a touchdown pass, the wildest orgasm he'd ever experienced. As he rolled off her and pulled her close, his thoughts moved beyond sex...beyond raw sensation to a realization that Marly was not only his lover but his life. "Let's go shower, baby. I think the toys are gonna prove a good investment."

"Oh yeah."

Next time maybe they'd try the vibrators. Bobby wondered how much stimulation a man could take. He guessed they'd find out soon enough. As they showered together, he wondered why he'd ever thought having sex under the bleachers did any more than cause the usual physical release. Come to think of it, he doubted that he'd ever given Tina an orgasm.

He'd been a self-centered high-school jock, and he wasn't proud of it. When they got back in bed, Bobby gathered Marly in his arms and thanked God they'd found each other. He wondered how he'd survive if someday he lost her the way Keith had lost his wife.

He was pretty sure he wouldn't—or at least that he wouldn't want to. "I love you, baby," he whispered, moving her hair out of the way and placing a soft kiss on her neck just below the hairline.

"Love you, too. Now we'd better sleep or you'll have trouble rolling out of bed for practice."

* * * * *

How long had it been since he got a decent night's sleep? Keith stumbled out of bed and into the nursery, stifling a string of curses when he figured out his son didn't need a diaper change or food—that he just wanted to play. Hauling Jack to his own bed, he lay beside him and talked in a mock-stern voice.

"Look, bruiser, you need to sleep all night. All the books say so. They also say I shouldn't put you in my bed and risk smashing you, but we've both got to get some sleep."

"Da-da-da." Jack chattered a reply, one Keith thought might be an attempt to say "Daddy", but he wasn't sure.

"Da-da to you, too. If we're lucky you're gonna get a nanny so your old dad can go earn us a living." It irked him that the housekeeper Jackie had hired two years earlier absolutely refused to add child care to her duties, but it seemed as if Bobby Anthony might have come up with a solution. "If we don't, I may be retiring before my time. You understand?"

Jack just drooled and kicked his heels on the mattress. Some bed partner! Not that Keith had any desire to replace Jackie in his bed. Not now. Maybe not ever. Still, he envied Bobby for having a hot, gorgeous woman to curl up with at night. A woman who loved football the way Jackie never did. "Come on, kid, doesn't your motor ever wear down?"

After fifteen minutes or so, Jack nodded off to sleep, leaving Keith wide awake, wondering what Tina Black looked like now. His vague memory of her was as a disheveled tomboy with mousy light brown hair and clothes that had seen better days. He didn't imagine she'd stir his dormant libido now, which was good. As he took Jack back to the nursery, he stopped a minute and looked at the last portrait he'd had done of Jackie.

The wind blew her blonde hair as she stood on a dock by the man-made lake behind their home, seven months pregnant with Jack. And she was smiling at something he'd said. A friend had shot the picture and given them an enlargement that Jackie had refused to have framed. But after she died, Keith framed it himself because it reminded him of the Jackie she never showed to anyone but him. Tell the truth, he hated the formal portrait of her that hung over the living-room fireplace — but he knew he'd feel guilty if he had it taken down and stored in the attic.

"We love you, Mommy." Jackie would never know how much Keith had loved her, or how empty his life was now that she was gone, even though their years together had been full of ups and downs, even a couple of separations when she'd gone storming off to her indulgent parents. He looked down at his son. "Let's get you back to bed now." His heart aching, Keith laid Jack in his crib and covered him with the blanket his boy had decided in the last few weeks was his favorite. Maybe he'd send Tina to the store to buy a dozen more just like it, because Jack was a beast when he didn't have that "blankie".

That is, he'd send her if she was willing to take on a bereaved widower and his baby while he tried to come back from his injury and take his place again as the number-one quarterback for the Maulers. He'd never realized until he risked losing that place that it defined him as much as it did. Oh well, he'd know soon enough. He crawled back in bed, tried not to think of what his backup was doing right now with Marly. Reminding himself he'd never been into voyeurism, Keith drifted off to sleep.

And he dreamed about a faceless woman. A woman who'd love Jack and like him. Someone who'd be proud of what he did on the field and teach his son to be proud, too. She wasn't Jackie, who'd barely tolerated his playing football when he could have taken a job with her father's company. Keith had no idea who he was seeing up in the stands, screaming when a lineman sacked him, telling Jack his daddy was going to be okay.

*****

The next afternoon Keith collected Jack from the office, where he'd become a distraction for the women who'd volunteered to watch him, and went downstairs where Bobby was waiting with Marly and Tina.

It struck him that Marly was the stereotypical perfect trophy wife for a quarterback on the rise, while the other woman looked more like the stereotypical girl next door. Not ugly, but no stunning beauty, her light brown hair touched her shoulders and framed her small, roundish face. Taller than Marly, she was more slender. Less voluptuous, he thought, revising his first impression. Both of them had on jeans and sweaters, only Marly filled hers out in a way that made men stop for a second look.

Tina looked like someone's mom. Keith had no trouble picturing her growing up in Hedgecock, living in a much simpler world than he had traveled since going away to college and marrying a millionaire's daughter. Good, he'd have no trouble keeping his hands off her, something he'd wondered about last night. If she'd looked like Marly, his dormant libido would have been more likely to come alive. "Are you-all ready to go get some lunch? I figured we might as well have it at my house, so I ordered some pizzas that should get there about the time we arrive."

* * * * *

Once Tina got in the backseat of Keith's car and started amusing Jack, Bobby led Marly to his truck. "We thought this would work better, so they can see how they get along. Besides, I like having you all to myself. There's been little enough of that since we got home from LA."

"Speaking of LA, how's that knee feeling?" Marly frowned, because she'd noticed Bobby limping again when he came out from practice. The one downside to having an athlete for a lover was that he was always getting dents and dings that caused him discomfort if not downright agonizing pain.

Bobby laid a hand on the knee. "It's okay. The trainer wrapped it again after I spent an hour in the hydrotherapy pool. Coach wouldn't let me take part in the contact drills this morning, but I did get to throw some. Keith looks a little rusty, but I imagine he'll be good to go by a week from Sunday."

That would be good for him, not so good for Bobby. "Does that bother you? You've been doing such a great job while he's been out."

"Yeah, it bothers me, but it's nothing I can't live with. Keith's a better quarterback than I am now, but I figure that seven or eight years from now, I'll be better than him. I came here expecting to get traded unless something bad happened with Keith, and there's no way I can wish anything horrible on him. He's gone out of his way to teach me a lot."

Marly hated the idea of living far from her family, but she wouldn't complain. After all, Bobby had come a long way toward being the hero her life rotated around, and she wasn't about to let him leave Memphis without her. "I know. If we move, we move. I'll survive not being within an hour's drive of my mom and dad."

That was the first time Marly had come right out and said that. Bobby had assumed she would, but he liked hearing her say the words. "We'll cross that bridge when it comes, but truth is, I'll probably be on the trading block pretty soon after Keith gets back to work. That will happen in a hurry if he offers Tina the job and she accepts."

Bobby was glad he had Marly persuaded that he had no sexual interest in Tina or anybody else except her. At least he hoped he had. The fact that some creep had dumped her the way she'd finally told him made him want to kill the guy if he could find him—or wrap her in his love and make damn sure nobody ever hurt her again. "Want to get married soon?"

"Mom wants a year to plan the circus she has in mind." Marly pouted, obviously not thrilled with the idea of Ringling Brothers coming to town to help celebrate her marriage, to him or anybody else.

"I bet we can persuade her she wouldn't like the media circus that probably would happen if you marry me in Memphis. I'd like to do it quietly, with just your family and my mom and a few friends of ours from the team. Since I've been playing every week, I've developed a phobia about reporters." He had a sneaking suspicion Marly's mom's idea of a wedding would intimidate his mom and everybody from Hedgecock who might attend, and he didn't want that.

Especially since he was pretty sure Marly wasn't enthusiastic about a huge blowout, either.

"You know, we could do it here or in Hedgecock, except there aren't enough hotel rooms there to handle even a few out-of-town guests. Or I could do the way a lot of players do and buy out a resort for a weekend and invite our guests there."

Marly sat a few minutes, obviously thinking about the choices he'd suggested. "Going to Cabo or some resort like it would seem copycat, and I like to think we're original. I vote for here, a small wedding for less than a hundred people, at my parish church with a reception at Dad's restaurant."

No, Marly wouldn't want to follow anybody else's pattern, and she seemed too frugal anyway to okay him spending fifty thousand or so to haul fifty or sixty guests to some popular Mexican or Caribbean resort. As far as her suggestion to do it here went, Bobby wasn't too big on a church affair since he hadn't been to Mass since he was too small to protest going, but it obviously meant something to Marly, or more particularly to her parents. He really didn't want to get married in Hedgecock. He'd moved on from there when he left for college, and the only thing that drew him back now was his mom.

"I wouldn't mind that. You can blame me for nixing the huge blowout if you want to. First thing, I don't want to wait a year. Second, I have no desire to go on display for Memphis' most intrusive reporters, especially since I'm sure I'll have been traded long before a year's up."

Marly smiled. "I know you aren't very religious, and I'm not either. But Mom and Dad will be happy if we get married in church. And I think I can make them believe I don't want the hoopla either. My best friend from college had a three-ring-circus wedding last year, and the marriage didn't last six months."

After he pulled into Keith's driveway and stopped the truck, Bobby leaned over the console and gave Marly a grateful kiss. She was so beautiful, but that wasn't important. He'd found his soul mate and he wasn't about to lose her over anything—particularly something as unimportant as the ceremony that would join them for the rest of their lives. "Let's go in and see how Keith and Jack are doing persuading Tina to come take care of them."

* * * * *

"They're in the game room. Mr. Connors said to send you in when you arrived. Just follow the noise. You'll find them." The middle-aged woman who answered the door wore a black and white uniform that reminded Marly of what female servers wore in four-star restaurants that boasted microscopic servings at obscene prices. She didn't look any too happy when she answered the door and invited them in.

Mr. Connors? She'd never imagined Keith would have servants who called him "Mister". The formality just didn't seem to fit with what she knew of him, or the way he'd acted toward them last night. She and Bobby turned the corner and laughed out loud when they found Tina and Keith on the floor with Jack. Their mouths, even the baby's, gave evidence that the pizza was already here and had been at least partially consumed. Both adults looked happier than Marly had ever seen them as they clowned for Jack's amusement.

"Come on, join us. There's plenty of pizza on the bar, and drinks are in the refrigerator. Tina and I just found out Jack likes pizza crust. She says it's good for teething."

Marly wasn't all that sure she'd have tried feeding pizza to a baby, but then she guessed Jack was old enough to start trying some adult foods. "It looks like he's having fun. You guys, too." She put two slices of pepperoni pizza on a plate and handed it to Bobby. "Here you go. Plain, vanilla pizza. Just the way you like it." She'd laughed at Bobby the first time they'd eaten at her dad's restaurant, because he'd carefully picked all the visible ingredients besides the meat off his serving before devouring it. Smiling at the memory, she served herself a slice of the pizza that looked to have every imaginable topping on it. "This looks good."

Bobby handed her a soda and took a beer for himself. "I haven't figured you out yet, baby. You like beer with ribs but you want soda with pizza. I always heard pizza shouldn't be eaten without beer."

"Real Italians drink wine with their pizza." Marly didn't much care for the Chianti that was traditional with southern Italian food either, but she figured her dad would cringe if she didn't say it.

"Ugh," Keith said, looking up at them as he and Tina took turns pushing toy cars back and forth for Jack to roll back to them. "I can't stand wine of any kind. Give me a beer any day, or even a soft drink."

Tina looked at him. "Uh, Keith, if you don't like wine, why do you keep a huge refrigerator full of it in the kitchen?"

"For guests," he said shortly. "Bobby, do you think your knee will be up to playing this week?"

"I guess." Bobby sounded as confused at the sudden change of topic as Marly felt. "How's the shoulder feeling after the workout today?"

"Sore. But I could play if I had to. I imagine that if I don't get back on the field pretty soon, I'll be out of a job. You've done amazing things considering this is your first year."

They chatted for a while, until a pungent odor let Marly know Jack needed a change. "Shall I take him upstairs and do the honors?" she asked Keith.

"No. Let Tina do it. I've shown her around the house, so she knows where to find his stuff."

Tina grinned. "I think I can find his room again. Come on, little guy, let's go get changed."

As Jack left, giggling in Tina's arms, Marly figured this was going to work. Sure, Tina didn't seem to fit in this elegant mansion the way the housekeeper did, but then neither did Keith. "Seems you're getting along pretty well," she commented to Keith when he moved off the floor onto a bar stool.

"She's easy to relax with. And Jack already seems crazy about her. My only worry is how she'll get along with Mrs. Gardner."

"The woman who answered the door?" Bobby's tone hinted that he doubted the housekeeper much liked anybody.

"Yeah. Jackie hired her when we first moved here. All the good I can say about her is that she keeps the place straightened up. I'm fairly sure she thinks I'm some sort of a caveman since I wander around the house in cutoffs and T-shirts instead of whatever it is she thinks the master of the house should be wearing."

Bobby washed down the last of his pizza with a big slug of beer. "I'd fire her. Having the hired help look down her pointy nose at me would be the last straw."

"Now, Bobby," Marly chided gently. "There is something to be said for a clean house, and I can't see you actually cleaning yours, even though you are pretty neat for a guy."

Keith's laugh sounded forced. "I'm not very neat, so I need someone to pick up after me. Mrs. Gardner's not all that bad. She's always stayed out of my way as much as possible."

"What if she's not nice to Tina?" From the little Marly knew, Tina had lived a hard life. She deserved some peace if she was going to take this job.

"Then I'll fire her and let Tina hire a cleaning woman she gets on with. I can live with a mess before I'll make Jack do without her. He loves her already, and it's only been a few hours." Keith sighed, as if making that decision had taken a load off his back. "I shouldn't have gotten upset when she mentioned the wine collection. It was Jackie's. She liked 'fine dining', as she called it. It's hard when I have to think of her."

"I imagine it is." Never having known Keith before, Marly was surprised at his sensitivity, but she understood it. After all, he'd lost Jackie and now was floundering around, trying to make a go on his own. "When do you want Tina to start?"

"Now."

"Is she okay with this? After all, she's just gotten here, and she might need some rest before taking on Hurricane Jack." Bobby grinned, as if he could picture the havoc Keith's eight month-old terror might instigate with a tired, new nanny.

Keith smiled. "I talked with Coach Lyle, and I'm going to stay home with them for the next two days. Between us, Tina and I should each be able to get a bit of rest, and I won't have to subject poor Jack to Mrs. Gardner. I never saw another woman who seems to despise babies the way she does."

Marly laughed. This was going to work out. She knew it. "We'd better go home and get Tina's stuff," she told Bobby. "Not that I'm anxious to lose our houseguest so soon."

He bent over and whispered in her ear. "Liar. I know you can't wait to get home so we can play with our toys." Then he turned to Keith. "We'll go get Tina's luggage and bring it over here. I'm pretty sure she hasn't even unpacked."

Chapter Nine

By Friday, Tina had settled in and Keith was back at practice. Bobby thought he looked rested for the first time since they'd gotten to training camp back in August. Coach Lyle had given Bobby the start but told him Keith would be taking over the following week. They'd talked for a few minutes in the parking lot before getting in their cars and heading home.

Not that Bobby hadn't expected this. He knew he'd soon be traded to a team whose starting quarterback had bombed out or gone down with a season-ending injury at mid-season, and whose backup was a dud. But he wouldn't be going alone, so it was okay.

He imagined taking Marly to the frozen North, or the balmy South, or anywhere in between. Even to the West Coast. It wouldn't matter, as long as he had her with him. When his cell phone rang, he smiled at the sight of Marly's name on the LCD screen and turned on the speaker phone.

"This week will be my last start. Coach just told me Keith will be ready in time for next week's game."

"Then come home, honey, and I'll console you. My practice was over early, so I wanted to get some planning done for our big day. I let Mom talk me into wearing a white dress, but I nixed the veil."

"Hussy. You know you're no wide-eyed virgin. But go on, wear that white gown, not that I think you can persuade even your own parents that your big jock fiancée hasn't sampled you pretty thoroughly before the wedding." Bobby loved to tease her, even when she bristled and let her hot Italian temper show. "Just remember, baby, I like you best when you're wearing nothing at all." Blood rushed to his sex as he recalled the game they'd played last night, with vibrating dildos and cock rings and the sexy-smelling heated oil they'd spent hours massaging into each other's bodies.

"Oh, I forgot to tell you. Mom and Dad want us to come over for dinner. They've got something they want to give us."

Bobby pictured some antique that was a family heirloom, or maybe a cookbook with all of Dom's secret recipes. "I'll manage the appropriate reaction, whatever it may be."

But Marly wasn't so sure. Her parents had given her older brothers houses when they got married, which was probably the only reason they'd stayed in the old neighborhood. "It might be a house, you know."

"Nah. They wouldn't buy us a house when they know we'll likely be living somewhere else but here. Would they?" His voice had an edge, as if he figured this was somewhat likely.

"Remember they bought houses for my brothers."

"Your brothers didn't make several million bucks a year when they got married, did they?"

"No, but—"

"No buts. They can give us whatever they want to, other than a house. I'll buy that for us, and I doubt it will be here in Memphis."

"You don't want to live here in the off-season?"

Bobby groaned. "No, baby. I want us to make a year-round home wherever it is that I end up playing. We can visit your folks whenever we want to. They've got plenty of room to put us up for a week here and there."

Marly was torn. Her parents had given in on the wedding plans. They'd taken Bobby in their open arms and treated him like another son. She knew they really wanted to keep their kids nearby for family meals and outings, and it hurt to know

Bobby was so emphatic about keeping families at a distance. Her family, that is, she thought uncharitably, because she figured he'd move his own mother in with them at the drop of a hat unless her romance with the Hedgecock banker ended up with a wedding, as Marly hoped it would.

"Is this going to be a problem?" His voice sounded cold over the phone, as though he wasn't anxious to humor her and keep them close to Memphis.

"I don't know. I've always thought we'd come back here, that this would sort of be our second home...that we'd live here once you retire."

"Baby, I've just started. I'm hoping retirement won't come into the picture for at least fifteen or sixteen years. Besides, what makes you think I wouldn't want to go back to my own hometown?"

That made her furious. "Bobby, you've said a million times that you'd never want to go back and live in Hedgecock. You've never even taken me there for a visit with your mom."

"And I don't," he ground out. "But I don't want to live under the collective noses of your family, either. You want a place in Memphis, fine. We'll pick a place out close to Keith's place, or buy a bigger condo in the building where we live now. Why this sudden urge to stay close to Mom and Dad?"

Marly didn't know. Maybe it was the wedding. Or maybe it was all the changes piling up on her life at once. "I don't know," she said after trying to figure out for herself what had her emotions on a roller coaster. "I don't know why we're arguing. Mom and Dad might have decided to give us that atrocious brass coat rack they got from her grandparents when they moved to a retirement home."

"I don't want that, either." Bobby chuckled, though, so Marly thought she'd probably lightened his mood a bit. "I guess it would be easier to haul around the country than an entire house, so I might be inclined to accept it graciously. By the way, I'm pulling into the parking garage now, so you might want to get naked and meet me at the door."

* * * * *

From the look on Bobby's face, Marly figured he hadn't actually expected her to do it, but Marly greeted him wearing nothing but a smile. "I'd just finished my shower when I called you. I didn't have time to get dressed."

Bobby scooped her up in his arms and carried her to the sofa that faced the bank of windows overlooking the river. "Think somebody might see us?" he asked as he shucked his clothes and scooped her onto his lap. "The idea excites you, doesn't it, baby?"

"You're a bad, bad boy. If you didn't keep me so hot all the time, I'd punish you." She nipped at his neck, leaving a growing bruise. He'd be mad about it in the morning, but he'd wear her mark the way she wore his, on her finger all the time and frequently on intimate parts of her body as well. "But I find all I want to do is love you."

"Then let me inside, baby. I had a hard day at practice so you'll have to put out most of the energy." He lay back and dragged her over his hard, tough body. "Climb aboard. Every time I listen to your voice I get hard. It's all your fault."

She knew the glow would wear off eventually, and that Bobby would come home intent on sleeping or relaxing in the hot tub instead of this, so she'd enjoy it while it lasted. Stroking his warm skin, circling his nipples with her fingertips, she touched him with more love than explosive lust. He felt so good inside her, his sex throbbing inside her well-loved pussy. Not thrusting, just filling her with a slow-burning fire they might bank for later or let develop into a burning flame. Either one was fine.

Fine because she loved him. She even loved the fact that he'd wanted to be there for his old lover and to take care of his mother financially now that he was in the position to do so.

When she rode him like this, slow and easy, she couldn't work up the resentment that she'd felt at first when he assured her he wasn't going to live under her parents' loving thumbs and he wasn't going to let her do it, either. "That feels so good." While he wasn't moving much, he was getting her hotter with every teasing pulsation of his cock inside her.

As hot as she'd been last night when they played with toys until they were both dripping with sweat from all the forceful sensations, the pure lust of it all. "Want more?" he asked, but she just wanted to stay there, with him inside her, needing the closeness and feeling of belonging that seemed to surround them, her tired hero still determined to bring her the release.

"Just relax and enjoy it, honey. We've got the rest of our lives to experiment with kinky sex. Right now you're tired, and I want you to rest."

"You know, I think I love you more every day. And I know I've got enough gas left in my engine to give you a climax." Bobby raised his head and took her mouth, his warm breath sweet-smelling when he traced the seam of her lips with his tongue. The gesture seemed so generous because the effort it cost him to lift his head was unmistakable.

"I don't need one now. Let's go in the bedroom and I'll give you a rubdown. Then you can get an hour or so of sleep before we have to see the folks."

"Thanks, babe. The feel of your hands on me will soothe away the aches and pains."

More like it would ease the tension, Marly thought as she recalled their earlier conversation while Bobby was driving home. "You know I'll follow you anywhere," she said as she massaged pungent oil into his throwing shoulder and back. He rewarded her with a muffled sigh. "Go on, go to sleep. I'll be quiet."

Soon his taut muscles loosened up and he started to snore softly. Marly lay beside him, soaking in his warmth. Nobody was going to come between them, not even her own well-meaning parents. Or her own fragile ego wondering when she'd lose Bobby. "I trust you, my big handsome jock. Really I do."

* * * * *

Marly knew right away that Mom had planned something special. The aroma of homemade lasagna surrounded her and Bobby as soon as they opened the door, and when they went into the kitchen she noticed four prime steaks on a platter waiting to be cooked on the Jenn-Air grill.

Mom was calorie-conscious. She might serve either the steaks or the lasagna with the huge antipasto tray for an ordinary dinner, but not both. So Marly figured she had to consider this night a very special occasion. "We can't stay late, Mom," she said by way of warning. "Bobby had a rough practice today."

"That's okay. Marly, will you show Bobby to Dad's den?"

Oh no. Daddy's private place where kids are invited only for very solemn occasions or lectures. "Sure. Come on, Bobby. Brace yourself. We only get invited in here when something serious is going down."

"I think I'll survive." He grinned as he got up and followed her down a narrow hallway to a room at the back of the old house.

"You may be surprised. But remember I'll still love you whatever happens."

For a long time Marly stared at the closed door, wondering what was going on inside. When she didn't hear shouting or the sound of flying objects, she went back to the kitchen. "What did Daddy want with Bobby?"

"I'm not sure. Here, taste the marinade. I think it's a little too acidic."

"It tastes fine, Mom. Just like it always does." Marly wondered why her mom always kept quiet when her dad critiqued everything about their meals. "I'm glad Bobby isn't in the restaurant business. He eats everything set before him and doesn't say anything negative."

"Good for you, *bella*. All men have their little eccentricities. A lot of them are worse than your dad's tendency to criticize every bite he puts in his mouth. It may take time for those little things to surface, because during the courting period, they're trying their best to reel a girl in."

What irritating habits might Bobby be hiding? Marly thought about his practice of never leaving anything lying around. She figured that if that was his only quirk, she could live with it. "Bobby never leaves anything out of place, but he doesn't complain when I do."

"Sooner or later he will. I bet he cringes every time he comes here and sees coats and boots strewn around the front hall. You'll slip and leave something where it doesn't belong, and eventually he'll explode over it, just like Daddy does with some of the dishes I cook."

Marly smiled. Mom was probably right. Still, Bobby hadn't appeared to have a problem dealing with the mess in Keith's game room the other day. "Can I help with anything?"

"Yes, you can set the table while I grill these steaks. I imagine your dad and Bobby will be coming out here any minute."

They did, and Marly didn't notice any blood. Surprisingly, they were talking pleasantly about this Sunday's game. The meal went well, even though Marly felt like holding her breath, waiting for someone to bring up The Gift.

Mom brought out tiramisu for dessert, and when she did Dad handed Bobby an envelope. "For your first home," he said as though he'd never once thought of giving them the deed for a house he and Mom had chosen.

"Thank you, Dad." Bobby slid the envelope into Marly's hand without opening it. "We both appreciate your generosity."

On the way home he told her how he'd persuaded her dad to forget about giving them a house around the corner and put some of the money he'd planned to spend into a down payment for the place they'd someday buy or build.

"It wasn't easy, believe me. I finally had to say flat-out that I felt a man should buy his own home, and that seeing as how I make more than I can possibly spend, it would be unfair for him to buy me a house when he had two boys who might need the money at some point."

"I wouldn't have believed you could do it." Marly squeezed his thigh, still having trouble picturing Bobby changing her stubborn father's mind.

* * * * *

Keith was back leading the Maulers for the second week now. Bobby was expecting to be traded any day. Just two weeks were left until his and Marly's wedding. And life was incredibly hectic.

He'd never realized how much planning went into a ceremony and reception for just twenty or so guests, but Marly was pretty much at the mercy of her mom every day when she didn't have cheerleader practice. His urgent assignment now was to call his own mother and find out what she planned to wear. "Why don't I just send you to one of the nice boutiques here in town and have you pick out something for Mom?" he asked Marly who shot him a disbelieving look.

"She'd kill you. She'd kill me. Every woman wants to select her own clothes. Don't they have any stores in Hedgecock?"

"Not that you'd consider dress shops. There's a general store where they sell jeans and shirts." Mom would have to come a few days early and shop here, or make a trip to San Antonio, and Bobby wasn't sure she could get the time off work, or that she'd let him pay for her outfit. "I'll call her. Why couldn't we just do this casual?" Fortunately he already had a suit, the one he'd bought to wear to games when he might have to meet reporters afterward. He was pretty certain his mom had nothing suitable to wear to the shindig Marly's mother was engineering.

He was pleasantly surprised when Mom told him she already had the perfect dress, shocked when she admitted she was getting married, too—to Mr. Tate from the bank. They weren't doing anything special, just going to San Antonio for a long weekend and getting married in the chapel at St. Mary's College. "We'll be married next Saturday and spending a few days playing tourist at the Alamo. This will work out fine, so we can come the next weekend to be with you and Marly."

"I love you, Mom. Be happy. You deserve it after all those years, keeping me on the straight and narrow." He shut off the phone and turned to Marly. "That was a lot easier than I thought it would be. She and Mr. Tate are getting married this weekend. I had no idea they were serious about each other. She said she already has a dress to wear."

"The color, Bobby. What color is your mother's dress? My mom wants to know right now."

"Royal blue." Why the hell should colors matter? He was trying to let the idea of his mom marrying Mr. Tate sink in. Not that he objected. Mom couldn't have found a better man in Hedgecock if she'd tried.

Bobby shook his head as he watched Marly use the speed-dial. Women! He should have figured out they were all obsessed with coordinating colors when Marly had rifled through his tie rack the other day and promptly gone out to get him one she thought went better than any he already had with the dark-gray suit he'd had to have tailored for the wedding. Damn, he hadn't needed a new suit, but Marly had insisted and he'd dropped another few thousand having another one made. It wasn't as though he wore suits every day, or that he could saunter into any store and buy one off the rack.

Thank God the madhouse would soon be over. Bobby's agent said a deal was almost done with the Orlando team, and he almost looked forward to getting away from the madhouse here. "George Woodley didn't call me on the house phone, did he?"

"No. Was he supposed to?"

"I thought he might." Though Marly insisted she'd be okay with them moving right away, he didn't want to remind her that would almost certainly be happening. "I think we ought to ditch this wedding and go elope tomorrow. I bet we could still get a license if we hurried down to the courthouse."

"No. Not that I wouldn't like that, too, but I'm not going to let my mom down. I'm disappointing her enough as it is."

"I know, baby. Just keep reminding her that you're marrying a pro quarterback and that reporters would be an annoying fact of life if we went for a huge wedding."

* * * * *

Time flew when you were having fun. It also seemed to evaporate when you didn't have a moment to yourself. Marly could barely take in all the changes. They were getting married and moving to Orlando two days later where he'd be starting for a team that had lost its last six games behind a hapless quarterback who no longer had a job. Yesterday she'd flown to the land of 24/7 entertainment and chosen a furnished apartment from several empty ones owned by the team owner there. Then she'd flown back here and gone to the shower Liz Grady had hurriedly arranged.

Bobby was with his mom and her new husband in the condo while she was staying here at home for the last few days—her dad's idea, not hers.

She rubbed her aching pussy, recalled the few times they'd made love here in the ruffled four-poster. As crazy as it had looked, having her big, burly jock surrounded by the trappings of her youth, it had been good. Good thing they were getting married tomorrow. Reception or not she intended to grab her new husband and take the edge off her starved libido the minute they left the church.

Meanwhile she took out the vibrating dildo that didn't hold a candle to the real thing and tried to imagine it was Bobby inside her.

* * * * *

It was about time. Bobby stood at the front of the chapel, Keith at his side. The sounds of organ music filled the place, and ruby-colored light flowed through stained-glass windows. His mom and Mr. Tate were already seated on the front row, and a handful of his Mauler teammates dotted the aisles. Tina sat near the back with little Jack, looking content as she rubbed her cheek on the baby's shock of blond hair.

He caught himself starting to tug at his tie and willed himself to stay still. As the music started getting louder, he tried to look appropriately serious. He saw Liz Grady in the doorway, watched her glide down the aisle and take her place on the other side from Keith. She was one beautiful, sexy woman, but she didn't hold a candle to Marly, who stood in the entryway with her father. She looked like an angel in something white and soft-looking, and her long hair flowed over her bare shoulders like a dark curtain. The diamond studs he'd handed to her mom last night twinkled in her ears. She lifted her bouquet, a big white orchid surrounded by some of the same little white flowers that were in his boutonniere, and shot him a smile that sent blood flowing quite inappropriately to his groin.

Later, buddy. He tried thinking of something un-sexy, of the priest who'd reluctantly agreed to marry them without them going through months of counseling, and who undoubtedly was staring down disapprovingly from the altar. He took a deep breath and watched her come to him until he reached out and took her hand. What had seemed otherworldly suddenly felt right.

Marly felt his heat, even though they stood a few inches apart. Her heart was overflowing. As music surrounded them and dappled sunlight sent rays of color over them, she knew this was right. Words flowed over them, somber and melodious, words that registered only on a visceral level because Bobby was all she could focus on in her conscious mind. Her Bobby, not the budding star signal-caller she'd wanted at first, but the loving, decent man she'd come to love. A little demon whispered in her ear that her future husband's talent off the field was pretty awesome, too.

She had to jerk her brain back to the ceremony when the priest began reading the traditional vows Bobby had balked at until he gave in to please her and her parents. Trying to keep her hands from trembling, she watched him slide a diamond-studded band beside her engagement ring. "I love you, baby," he whispered when she slid a simple, wide gold band on his left ring finger.

"I love you, too."

The priest cleared his throat. "You may now kiss the bride." She loved Bobby's audacity when he took her in his arms and gave her a kiss that sent longing clear to her toes. "It's my pleasure to introduce Mr. and Mrs. Robert Anthony."

Marly didn't hear the benediction, because her ears were ringing from that hot, wet kiss. When the music rose, she watched Keith take Liz's arm and hurry down the aisle before looping her arm through Bobby's. He must have been in a big hurry, because she could barely keep pace with him as he hurried them out of the chapel.

"Let's find someplace and make love." His grin was positively evil, as if he didn't intend to wait one minute to consummate the vows they'd just made in front of God and all their families and friends. "You mind if the driver knows what we're doing?"

"Not really. I imagine everybody will know. After all, they've all been conspiring to keep us apart for the last week. Come on. If he's shy he can always park and take a walk."

* * * * *

"Take your time getting to the reception," Bobby ordered as he shut the panel dividing the passengers from the driver's seat. Then he pulled Marly onto his lap. "Look, we've got privacy, sort of. Open up for me. And help me find your hot little pussy in all this fluff."

"You're bad. But I love you. I'm also so horny I'm going to die if you don't get inside me this minute." She struggled with his belt and zipper, finally freeing him and shoving his pants out of the way. "The panties have an open crotch. See, I thought ahead."

Yeah, she had thought ahead. Her cunt was wet and hot and ready for his first thrust. So ready that he felt the imprint of her fingernails through his suit jacket and shirt. "Like this?" he asked, lifting her at the waist and slamming her hard onto his swollen shaft. "I think the priest may have noticed my hard-on."

"Did you care?"

"No. I just didn't want to embarrass you if the guests figured out how desperate I was to get inside you."

"Like your mom?" She slid a hand between the buttons on his shirt, and her playful antics damn near made him come on the spot.

"No, Mom has known for a long time that she raised a bad boy. She tried, but she couldn't make me restrain the testosterone that started flowing way back when. Come on, baby, ride me. Come for me. I'll try to wait, because I don't have a condom with me and I don't want to get your dress all messed up."

She kissed him, her tongue darting in and out of his mouth. "How about letting me get you off? It's not fair, you having to wait any longer."

"Okay. But first you have to come for me." He lifted her again and again, each time sliding harder and deeper in her delicious cunt. "Squeeze me."

When she did, she began to convulse around him. He had to quit breathing to keep from coming inside her. But he didn't. Instead he let her slide off him and go to her knees. Her pretty mouth took up where her pussy had left off, taking him deep down her throat then retreating to lick and suck his cock. "God, baby, I've missed you. I don't think I'll ever let you out of my sight again." Maybe there was some way he could finagle his new coach to let him take her with him for out-of-town games.

But not now. Pressure built in his balls. His muscles tensed. "I'm coming, baby. Swallow hard or you'll mess up your makeup."

She did, and somehow they managed to straighten their clothes and look reasonably respectable when they arrived at their reception. "We've banked the fires, brand-new wife. Now let's go enjoy our party."

Epilogue

"Those two seem made for each other," Bobby's mother told Keith as he showed Jack off to her. She'd noticed how this other hometown hero had stayed close by Tina even though the sexy-looking maid of honor had tried awfully hard to lure him away.

Keith smiled, but she noticed his eyes held sadness. "Yeah. They do. I'm glad they found Tina for us," he said, his gaze settling on her and his adorable little boy. "She's been a lifesaver."

"I'm glad, too. She needed something to do, somewhere safe where she wouldn't worry about her perverted stepfather coming after her."

"You don't need to worry. I'm not about to let anyone hurt her."

They chatted a few minutes while Caleb spoke with Marly's father. "I bet they're talking about the market. Cal can't seem to get it off his mind these days."

"I know all about that. I worried all the time until I quit trying to manage my investments this fall and turned them over to a professional. Not that he's been doing a whole lot better lately than I might have done myself."

Bobby's mom nodded. "Cal set Bobby up with somebody he trusted. My boy told him he wanted to play football and let experts manage his signing bonus."

"Good idea. I wouldn't ever have tried to do it myself except for the fact my wife, or rather my late wife's father, insisted on it." Keith shook his head. "Good thing Bobby already made arrangements for investment management, or his in-laws might have had ideas he couldn't very easily ignore."

"You must have gotten married young—not that twenty-two's any great age to be starting a family, but I can't complain because Bobby was three years old before I made it to twenty-two."

"I did. I was twenty and Jackie was a year older."

"You two waited a long time to have little Jack." Melanie clapped her hand over her mouth. "I'm so sorry."

Keith took her hand, tried to smile. After all, Melanie Anthony had been a ray of sunshine among a lot of the old crones who'd worked at the high school when he was there. "It's okay. We tried. Jackie wanted a houseful of babies, but it didn't work out. Finally we had Jack, but something went terribly wrong and she died." It surprised him that he got the words out without fighting tears. The hurt was still there, still deep and painful, but at last he'd managed to talk about it.

They chatted a few minutes about Colin Zanardi, the first of the Hedgecock High quarterbacks, and Dave Delaney, who'd been Keith's own hero back when he was a little kid and Dave was tossing passes over on the field. "Dave's got Hall of Fame credentials, but he's hit the skids. Too much partying, too many grasping wives. I hear his latest wife walked out on him and took their two kids with her. He's playing for Colin now, down in Savannah."

Keith hadn't been back to Hedgecock since high school. He doubted if anybody would have held that against him since his mom had remarried and moved to Colorado right after his graduation. He remembered Dave telling him he'd never looked back either. Somehow it seemed sad. He'd made a lot of memories at the old school, and he should have been giving back. *Pay it forward* was the mantra of most NFL stars, and he'd failed to spread some of his wealth, and his knowledge, back to his roots. "You know, we should all be ashamed because we haven't gotten together and done something to help Hedgecock."

"Well, it's never too late," Melanie said. "The school needs new bleachers and concession stands before they fall completely apart. We've been planning a reunion to raise money for that, a festival celebrating all the Hedgecock quarterbacks. It should work if all you boys would come back for a couple of days and draw in folks with money from San Antonio, maybe even Dallas and Houston. "

"We could always do a football camp." Keith held one here each year for high school athletes. He always had fun, and he thought the kids did, too. "I might be able to set one up in Hedgecock, but I doubt many of the families could afford the tuition and fees."

"I doubt it, too. That's why we were thinking of incorporating a weekend camp with the reunion, so the camp would draw kids from farther away. Times are hard these days. Even your sister's having a rough time, raising your nephew on her own."

"Maybe that would work. If you want, I can talk to the others and see what they suggest." He made a mental note to send money to Diane and insist this time that she keep it, for Dylan if not for herself. Never mind that they'd grown apart, largely because Jackie hadn't been able to stomach Hedgecock or anything in it. He'd stayed away because of her, but now there was no one to stop him if he wanted to reconnect with his roots.

"Let's keep in touch," he told Melanie before seeking out Marly's parents and thanking them for the most enjoyable gathering he'd attended in months.

Mrs. Ragusa checked her watch. "I wonder when the newlyweds will arrive in Orlando, I already miss them and they haven't been gone much more than an hour."

"Bobby told me the plane would land around midnight our time. That would be one a.m. there. I imagine they'll call you when they arrive." Keith imagined calling the parents would be the last thing on Bobby's mind, probably Marly's, too. It seemed they could barely keep their hands off each other. When Keith tried to remember when he'd been so hot and so carefree, he couldn't. He guessed those times had been replaced in his memory with the carefully timed matings that got more frantic every time Jackie had insisted on attempting another pregnancy. This was too happy a night for him to think about the fact his only child had been conceived in a cold, sexless laboratory, or to consider his lack of interest in sex since his wife had died.

He looked around the room, found Tina waiting alone near the door. "We'd better get going and put Jack to bed."

* * * * *

Where Memphis had the air of an old but feisty lady, Orlando seemed like a never-ending kaleidoscope of activity. Tourists still milled on International Drive when the limo brought them to the hotel where he'd made reservations. Bobby couldn't care less about anything else but getting to their suite and going to sleep in Marly's arms. His ring felt strange on his hand, until he thought about Marly putting it there.

He kept Marly close as he checked them in. Anywhere else the lobby would have been deserted, but not here. He felt the stares, wondered if the people were gawking at his beautiful wife. They might be sizing him up, if they recognized him. In any case he didn't like the attention, not now when every sane person should have been sleeping.

"Hurry up, for God's sake," he growled at the sleepy clerk. He scribbled his name on the credit card receipt and grabbed the key card out of the man's hand as soon as he offered it. "Doesn't anybody sleep around here?" he said to no one in particular.

"You act like you need some sleep." When they got in the elevator Marly stood on tiptoe and gave him a kiss.

"I do. Some wedding night this is gonna be, with me having to show up at the stadium by eleven for a game. I can just imagine how it will go, since I've never practiced with this team. Sorry, babe. I didn't know this trade would happen before the wedding. I'll make it all up to you."

After he opened the door to the hotel's bridal suite, he lifted Marly and set her down inside. "This place is supposed to have a Jacuzzi. Let's go soak for a while before we go to bed."

Hot water bubbled around them as they cuddled near a strong jet in a corner of the sunken tub. Its whooshing sounds kept them alert, but Marly could literally feel Bobby's exhaustion. Hers too, even though she'd gotten more rest than he had. "Let's go to bed before we go to sleep in here and drown. Don't worry about tomorrow, you'll do fine."

He dragged himself to his feet and climbed out of the tub. "Don't bet on it. I've never gone in and played an actual game with players I've never even seen on tape before. Come here."

When she stepped out of the tub, he wrapped her in a huge, soft towel. "Thank you for marrying me and hanging in for all the curves in the road. I promise this all will work out."

"I know." And she did. He had a career to build, and she was here to help him. "Let me give you a quick rubdown. Tomorrow or the next day will be soon enough for us to find out if sex is more fun with wedding bands and a marriage certificate."

"Okay. You can stay here and sleep through the game if you want to. I'm sure I won't be breaking any records unless they're for the most interceptions or something equally as bad."

"You won't. And if you do you'll just be getting those miserable stats out of the way. Relax, let me love you the easy way tonight." Spilling some of the now-familiar-smelling oil on his back, she deliberately made her touch slow, gentle. A soothing touch, one to draw out the tension and let him sleep.

Water still swirled in the hot tub after they got out, and the fragrant bath salts hung in the cool, damp air. For a long time after Bobby drifted off to sleep, Marly lay beside him, watching the slow, rhythmic rise of his breathing and wondering how she could have been so lucky as to make this hot jock want her, not just for her body but for *her*. For the sexy cheerleader, but also for the slightly insecure woman who had so much trouble believing he wanted her for always, not for just a fast, hot fuck.

He'd told her that first night that he was looking for more, and now she was persuaded. Who but a man who loved her would have let himself get caught up in planning for a quick wedding, even though he'd surely suspected the timing might have coincided with this trade? "You're my love, my lover…for always." Snuggling close to her Bobby, she finally slept.

The End

FORWARD PASS
❧

Dedication

To Joey W. Hill, the best writer friend and critique partner on Earth, for her keen eye, her frequent nudges at me to let my story people's emotions fly. And to Jaid Black, who in her wisdom got us together to critique each other nearly seven years ago. I hope I've helped Joey's beautiful stories one tenth as much as she's helped mine.

Trademarks Acknowledgement

The author acknowledges the trademarked status and trademark owners of the following wordmarks mentioned in this work of fiction:

Cadillac: General Motors Corporation

Coke: The Coca-Cola Company

Escalade: General Motors Corporation

Lexus: Toyota Jidosha Kabushiki Kaisha TA Toyota Motor Corporation

Louis XIII Fine Champagne Cognac: E. Remy Martin & Co.

NFL, NFL Network: NFL Enterprises LLC

Photoshop: Adobe Systems Incorporated

Porsche: Dr. Ing. h. c. f. Porsche Aktiengesellschaft Corporation

Super Bowl: National Football League unincorporated association

Target: Target Brands, Inc.

The Weather Channel: The Weather Channel, Inc

TiVo: TiVo Brands LLC

Forward Pass

Author's Notes and Glossary

I'm a rabid football fan, or rather a rabid fan of several generations of quarterbacks I've watched play on TV and in person. This fandom caused me to come up with an idea for the Gridiron Lovers, a series of erotic romances about four star quarterbacks who just happened to have grown up in the same small west Texas town and who went on to fame and fortune as professionals. All of these guys and their teams are fictional, and any resemblance to an actual NFL player or team past or present is purely coincidental.

The four books' titles apparently need some explanation for readers who haven't been watching games every fall since…well, for quite a few years. Suffice it to say, I've watched every Super Bowl since number three, when Broadway Joe Namath came through on his guarantee of a win for the New York Jets. I was just a baby then (wink-wink).

So here we go. Mind you, these definitions may not all be technically correct, since they're based on my personal observations and comments I've digested from the media personalities who call the games on TV every Sunday from August through December and early January. Take a minute and read these pages first, or as my Aussie editor says, you may become totally confused.

Naked Bootleg. This is a play where the quarterback takes the snap, fakes a handoff to a running back but keeps the ball. He runs the opposite direction from the runner without a lineman protecting him—this makes the bootleg "naked"— and either passes to a receiver downfield or runs downfield himself. I thought it was a great play for Bobby Anthony to make during his first NFL appearance, as well as a sexy-sounding title for the first Gridiron Lovers book.

Forward Pass. The quarterback drops back from the line of scrimmage and throws the ball forward to an eligible receiver downfield. Eligible receivers, I think, are the backs, tight ends and wide receivers. Keith Connors is a master of the forward pass on the field, but he's pretty hot in the bedroom, as well.

Clutch, as in *Hot in the Clutch*. A player, usually a quarterback, who's especially good at coming through with points when the team needs them most. Dave Delaney's career is almost over, but he can still be counted on for a great play in the clutch, whether it's on the field or in a woman's bed.

Coach, as in *Coach Me*. The masterminds of the game, often former players great or average. Each team has several coaches, with the "head coach" in charge of it all. Colin Zanardi's playing days are over, but he's still in the game, not only with his team but also with the hottest of the local ladies.

Now for the glossary, which I'm putting in alphabetical order so you can refer to it as needed while you read:

Athletic waivers: A certain number of exceptions a college coach can use to recruit top athletes who don't meet minimum academic standards for the institution, which are determined by a combination of high school grades and standardized test scores.

Audible: When the quarterback calls out a change of the play at the line of scrimmage.

Block: What linemen do to keep defensive players away from the quarterback, as in "throw a block" or "miss a block".

Center: The player on the offensive line who snaps the ball to the quarterback when he's "under center" or "in the shotgun".

Clipboard: The object that all backup quarterbacks almost always have in their hands while standing on the sidelines; a backup quarterback's assignment, as in "carry the clipboard".

Depth chart: W chart that shows each player's status at his position—starter, second string, third string, etc.

Double coverage: Two defensive players are covering (chasing) one potential receiver for the offense at the same time.

Field position: The spot on the hundred-yard field where the ball is spotted—the closer to the defense's goal, the better the field position is for the offense.

First down: When the offense starts a series or moves ten yards down the field toward the opponent's goal—can be a longer or shorter distance if penalties are involved—and is then given four more tries to make another ten yards or a touchdown, or kick the ball away.

Fumble: When the football gets loose from whatever player had it in his hands and is fair game for any player, either offensive or defensive, to pick up and claim—called a fumble recovery.

Groupie: A woman who's obsessed with professional athletes and wants any athlete, but preferably a star, for a day or night's fun and games.

Handoff: When the quarterback takes the snap from the center and immediately hands it to a running back.

Huddle: A gathering of the entire offense around the quarterback, who gives them the play the coach has sent from the sideline or via a speaker in the quarterback's helmet.

Interception: When an opposing player catches a pass, thereby causing the defense to get the ball.

Linebackers: Defensive players who often break through the offensive line and go after the quarterback (there are three of them in some defenses, four in others); they also break up pass plays down field by stopping the receivers who are trying to catch passes and/or get additional yards after catching the ball.

Line of scrimmage: The point on the football field where the ball is placed.

Nose tackle: A defensive player who lines up in front of the center, usually a huge beast of a man who opens up holes in the offense so other defensive players can get to the quarterback (Note: this assumes the defense is what's called a three-four where the nose tackle and two defensive ends line up in front, with four linebackers behind them—the setup is different, although I can't explain how, if the defense is a so-called four-three with two tackles and two defensive ends in front and three linebackers behind them).

Penalty: A misdeed on the part of an offensive or defensive player that causes the team to be penalized from five to fifteen yards, and sometimes—in the case of a penalty on the defense—to create an automatic first down for the offense. Some of the reasons penalties are imposed are for holding, roughing the passer, unnecessary roughness, illegal motion before the ball is snapped, extra man on the field, or illegal formation.

Pick-six: An interception that the defensive player runs back for a touchdown.

Punt: Kick on fourth down, so the opposing team will get the ball as far as possible downfield; *punter:* the player who kicks punts.

Receiver, or wide receiver: An offensive player whose main function is to catch passes from the quarterback.

Running back: Offensive player who takes handoffs from quarterback and runs the ball, or who catches short passes "out of the backfield" and then runs for yardage.

Sack: When a defensive player gets to the quarterback before he passes the ball, and throws him to the ground.

Scout team: A team of non-starting players who study and then try to duplicate the plays of an opposing team while the first team practices against them during the week before the actual game (the backup quarterback usually runs the scout team, although sometimes that job goes to the third string guy).

Shotgun: A formation where the quarterback stands a good distance back from the center to take the snap.

Snap: The movement of the ball from the center to the quarterback.

Taking a knee: When the quarterback takes the snap and goes down on one knee instead of initiating a play as the time is winding down to zero at halftime or at the end of a game.

Three-and-out: An expression that describes an offensive series where the offense goes three snaps without getting a first down.

Tight end: Offensive players who generally line up at the ends of the offensive line (if there are two of them in for the play) and who block as well as catch passes.

Turnover: The offense gives the ball to the other team because of a fumble or interception rather than after three-and-out or a touchdown.

I hope you all enjoy this series as much as I've loved putting it together.

Ann Jacobs

Ann Jacobs

Prologue
☙

For the first time since Jackie died nearly eight months ago, Keith Connors felt a heavy weight of responsibility start to lift off his shoulders. Finally, after six months of looking, he'd found a nanny he could trust to take care of Jack. And from his own postage stamp-sized hometown, no less. Tina Black had the confidence of Keith's older sister as well as recommendations from rookie Maulers quarterback Bobby Anthony and Bobby's mother, who'd known Tina well while she'd been growing up in a town too small for anyone to have any serious secrets.

Now Keith could get back to the field and concentrate on playing football. Much more time away and he'd have lost his starting slot to Bobby. He knew now he'd been a fool to suggest that the Maulers draft the talented rookie from Hedgecock County High this spring, but in those first dark days after Jackie's death he hadn't known if he could, or even if he wanted to go on playing. Plus, Bobby was a good guy who'd deserved the shot and Keith wished him well in his NFL career.

On the way inside the house Jackie had chosen soon after they moved to Memphis, he paused in the foyer and looked at her portrait—one her parents had commissioned and given them when they'd moved in more than nine years ago. The portrait was beautiful, but it wasn't Jackie as he wanted to remember her. It looked too much like the Jackie she'd become before she died—brittle, cold and so determined to have her way that she'd ended up dying, leaving him lost without her.

Keith turned away from the lifeless painting. He'd spent plenty of time grieving, wondering how he'd ever go on living and bring up the little boy his wife had wanted so desperately.

Now he wouldn't have to face the weekly calls from her mother, offering to take Jack and raise him so he could keep on "playing children's games" as she generally referred to the career that had made him a multimillionaire before his twenty-second birthday. And he wouldn't have to listen to his own mom's worried voice almost every day, asking if he was ever going to find the right nanny to take care of her grandson.

Glancing to the right, at the formal dining room he hadn't been in since the day of Jackie's funeral, he continued through the entryway past a curving staircase to the game room and bar where he spent most of his time at home. As he stared out the window and watched a brisk October wind making ripples along the usually calm shoreline of a man-made lake, he tried to picture the young woman who'd be arriving anytime now to take care of Jack.

Funny, though she'd come with Bobby to meet him and his son just two days ago and he'd seen her again this morning at the team's training facility, he was having a hard time remembering what she looked like. The first time, he'd been most captivated by how Jack had responded to her. He remembered her on her knees in the nursery, lifting his laughing baby in the air while Jack latched onto her hair with both his tiny fists. She'd been young, he remembered that. Just twenty-two, and unlike most women he encountered, she seemed shy around him. That was okay, because she exuded a strong sense of self-confidence when she handled his son. Jack obviously had loved her at first sight. When Bobby's fiancée had brought her over to meet him and Bobby after practice, his impression had been that looks-wise, Tina didn't hold a candle to Marly.

He'd scoured his memory, but the only impression of Tina from Hedgecock, Texas, where they both grew up, had been a young shadow of a girl hanging to the back of the group of boys who used to like pestering him to throw a football with them. His sister Diane had coolly reminded him that she'd been best friends with Tina's mom and that Keith had also run into Tina when he occasionally came to her house to get a ride home from Diane after practice.

Yeah, Diane was still pissed about how he'd turned his back on where he grew up. He'd shoved a lot of childhood memories of Hedgecock deep in the back of his mind. Though he remembered the Black family's modest frame house a stone's throw from the school, and he could still picture a tire swing in the backyard and almost taste the homemade cookies he'd eaten in Tina's mother's kitchen.

Hedgecock hadn't been so bad. He'd just wanted to get the hell away from there so much, away from the empty, dead-end lives so many of the men working the rigs had. He hadn't wanted that to be his future.

Tina was only twenty-two now, but she apparently had taken care of her mother until her death a few months ago. Despite her problems with him, Diane spoke highly of Tina's sense of responsibility, which gave Keith a degree of comfort.

It helped, too, that Bobby recommended her. Some problem had come up back home, bringing Tina to Memphis, but Bobby had assured him it wasn't anything that would interfere with her being a nanny. The two had been close friends since they were kids, and Keith imagined they'd been lovers too. If so, that was in the past. Keith couldn't imagine Bobby's fiancée putting up with him messing around now, just weeks before their wedding. Marly didn't strike him as a woman willing to share her man. Tina would have had a hard time competing for Bobby's attention with the incredibly sexy Marly, anyhow. And that was fine with Keith.

In the past few months he'd interviewed at least a hundred women, most of whom seemed more interested in sleeping with him than taking care of Jack. Tina's appearance hadn't stuck in his mind, but her attitude impressed him. She didn't seem like the type to chase him around the house, trying to seduce him. If anything, he'd sensed a "don't touch" attitude about her that he'd have wondered more about if only he weren't so relieved to be getting his life back in order.

Picking up the phone, he speed-dialed his mom to let her know Tina had agreed to be Jack's nanny and that she'd be moving in later today. Afterward he hesitated then called Jackie's parents too, bracing himself as he dialed the number for the inevitable tears and thinly veiled accusations that accompanied every contact he'd had with them since Jackie's death. Nothing he could say or do would bring her back or make her parents believe she hadn't died entirely because he was a selfish bastard.

Once he got off that difficult conversation, he took a deep breath. After the struggles and grief of the past months, he felt sure Tina was going to be the first good thing that had happened to him and Jack in a while. It almost felt like a new beginning. A good one.

Chapter One
A month later, after a tough Maulers loss

℘

Why the hell hadn't he just retired when Jackie died? Or, if not then, when he took the hit that had kept him off the field six games of this miserable season? His shoulder still ached, a constant reminder that he was nowhere near invincible.

Keith heaved himself out of the ice tub and shivered all the way to the shower, where he thawed out under what felt like fiery needles pounding at his abused body. Yesterday's game had been brutal, but not nearly as much so as the ass chewing he took from Coach Lyle before the team meeting this morning.

He fucking knew he was rusty. It didn't take his genius coach to point that out, only a glance at the stats that said he'd thrown three picks and only one touchdown against a surging Savannah team the Maulers should have beaten. He'd work out the kinks before the last three regular season games though, and Coach damn well knew it. Keith hadn't needed to be bellowed at as though he were a green rookie.

It would serve Coach right if he had to play Ellis Tripp at quarterback. After all, the team had traded talented rookie Bobby Anthony away right before the late October deadline, so the thirty-eight-year-old journeyman would be Coach's only choice if he benched Keith the way he'd just threatened to do. Ellis, fine friend and backup that he'd always been to Keith since his rookie year, hadn't played a regular season down in at least three years. Ellis would show Coach what rusty really was, Keith thought uncharitably.

Still fuming inside at his coach as well as himself, Keith dressed and headed home. Maybe playing with Jack for an hour or so would help him cool off and concentrate on getting his mind right for another night of studying film, a day off tomorrow that would involve more film study for next Sunday's game, as well as a public service appearance Coach Lyle had dumped on him as punishment. At least it seemed that way, because the coach had tacked on his order for Keith to show up at the team's pre-Thanksgiving turkey giveaway at the end of the tirade, almost like an afterthought.

His gaze taking in the last of the fall colors dotting trees along the river as he drove, Keith let his mind wander to his son. And, as he'd found himself doing a lot lately, it also wandered to Tina.

She'd been a godsend and more. He hated to say it even to himself, but she was more loving and giving to Jack than he imagined Jackie would have been. One thing for sure, Tina made him want to be a better dad, seeing the difference her stability and nurturing had already made to the baby's life.

But it was the mystery of the woman, not the efficiency of the nanny, that had been creeping into his brain of late.

He didn't know why. Tina certainly hadn't made any advances toward him. As a matter of fact, he suspected he put her on edge when they were in the same room and Jack wasn't around. It wasn't anything she said, only that air of reserve that perversely made him notice how attractive she was, in a quiet, unassuming way. He wasn't used to women acting as though they were hesitant to get close to him, and Tina gave him that impression. She even acted skittish when their paths crossed by accident.

Just yesterday when they almost bumped into each other on the stairs while she had a hamper of clean clothes in her arms, Keith had reached out to steady her when she looked as though she might fall. The momentary look of panic in her blue eyes as he caught her arms bothered him. He certainly didn't want her to be afraid of him. Yeah, he was incredibly grateful to Tina for making it possible for him to concentrate fully on the career he'd nearly walked away from one bleak day last January.

He found himself wanting to put her at ease with him, wanting her friendship for himself as well as the love she showered on his son.

* * * * *

Something was bothering Jack's dad. Tina sensed it, though Keith was going through all the right motions, playing with the baby on the carpeted nursery floor and riding him piggyback before helping feed him an early supper. She hoped it wasn't something she'd done to upset her moody employer.

Of course it wasn't. Tina scolded herself for her lack of self-confidence. If Keith was angry with her, she was certain he'd have said so. It must have been something that had happened while he was at practice. And she'd guessed from his silence and his scowl last night that he'd come home unhappy about yesterday's game. If she hadn't watched most of it on TV, though, she never would have known he'd thrown two or three interceptions or that the Maulers had lost, because he hadn't uttered a word about the game while helping tuck Jack in his bed.

She'd never known anybody before who was so close-mouthed about his work. Even Bobby, who'd been preoccupied with Marly and his upcoming wedding during the few days she'd been their guest, had given what amounted to a daily report about what he'd done at practice during the short time she'd been staying with them.

It was as though Keith had two lives, one here with Jack, the other as the Maulers' quarterback. He didn't have teammates dropping in, the way Bobby and Marly often did. That had been fine with her at first, not having a lot of guys around. But it didn't seem natural, either, for him to isolate himself in the house, even from Mrs. Gardner, the housekeeper who'd apparently worked there ever since he and his wife had moved in years ago.

As far as she knew, Keith didn't have a girlfriend. Of course, it had just been nine months or so since his wife died. Still Tina imagined he had to be lonely. He was so handsome, so tall and muscular, most women would fall all over themselves to have him notice them. A lot of them probably made a point to run into him every time they had half a chance.

He wasn't happy. That was easy to tell from observing him in person and seeing him in TV ads looking happy and sexier than any man she'd ever known. He made his living playing football. The season was under way. One would think he'd talk about practice, or games, or his teammates, but during the month she'd been there, Keith had never talked about his work at all.

"It seems like you may have had a rough morning," she said just to break the silence.

"Yeah. Trust me, you don't want to hear about it." When Jack began to fuss, Keith set him in the playpen then paced restlessly around the room. It couldn't have been good for him to bottle up whatever was bothering him. And it wasn't good for the baby either. Tina was sure Jack picked up on his daddy's moods, because the little guy had been uncharacteristically fussy all day.

She curbed a sudden urge to go to Keith, comfort him the way she would little Jack. She smiled at him instead, met his somber gaze. "Try me."

Did she really want to know? Keith paused, looked Tina in the eye. "I didn't play worth crap yesterday. Coach bounced plenty of words off me this morning, most of which I won't repeat in front of my kid, reminding me just how bad I was. If he hadn't traded Bobby away last month after my shoulder healed enough so I could play again, I'm certain he'd bench me."

Tina met his gaze, her expression serious. "With all the awards you've won, I doubt your coach would do that. Would it help to talk about it? I've been told I'm a pretty good listener. Jack and I watched the game on TV, so you don't have to rehash every play."

She sounded sincere enough, so he sat on an upholstered window seat near the baby's crib and rested his chin on his knees. "I'm not used to this. Jack's mom had a rule, no talking about my job once I was home. Unless you're seriously interested, we can keep that rule in force."

"No. I'd like for you to tell me. The game wasn't what fans hoped for, but I thought you did plenty of good things." She smiled as she recounted the ninety-five-yard touchdown drive he'd led, and a couple of long passes he'd thrown well only to have his receivers drop or fumble the ball. "I'm not an expert on football, but even I could tell that one of those interceptions was your receiver's fault. He let a perfectly thrown ball go right through his hands."

"You really do like football, don't you?" That shouldn't have surprised Keith, he guessed, as he recalled that skinny little girl following a bunch of the boys who'd always pestered him when he was a teenager. "You know, I remember you hanging back behind Bobby and those other boys who always followed me around when I was playing high-school ball. Did you want to get me to throw you the ball, too?"

"A little." The flush on her cheeks made her look downright pretty.

"I bet you did. Did you ask Coach Williams to let you play when you got to high school?" He doubted she did. She was much too delicate to risk getting smashed by a bunch of rowdy high-school jocks.

"Not me. I went out for cheerleader and made it only because there weren't that many girls to compete." She grinned. "My sophomore year, there were only twelve girls compared with sixty or seventy boys in the entire school. There was real good boy-hunting there for a while." She paused, shrugged. "Unfortunately, the good hunting didn't last. The next year's freshman class was mostly girls."

"Nature sort of averages things out over time. My class had more boys than girls. I remember how getting a date sometimes took some serious pre-planning."

Tina laughed. "I doubt you ever had trouble getting a date."

"Well, I *was* the team's starting quarterback." Keith shot her a grin. "That had to have counted for something."

"I'm sure it did." She paused, as though visualizing the game that had led into this reminiscing about long-ago days back home. "I don't think you should feel guilty about yesterday's game. Your receivers didn't play well. And that one guy should have caught your first pass that got picked off."

"You're right about that." Thinking about how Willis had dropped that well-thrown ball reminded Keith how hard he'd fought to keep the man out of the lineup, partly because he was a disgrace to pro football but largely because he'd spent the last few weeks sitting out, or rather sitting in a Los Angeles jail, until a judge finally set bail and let him walk, pending a trial that wouldn't take place until next spring. "Coach Lyle shouldn't have let him play."

"Bobby mentioned something about him and his buddy getting drunk and beating up on a couple of women while the team was out west for a game. I don't understand why the league lets players who act like that go on playing."

Keith didn't understand either, even though he could see some merit in the commissioner's position of waiting for the law to punish errant players instead of doing it based on a player merely having been accused. "Innocent until proven guilty," he said, shaking his head. "Still, even if Willis didn't do what he's accused of, he got out of shape, sitting in a jail cell for all that time. Just like I got rusty while I rehabbed my shoulder, as Coach so kindly pointed out to me this morning."

Tina bent over Jack's playpen, rearranged the blanket over the baby's well-padded butt. Then she curled her feet up under her in the rocker where she usually sat to give him his bottle. Looking over at Keith, she smiled. "I bet he didn't even consider the difference."

"Huh?"

"What I meant is that you're a little rusty because you got hurt and missed a few games. That wasn't your fault. Your receiver's not playing for a few weeks was because of his own doing."

She looked pretty when she smiled, all soft and pink and touchable. The way her blue eyes flashed, he felt her indignation—a righteous anger that warmed him and swept away much of the resentment he'd been harboring since the talk with Coach Lyle.

Jackie would never have understood. She hadn't wanted to share the part of his life that belonged to football, and she'd resented every moment the game took him away from her. Even so, he missed her, wished...

Hell, he didn't know what it was that he was missing. Sex? There'd been little enough of that during the pregnancy that began in a sterile lab and ended in tragedy. Companionship? Sure. He'd loved Jackie, liked having the most beautiful woman he'd ever met smiling up at him. He just hadn't loved her enough to give up football and take her dad up on his offer of a cushy executive job he'd neither wanted nor deserved. He hadn't loved her snobbery either— her way of judging everybody she met by the length of his pedigree or size of his bank balance.

Fuck, he wasn't about to feel guilty for talking football with his son's nanny. Or for enjoying a quiet afternoon with another adult who seemed genuinely interested and sympathetic. It wasn't as if he were seducing Tina, treating her like one of the groupies who crowded around him before and after every game. She was Jack's surrogate mom, too young and unsophisticated for him to think of as a potential lover even if he was looking for one, which he wasn't.

With quiet amazement, he realized he wanted to get to know Tina better. What she offered Keith was an easy friendship he wanted to explore, one he'd never experienced with another female. He wanted to get to know her better, spend time with her apart from the hours they shared each day with his son. *Whoa.* Keith took a mental step back, told himself to take it easy.

She looked at him, smiled. "Am I right about how that chewing-out made you feel?"

Tina had hit his emotional reaction to that chewing out squarely on the head. "Yeah, you're right. The unfairness of it had me furious. I've given almost ten seasons to the Maulers. I've played hurt, never missed a game until I got my shoulder separated right after Labor Day. I've taken the team to a Super Bowl, been league MVP twice. I didn't deserve to get my ass raked over the coals for one bad game. And I especially didn't deserve to be ordered to show up tomorrow for the team's annual Thanksgiving turkey giveaway."

Her smile broadened. "No, you didn't. Don't you feel better now, after letting it all out?"

"Yeah. Thanks. I can almost pleasantly anticipate signing autographs tomorrow. How about you and Jack bundling up and going with me? I'd like the company." What he'd like was to have Tina and Jack at his side, insulating him a little from the groupies who'd hopefully back off from the usual pawing and propositioning if he had not only his baby boy but also a woman at his side. He found himself looking forward to mingling with teammates outside practices and games, something Jackie had never been willing for him to do.

"We'd like that."

"Good. I'll go work out in the morning then come get you and Jack around lunchtime."

"All right."

Tina didn't say a lot, but when she did, he realized it was sincere and honest. It made him wonder if his invitation was sincere and honest the same way, or if somewhere along the way he'd started thinking about the nanny who took such good care of his son taking good care of his dad in a similar, but much more adult way.

Get that out of your head, Connors. You need a great nanny more than you need a good fuck. But he couldn't help noticing her smell, her hair as she bent over the playpen again, the supple way she moved. And wondering why, when he could have his choice of supermodels, this quiet, kind woman was starting to draw more and more of his attention...

* * * * *

Before noon the next day, Tina was searching through her closet for something decent to wear. Jeans and something warm on top seemed in order for spending several hours outside on a chilly November day, but all her sweatshirts and heavy sweaters looked more suitable for raking leaves outside than for going to some outdoor event.

Darn it, she wanted to look good for Jack. *Don't lie to yourself, Tina, it's his daddy you're trying to impress.* She was crazy, thinking Keith Connors would look at her *that* way, no matter how she wrapped the package.

Then she realized someone had come in, tensed momentarily and let out a little yelp. Concerned, she turned toward Jack, who'd been playing with a ball on the carpet in her bedroom, saw a pair of big, booted feet instead. She followed them up a pair of muscular jeans-clad thighs to see Keith holding his son in his strong arms.

He peered inside the closet. "I hope I didn't startle you."

"Oh no. I just..."

"You thought somebody got past the security at the gate? It won't happen, I promise."

"It's okay. I shouldn't be so jumpy. You look great." Tina looked up, noticed he was wearing what looked like the top of a red-and-black Maulers home uniform, minus the shoulder pads. Not that he needed them, of course.

When he stepped inside the closet and shot her a questioning look, her skin prickled. His body heat filled the small enclosure. It felt to Tina like he was using all the air, making it hard for her to breathe.

"Looking for something?" he asked.

"Something to wear today. I think I need to stop by Target on the way to wherever we're going and buy some decent sweats. All the ones I have date back to my high-school days." The words tumbled out as she clambered to her feet. She couldn't stop them even though she knew she sounded like an idiot.

He dropped a Maulers jersey and a black hooded undershirt onto the chair beside the closet door. "Will these do? I stopped by the front office and grabbed some stuff on my way out."

He'd thought about her, brought her some team gear. A gift. For a minute she stood, speechless, staring up at him and Jack. She loved that he'd…but no, she shouldn't be having him buy her clothes. Finally she found her voice. "Thanks. But you didn't have to. You pay me well enough that I can go buy clothes when I need them."

He looked sheepish. "I know. But I thought you'd look cute in Maulers colors, so I grabbed some for you while I was picking up some baby stuff for Jack."

"I'm sure he'll look adorable. He always does." Keith had called her "cute". She didn't know whether to be flattered or insulted, but she decided "cute" was good when it came from Keith's lips.

"So will you. How about us getting you two dressed, and we can stop by the Fifth Quarter for lunch on the way to the stadium. Several players will be there."

"That sounds good. But we'd better take some baby food for Jack." Tina had heard Bobby and Marly talk about the spot where a lot of the Maulers hung out after games, and she imagined burgers and ribs were probably the usual fare customers washed down there with pitchers of draft beer.

Keith grinned as he lifted Jack high in the air. "You're right. Guess this one's not quite ready for grown-up junk food."

"All right." It would be nice getting out of Keith's house, as gorgeous as it was. Tina picked up the black fleece shirt and a red-and-black Maulers jersey with Keith's name and number eight on the back. His jersey, not just a generic Maulers team one. She smiled, enjoying the fantasy of being his girlfriend and wearing his jersey for a second or two before crashing back to reality. "Thanks for these. They'll keep me nice and warm."

"You're welcome. I'll go get Jack dressed while you change, and start gathering up his stuff so we can leave. I worked out hard this morning and right now I feel like I'm about to starve."

Those two smiles, Keith's and Jack's, could have lit up midnight. As Tina slipped off her top and tucked the soft undershirt into the waistband of her jeans, she let herself fantasize once more that her smokin' hot boss might have some slight interest in her other than as the caretaker for his son. Just for a minute though. She slipped the oversize jersey over her head and smoothed it over her too-skinny curves. *You're Jack's nanny and that's all you'll ever be,* a voice inside her head whispered nastily.

Maybe, but I'm not going to think about that today. Today Tina was going with her boss and his baby to a Maulers team event, and she intended to enjoy every minute of it. She filled Jack's diaper bag and toted it downstairs while Keith took care of the stroller. It was almost as though they were taking off for a family outing, she thought as she turned her head and looked in the backseat of Keith's Lexus to make sure Jack was securely fastened in the car seat. Then she quelled the thought. She'd been thinking way too much about things lately — things that would only bring her heartache, not to mention possible unemployment.

Chapter Two

In the years he'd been playing for the Maulers, this was only the third time Keith had been inside the Fifth Quarter. It felt right, bringing Jack here to show him off to fellow players who'd stopped in for lunch before the turkey giveaway. "Hey, Dan," he said when he spotted running back Dan Morales sitting in a quiet corner booth with a small, dark-haired woman Keith assumed was his wife. "Mind if we join you?"

"Sit down. Myra, this is Keith Connors."

Keith took the hand Myra offered. "I take it you're Dan's wife?"

"Yes. For nearly five years now. This must be your little boy," she said, shooting a big smile at Jack, who was holding onto a handful of Tina's hair while she held him and a waitress set up a high chair.

"Tina, meet Dan and Myra Morales. Tina's Jack's best girlfriend, and my lifesaver." While Keith rescued Tina's hair from his son's determined clutches, he couldn't help noticing her soft, smooth earlobes. He couldn't blame Jack for wanting to hold onto the silky strands of light-brown hair either, even though the baby was being a little too enthusiastic about it. "Hey, kid, let go of Tina's hair so we can put you in this high chair."

Tina laughed at something Myra said—something about Keith not having spent much time around teammates that had sounded like an accusation thinly veiled with humor. "Tina, slide on into the booth, I'll take responsibility for Jack while we eat." When she did, he took the spot beside her.

Myra and Dan had looked a little surprised when they joined them, but Keith was gratified that they seemed cautiously welcoming. For years he'd felt something missing in his relationship with teammates and particularly their wives—but to keep peace at home he'd avoided socializing with his fellow players as much as possible. What the fuck was he supposed to say now? If he blamed Jackie they'd think he was a prick because she couldn't defend herself from the grave, not that she ever would have bothered. If he didn't... Well, most of the guys probably thought he was an asshole anyhow, at least off the field.

As if she sensed his discomfort, Tina reached over and took his hand. It felt good, so good he wanted to lace his fingers through hers, prolong the moment. But he didn't. Instead he froze. As though she realized her gesture was a bit familiar, she laid her hand back on the table, her expression worried.

The air seemed unnecessarily charged. He saw a knowing, speculative look on Myra's face and didn't want her to assume anything bad about Tina, so he quickly threw in an explanation he hoped would clear the air. "Tina and I go way back, since we were kids."

That comment seemed to relax her some. He wondered how she'd react if he put a familiar hand on her thigh, enjoyed the lean feel of her beneath the denim, something casually intimate people would do. "Don't we?" he asked instead, caressing her with his voice.

"Yes. Since I was in first or second grade and he was a high-school football hero." Tina smiled, seemingly more at ease now. "Keith wanted to show his little guy off to his teammates, so he brought me along to be an extra pair of hands. Not that I mind. I love football, and I'm thrilled to meet some other Maulers stars." Her smile at Dan brought out a hint of a blush on the swarthy tailback's face. "And you too, Myra. Do you have any children?"

"Not for another month or so. I don't imagine you told Keith we're expecting." Myra gave Keith a careful, quick look that made him wonder how hard his teammates had tried to keep their mouths shut about kids, wives and pregnancies when he was around, things they'd known had been stress triggers in his personal life. Damn, they'd been a hell of a lot more sensitive to him than he'd been to them.

"Now, Myra..." Dan shot a "shut-up" look at his wife. "I'm sorry, buddy."

"No problem. I appreciate everybody's concern, but I'm okay. Nobody needs to tiptoe around me. Tell the truth, I wish you'd all talk about your kids occasionally so I'd have an excuse to talk about Jack." Tina's smile hinted that he'd handled the awkward moment okay, and that made him feel better.

Tina made him feel better. What the fuck? He wanted that casual physical contact she'd offered. Looking into her eyes, he grabbed her hand, laid it on his thigh and covered it with his own. *Yeah. I liked you touching me, and I hope you don't mind me touching you back.*

A light flush touched her cheeks. She swallowed but didn't lose the eye contact that felt comfortable, reassuring...just the least bit arousing if he were to be completely honest with himself. Suddenly the feelings inside him were getting too intense. Almost frightening.

He turned to Myra and Dan. "What say we order something to eat? I threw the ball with a couple of receivers on the practice squad this morning, and the outdoor workout got me ravenous. Tina, what would you like?"

For a minute Keith watched her read the handwritten menu above the bar, imagined her declining to get anything, as Jackie would have done if he'd brought her to the family-run sports bar and grill. Then she saw something and grinned. "It's been too long since I got to eat some good old-fashioned barbecue. I'll have a sliced beef sandwich with coleslaw and fries. And a Coke."

"Myra?"

"We ordered before you got here," Dan said, his tone apologetic.

Keith motioned for the waitress and ordered for himself and Tina. "Go ahead and bring theirs first if it's ready. You might as well make it a pitcher of Coke." Glancing at the bar, he saw the team's two bad boys ordering shots and beer. Although he didn't actually have the authority to stop them, he didn't want the day spoiled for everybody so he lowered his voice and spoke to the waitress. "You see those two guys at the bar?"

"Yeah. The two with big mouths and no manners?"

"That's them. Do me a favor and tell the bartender that Keith Connors suggested he not serve alcohol to them."

The waitress nodded then stopped by the bar on the way to putting in their orders. Keith sat back, enjoyed the light pressure of Tina's hand above his knee. It felt comfortable. Warm and reassuring, as much so as Jack's grip on the little finger of his free hand. Not exactly arousing, just...right.

He was enjoying himself and imagining, unbidden, having some of the guys and their wives over, or meeting them like this more often, the way he'd always thought relationships with his coworkers ought to have been. The picture looked pretty damn good, with Tina a big part of it.

"Why'd you tell the waitress no beer?" Myra asked. "I can't drink because of the baby, but that's no reason everybody else can't enjoy one or two."

Keith tensed. "I overheard Willis and Mort ordering shots and a pitcher. I wanted to make sure they don't get any. I'm sure you heard about what they did the night the team got to LA."

"Yes. I heard. The only way I could not have found out about that was if I'd been buried in some underground cave with no TV or radio." Myra shook her head. "Those guys..."

"Then you probably understand why I don't want them getting in trouble again, especially when they have to show up at the turkey giveaway." Willis and Mort might pitch a fit, but it wouldn't be as bad as listening to Coach Lyle read the entire team the riot act if anybody showed up at the media event anywhere close to being tanked. "Are you expecting a boy or girl?"

Myra smiled, the first genuine look of pleasure Keith had gotten from her since they arrived. "A boy. He's due the last game of the season, so we hope he comes a few days early or late."

"That would be nice of him." Jack had arrived early, but still after the Maulers had been eliminated from last season's playoffs. It stung, the memory of losing Jackie, of not knowing how he'd manage to care for his tiny, helpless baby. But when Keith concentrated on the warm weight of Tina's hand on his leg, the mental anguish started to go away and he made a conscious effort to smile. "We can't afford to have Dan missing any games if it can be helped."

"Uh-oh. Here comes Willis." Dan put an arm around Myra, as though that might protect her from any nastiness that might be coming.

Willis stopped in front of the booth and shot Keith a dirty look. "Look, Mr. Perfect. I ain't drunk. Haven't even had a drink yet. Who the fuck do you think you are, telling the bartender not to serve us?"

"Watch your mouth. There are women and children here." Keith struggled to hold on to his temper, while his fingers were itching for a chance to rearrange Willis' smart-ass face. "I was doing you and your pal a favor. You're already in Coach's doghouse, and if you show up drunk at the stadium this afternoon you might as well clean out your lockers."

"Hear you're chewin' doghouse bones too, golden boy. Coach didn't like them picks you threw last Sunday."

Keith felt Tina getting tense, saw her eyes darting to Jack who was less than a foot from Willis. He wouldn't let anything happen to his baby or to her, but he understood how living with an abusive stepdad might have made her jumpy around nasty-mouthed men, and Willis definitely was that. He put pressure on her hand, reached over and touched Jack. *It's okay. Everything's under control. I won't let anybody hurt you or Jack.*

He scowled at Willis, even more furious because he was frightening Tina. "If I were you I'd watch what I do and say. If I had my way, both you and your pal Mort would be long gone. I kept hoping the judge out in LA would decide you should stay around until your trials. By the way, you weren't playing any too well yourself last weekend."

"Stuff it. If I want a beer I'll find me one. Enjoy your lunch." With that Willis stomped off. Keith didn't see him leave but assumed he had taken his business elsewhere, since he didn't make any more appearances at their table.

Slowly, he felt Tina's tension lessen until her fingers finally relaxed against his thigh just as the waitress brought their food. Keith dug in, surprised at just how comfortable he felt, surrounded by teammates, Tina and his baby boy. He found himself almost looking forward to signing autographs...and showing off his family.

* * * * *

He hadn't intended to show Jack and Tina off quite so visibly, Keith decided that evening after taking back-to-back phone calls from his mom, Jackie's mother and Bobby. When he grabbed the remote and replayed an NFL network piece about the Maulers' annual community service project, Keith understood what had everybody taking notice.

He, Tina and Jack really did look like a happy family in the short segment that made its way to network TV. He rewound the TiVo, replayed it again.

His mom mentioned how happy he'd looked in a shot where he had his free arm around Tina while she held Jack and he signed an autograph for a young fan. Jackie's mother apparently had seen him having fun with his baby and a strange woman when she felt strongly that he ought to have been teary-eyed and grieving, and anywhere but at the nationally telecast event. Bobby had seemed almost as protective as a father or big brother might be toward Tina, apparently having sensed a man-woman connection that Keith himself hadn't consciously felt at the time the video was being shot. Of course he realized after the fact that him having his hand on Tina's jeans-clad thigh while they knelt and played with Jack hadn't exactly looked like a nanny-employer kind of move.

He lay back against the pillows and flipped off the TV. Morning and a full-pads practice would roll around too soon. Keith tried to ignore the tightness in his shoulder and closed his eyes. Remembering the day, and the joy he'd felt while mingling with fans, he realized what a huge part Tina had played in turning the chore he'd dreaded into a pleasurable experience.

When they'd come home, he hadn't been able to resist brushing his lips across her soft, sun-kissed cheek when he bent to kiss a sleepy Jack good night.

His bed felt cold in spite of the down comforter he'd pulled up to his chin. Empty. Keith drew an extra pillow to his chest, seeking…a woman's warmth he hadn't consciously missed since Jackie died. At least until now. Sex wasn't what he missed, at least not as much as he yearned for the company of a warm, female friend.

Or maybe it was. A lazy twinge of arousal made its way through his veins. Keith squeezed his eyelids shut, tried hard to visualize Jackie. But the picture in his mind was Tina, laughing at Jack's baby antics. Soft, sweet Tina, whose comfortable presence beside him had evoked emotions he hadn't felt for years, since long before Jackie died.

It had to have been the day, the excitement of the fans and the reassuring sense of grounding Tina and Jack provided in the atmosphere that could easily have bubbled out of control. If not for them, Keith might have bought into the quarterback myth and taken up offers from a few brazen groupies—or worse, he could have shrunk inside himself and made a mental escape from the festivities. Smiling at the memory of having Tina at his side, holding Jack and chatting easily with some of his fans, Keith hugged the pillow and tried to clear his mind.

You look like you're in love. Keith's mom was a romantic, her main concern his emotional well-being. She made no secret of her fondest wish—for him to find a new lover who'd make him happier than Jackie ever had. But Mom was wrong. Keith wasn't in love with Tina, just relaxed and happy with a newly found friend.

Wasn't he?

It looks as though you've found yourself a new lover. What Georgia Bern said first wasn't all that different from his own mom's words, but her tone had been terse, as though she thought he'd done something very wrong. She also had made some snide remark about him getting awfully chummy with Jack's nanny at home—something she hadn't learned from the video or from him. After a few minutes' consideration, Keith figured Georgia probably milked Mrs. Gardner for information.

He made a mental note to have a chat with the housekeeper. For a long time he'd been cutting Georgia slack because she'd lost her only child, but it pissed him off that she seemed to think he should have buried not only himself but also her grandson along with Jackie. And it made him goddamn furious to think Mrs. Gardner was spying on him and giving his mother-in-law reports about what went on inside his house.

But Georgia had made him admit, at least to himself, that he had some need for Tina that went beyond her taking care of Jack. Fortunately Bobby's obvious concern for Tina's well-being tempered the sudden arousal that had slammed into Keith's belly when he took second and third looks at the picture of the three of them looking so happy and carefree. He promised himself he'd ignore the sexual attraction, that he'd be Tina's friend but not let his hormones push them into a relationship that might end up with her getting hurt.

After all, as Bobby had mentioned earlier tonight, Tina had gone through a lot in her short life, and it wouldn't be fair for her to fall hard for him unless he saw possibilities for something more together than a brief affair. Keith wondered briefly what difficulties Bobby had been talking about then decided he didn't need to know. He wasn't ready for another lifetime commitment yet. He might not ever be.

* * * * *

Every once in a while when they played with Jack or watched game tapes over pizza and beer, Tina got the feeling Keith was starting to see her as a woman, not just a friend who happened to be female. Occasional yearning looks, fleeting touches that seemed almost accidental, brief hot glances that disappeared almost as soon as she noticed, added up to make her wonder.

Of course she knew she was only dreaming. Keith Connors was miles out of her reach. He'd moved past Hedgecock, Texas, years ago, become a household name with football fans worldwide. He'd married a debutante, learned to move easily in social circles where Tina knew without trying that she'd stand out like a sore thumb. In case she hadn't been smart enough to know for herself that she'd never fit into Keith's life, Bobby and Marly both warned her every time they spoke on the phone, since that day Keith had taken her and Jack to the Maulers' public service event last month.

He wasn't leading her on. In fact, after the game yesterday he'd told her he was done grieving for Jack's mother—and that he intended to bring his long celibacy to an end. "I'm going to sample some of what I've been missing out on for a long, long time," he'd said as they ran the gauntlet of groupies outside the players' exit. Not that Tina could blame him. He'd married really young—younger than she was now — before his face and hot body had been plastered on TV ads and billboards to cause the frenzy of females chasing him at every turn. She just wished sometimes that he wanted to sample her.

They'd had good times, though. Warm, happy days when she and little Jack joined Keith in the massive dining room for Thanksgiving turkey, and when he began joining them for strolls along the lake behind his house. Even when he insisted she start bringing Jack to his home games, she felt right at home, getting to know his teammates' wives and girlfriends when she sat with them and cheered at every Maulers' play.

Some of the hard-eyed players like Willis made her nervous when they came in casual contact, but she wasn't afraid because she felt confident that Keith's protection would keep them from acting on their anger. She'd noticed almost from the first that she didn't have the wariness around Keith that she usually had around men. He was...comfortable, even though that seemed a strange way to describe the hottest, sexiest, best-looking guy she'd ever seen.

Keep your head out of the clouds, Tina. He's not for you.

Being sensible was hard, though, when she was beginning to anticipate Keith's smiles as much as Jack's. She'd stupidly begun keeping count of his casual touches like a schoolgirl.

Like today. They were out in front of the house, putting strings of lights on the evergreen shrubs in the front yard while Jack was taking a nap. Every time Keith passed her a new string, or when they had to brush bodies to connect a new set of lights, her body registered it like an embrace. A libido she hadn't recognized she had came to full, embarrassing life, nipples tightening against her bra, dampness soaking into her panties. She leaned forward against the ladder, where she'd been standing a couple of minutes, arguing with herself about whether or not to acknowledge these unfamiliar feelings.

"Are you okay?"

She gave him an absent glance and a smile. "Yeah. I guess I was doing a little daydreaming."

"Me, too." He put his hands at her waist, ostensibly to steady her down the ladder, but instead he turned her into him, reached up and cupped her head. Sliding his fingers through her hair, he claimed her lips. His big hands circled her waist, holding her steady when she'd have melted like a falling snowflake on this not-quite-freezing day. He didn't devour her. Instead he sampled her mouth, urging her lips to open for a lazy, sweet exploration.

He drew her close, so close she felt his arousal through the layers of their winter clothes. It wasn't insistent, just there, warm against her belly, reminding her he was male…a good male, a male who'd protect her, who'd never hurt her the way her stepfather had. When he released her mouth, he kept her close, rested his bent head against her shoulder.

"I guess I should apologize, but I'm not sorry." His damp breath warmed her throat while the heat of his body kept out the chill of the brisk wind whipping across the lake. "Merry Christmas, Tina."

He said he wasn't sorry, but Tina felt him draw back at little, emotionally. As if he needed to explain his action. "Merry Christmas to you, too." She steadied her hands on his muscular biceps, daring to look up at him, return his smile. "I'm not sorry either."

"It was an impulse, maybe brought on by the season, the bright lights. I don't think either of us is ready to take this further."

He wasn't. That was obvious. He might feel a certain desire for her, because of close proximity and their growing friendship. Most of the time, though, Keith treated her like a favorite younger sister. Despite the heat of his body next to hers, the quick beat of their hearts as they stood outside his house, she sensed this wouldn't go any further. He might want her, but he was fighting the desire. He wouldn't act on it with her.

As if she were damaged goods. No, Tina wouldn't go there. She wouldn't ruin this beautiful day by thinking of her stepfather or the rape. And she wouldn't let that one experience color the way she felt toward other men. There were plenty of other reasons, such as Keith not wanting to disturb her relationship with his baby, such as her being too young and green for him, that might make him think twice about initiating a sexual relationship with her.

He hugged her then loosened his grip on her waist and let her slide down his body to the ground. "I'm not sorry, but…it's getting cold out here. Let's go inside." Keith's tone made her think of warm beds and crackling fires, of his hard, fit body entwined with hers.

But she dared not dwell on what wasn't going to happen. Instead she stepped back, smiled up at him. "All right. It should be about time for Jack to wake up from his nap so we can take him around the gated community to look at all the decorations and lights."

When they turned to face the house, Tina thought she saw Mrs. Gardner staring at them from the French windows in the dining room. "I think Mrs. Gardner was watching us," she said as they carried the ladder to the garage.

"I imagine she was. She seems to enjoy spying more than she does polishing the furniture we never use." Keith set the ladder down, pulled Tina to him and hugged her, hard. "After the season's over, I'm going to have to let her go and find another housekeeper."

"I could…"

"No, you couldn't. You have enough to do, taking care of Jack. I won't have you taking on Mrs. Gardner's work, too." He bent, kissed the tip of her nose. "Thanks for offering, though. You know, you've already made yourself indispensible. I've got no intention of overworking you and losing you."

He wouldn't lose her. Tina had a feeling Keith knew it. Baby Jack had her wrapped around his little finger. But she was afraid Keith had, too. "You won't," she whispered, so quietly she doubted he heard her.

* * * * *

The last Monday in January, Keith tossed a travel bag into his car. After that far too brief kiss on Christmas Eve, he'd done what he'd told himself to do after that possibly unwise impulse and reined the relationship with Tina back to friendship. When he'd wavered, he reminded himself how having her as a nanny and friend had turned his house into a home, maybe for the first time ever. That was true, no matter how disloyal to Jackie's memory it sounded.

He itemized all the good things about her being his "friend". But he'd miss her as well as Jack this Super Bowl week.

Tina was…comfortable. When she asked if he'd like to play with his son, he never felt pushed. But he rarely said no. He found himself getting as much pleasure riding the boy piggy-back and pushing him in his stroller, while Tina walked along beside them, as he did playing ball or studying film for the next game. In the evenings, after Jack was asleep, they watched game film or talked about what had gone on at practice.

It was more than that. His feelings for Tina had crept up, from gratitude that she seemed to love his little boy and made juggling his responsibilities so much easier, to easy friendship to—although he'd tried hard to deny it—a desire to take the relationship between them to the next level. To see if what he felt for her was love or merely need born of long self-denial.

He'd even started expecting to see her at all his games, even ones that involved road trips. At his insistence, she and Jack had watched last week's division championship game from a warm luxury box in Pittsburgh's outdoor stadium while the Maulers eked out a three-point win during a nasty snowstorm. Knowing they were there had warmed Keith's heart even though his body had been damn near frozen.

Maybe he should have taken them with him this week. But Keith quickly discarded the idea. Super Bowl week in New Orleans was no place for a baby—and no place to take the young woman who was becoming more important to him each day. He'd use the time away from them to end his widower's period of grief and sample how life as a football hero could be, at the highest level. Bobby's frequent warning, "Don't mess with Tina's mind if you're not serious, she's been hurt way more than she deserves," rang in Keith's ears. But rather than anticipating a feast on augmented breasts, painted lips and women who knew how to turn a man inside out in bed, he was already thinking of what would happen if he found out that lifestyle truly wasn't what he wanted. He could come back and pursue Tina, with no worries about his motives. And that thought had his groin tightening in a way the groupie images hadn't.

He turned away from the car, looked at her standing on the steps. Then he went to them. "Take care, you two," he said, ruffling Jack's fair hair and nuzzling his cheek. Then, before he could talk himself out of it, he pulled them both into his arms and brushed his lips briefly but emphatically across Tina's inviting lips. "And wish us luck."

* * * * *

The first person he called when the game was over was Tina.

"We won." Keith imagined Tina curled up on the couch in front of the big-screen TV, flushed with excitement while Jack bounced up and down in his playpen by the bar.

"I know. You were incredibly good today. Congratulations on getting the MVP award." Her soft voice had him half hard in spite of his exhaustion. "Jack and I will have a celebration for you when you get home."

Keith let himself fantasize over a celebration that would involve just him and Tina, but only for a minute. The din in the locker room was drowning out their conversation, and everybody was yelling for him to get dressed and go talk to the waiting reporters.

"See you when I get home. Give Jack a hug for me." Keith figured, by the time he got home, he'd have a pretty good idea of what it was he wanted—the playboy life or...one woman who'd love him, appreciate his career and be a mother to his son.

Later. Dressing quickly, he went out to accept the accolades that meant far less than the joy he'd just heard in Tina's voice.

Chapter Three
New Orleans, Maulers' post-Super Bowl Celebration

"Way to go, Keith!" Bobby and Marly Anthony found the MVP quarterback surrounded by a horde of players, coaches and family members gathered for the presentation of league awards, including the Lombardi Trophy that Keith had hoisted on the field after the win an hour ago.

"Wish you'd stayed around long enough to earn your ring." Keith felt bad. Bobby had stepped in and won six of the Maulers' sixteen games while he'd been laid up with a bum shoulder.

Bobby grinned. "That's okay. I'll get mine next year."

Wishful thinking, Keith figured, because Bobby's new team was rebuilding and wasn't likely to have a winning season, let alone win its division, for several years. "You'll have to beat us to get it." Just as he'd had to beat the Savannah Rebels and his old idol, Dave Delaney, today. He had no doubt Savannah would be rebuilding next year since Dave had said he'd be retiring and the Rebels had no immediately recognizable replacement for him at quarterback.

"See you at the party later?" Marly asked.

"Yeah, I'll be there." He could hardly wait to start celebrating.

Today he felt alive. As though he'd come back to life and let go of the blue funk that had surrounded him since Jackie died. Nearly a year had gone by, and Keith was up for pretending his life was as good as he hoped his grin would look in a few minutes when he accepted the key to his MVP prize, a new Cadillac model of his choice.

"Which Cadillac are you gonna choose?" Bobby asked.

"The Escalade." Keith hadn't realized until now that he meant to hand over the MVP prize to Tina and Jack for their trips around Memphis. Right now, though, his main interest was in finding a girl to party with, a groupie who wouldn't expect anything but a good time celebration. "Is Liz around?" he asked Marly. He knew the Maulers had brought their cheerleading squad down for today's festivities, but he'd been too busy playing and planning his next offensive drives to notice the eye candy on the sidelines.

"She's here. She'd fall over if you'd actually go talk to her a little bit." Marly scanned the crowd, pointed out her friend. "See her? She's over in the corner talking with Ellis and his wife, and Jeff Gregory."

Jeff, their punter, looked as if he was already putting a hit on the hot blonde groupie, but Keith figured he'd have a pretty good shot if he went after her. After all, they weren't exactly strangers since they'd stood up with Bobby and Marly at their wedding a couple of months ago. Liz had told him then that she had a thing for signal-callers while dropping thinly veiled hints that he could take her home and enjoy a one-night honeymoon instead of collecting Jack and his nanny and spending another lonesome night in his own bed. "I'll go catch up with her after I do my thing on stage."

* * * * *

After they polished off a meal fit for kings, a band came out and the party began getting interesting. The music was loud, a mixture of New Orleans jazz, disco and raucous rap. Keith was finding it hard balancing one groupie on each knee while downing champagne as though the fountain at the center of the table was about to run dry.

He didn't remember the Maulers' post-Super Bowl party having been quite so wild three years ago when Jackie had been at the party with him, looking pretty scandalized. For certain, Jackie hadn't been gyrating on him then the way Liz

Grady and another Maulers cheerleader were doing now. He hadn't caught the redhead's name but his cock was getting well acquainted with her hot little pussy, through his slacks and whatever it was she had on under the barely-there dress that was hiked up over her thighs.

He tweaked one of her impressive, silicone-enhanced boobs. "Hey there, you. Unless you want to get fucked right here in front of God and everyone, quit the teasing." He freed one arm from Liz and lifted the redhead off him. Liz took over, straddling him and giving him a lap dance he wasn't likely to forget when the band started playing something that sounded strictly carnal. He thought he'd once heard the bump-and-grind cadence in a strip club some of his teammates had dragged him to after an out-of-town victory a few years ago.

In a way he was glad Jackie wasn't around to purse her pretty lips and drag his butt upstairs before things got rowdy. He was even gladder he hadn't brought Tina and Jack, because while Tina wouldn't have complained, he was pretty sure she'd have been hurt watching cheerleaders gyrate all over him the way Liz was doing.

He was wired, high on the atmosphere and buckets of vintage champagne. His offensive linemen were doing a conga dance around the table while their wives and girlfriends laughed over their drunken antics. Oh fuck. Liz knew how to move her ass against him, and she ground harder and faster when the guys started chanting encouragement.

She bent close and nibbled on his ear, never missing a beat of the stripper music. "You can fuck me anytime you want. Anyplace."

Would she have liked it if he said, "Here and now"? Having sex in public had never been one of Keith's fantasies. He'd even been shy about gettin' it on with his high-school girlfriend under the old bleachers at Hedgecock County High.

Something inside his fuzzy brain suggested he should feel some sense of sadness over his memories of Jackie, but right now he wasn't feeling any guilt or grief. Amazing what alcohol could do to dull emotions. Especially the copious amounts of champagne being served to celebrate the biggest win in football.

Liz felt hot, reeked of pure lust that had nothing to do with any other emotion. And Keith was pumped up as well as pleasantly buzzed and horny as hell. "Why don't we try dancing standing up first, you sexy thing?" He set her off him and stood, a little unsteady on his feet from the champagne bubbling away in his brain. "C'mere."

She was tall. And stacked like a brick outhouse, too, as one of his college teammates used to say. Her generous breasts burrowed into his chest when he wrapped both arms around her and swayed to the tune of some blues song about strangers fucking in the moonlight on a one-night stand. The song turned Keith's thoughts toward ending a long, sexless dry spell with this woman who so obviously was eager to sample Keith Connors, Super Bowl MVP and out-of-practice stud desperately in need of a few orgasms.

There was always a first time to indulge in the sort of debauchery some of his teammates enjoyed talking about pretty much all the time. The win had been a high unto itself, while the champagne and all the public foreplay had his hormones on fire. When the dance was over and they sat back down, Keith winked across the table at Marly and Bobby, who seemed not at all shy about indulging in some pretty obvious sex play of their own.

What the hell? He nuzzled Liz's smooth, silky neck and whispered, "How about sliding under the table and giving me a blowjob where nobody will see?"

She turned, placed a wet, champagne-flavored kiss on his lips. "I was hoping you'd ask. I've always wondered what an MVP's cock would taste like." Laughing, she slid off his lap and landed at his feet, on her knees. When she unfastened his belt and unzipped his slacks he had a brief second, time for one uncomfortable and unexpected thought about what the fuck he was doing here.

Then her full lips closed around him, and he forgot any reservations that might have been lurking in his fuzzy brain. *Yeah. Suck me, baby, suck me hard. Like that. Omigod.* He held out his glass, let Coach Lyle pour him more champagne from a giant bottle he was carrying around the ballroom. "Having fun, Coach?"

"Hell yes. My wife went upstairs, so now I'm gonna party." Coach did a double take. "What happened to the hot blonde that was on your lap a minute ago?"

Keith didn't know if he should laugh or cry when Liz's hand came up and touched his lips. "She's under the table," he croaked, figuring Coach knew anyway that he was getting some head there in the middle of one of the Hotel Monteleone's very elegant ballrooms. Marly was down there, too, blowing Bobby, or else she'd slipped away to the restroom. Probably Keith's first guess was right, from the ecstatic look on his former backup's baby face. "Don't stop now, honey," he said, knotting his fists in Liz's bright blonde hair. "You don't know how good that feels."

She paused. "I'm hoping I'll find out, though." Then she sank on him again, took him down her throat and swallowed. If she didn't stop he was gonna come, and right now he wanted to give as good as he got.

"What say we go up to my suite?" It had a hot tub and a king-size bed with a mirror above it. Right now he was more interested in the bed, but he figured they could have some more fun later in the hot tub. "Zip me up. Before you know it, we'll be naked and fucking like minks, if the elevators will cooperate." While she stuffed his throbbing cock back in his pants and zipped them, he grabbed a handful of the condoms someone had smartly included as part of the table decoration. He'd have picked her up and carried her, if only he hadn't already consumed more champagne than he should have.

* * * * *

Forward Pass

Liz was firm and female and all Keith needed to top off the most successful single day of his career. And she made him feel all male, a mindless animal, full of a driving lust that stirred him to fuck her fast and furious, give her everything she asked for.

"I'm not a tender little girl, Keith, you won't hurt me. Fuck me hard."

"Like this?" He grabbed her wrists and pounded into her like a jackhammer, bending to bite her neck, consume her mouth. She writhed beneath him, urging him on, screaming with pleasure as she convulsed around his cock, drew out his own climax. He yelled, a shout of triumph he'd never felt so strongly before then collapsed on her, spent. Their hearts pounded in unison.

Until now he'd never had sex without tenderness, without some form of affection beyond the animal need for a woman. Any woman. But Liz evoked that heat, the pure sexuality that was nothing less, nothing more than carnality at its finest.

Not wanting to crush her, Keith rolled over and dragged her so close he felt her heart pounding against his chest. "Thank you," he said, not knowing if he should change condoms and fuck her again or try for a show of post-sex affection. "Wanna relax in the hot tub?"

"Sure."

This was a fantasy, one he'd occasionally acted out in his dreams. But tonight it was real. A semi-nympho groupie was clawing at his back as hot jets of water poured over them. His cock was buried deep in her steaming cunt. She asked for nothing but his cock to pound her pussy so she could tell her friends she'd been fucked by the Super Bowl MVP the night after the big game.

It felt good. Weird, but very good. Surreal in a way, he thought as the fog of champagne was beginning to wear off. Lifting Liz off him, he stepped out of the tub and toweled himself off. "Come on, baby, let's go back to bed before we drown." He kissed her full on the lips, felt for the first time that this was wrong. That something important was missing from this scene. As fast as he'd fallen for her blatant invitation, he now felt cold.

He didn't know exactly when things shifted, maybe after they'd fucked two or three times, but he found himself staring at the mirrored ceiling while Liz blew him off again, his thoughts wandering somewhere else. To a young, quiet woman with silky hair who'd stood on a ladder on Christmas Eve. To the hopeful smile on her face, the soft touch of her lips.

Keith pushed that thought away, did what he needed to do. But when it was over this time, he rolled away, feigning a not completely fake exhaustion. The adrenaline was burning off, and his cock was no longer calling the shots.

Yeah, it was a great high, while it lasted. But he was no kid. Tomorrow was Jack and practice and bills to pay, the ups and downs of every day. He needed a companion, someone to share his life, not just a hot chick to blow him. If he'd had Tina beneath him in a bed, after he brought her to a screaming orgasm he'd want to hold her in his arms, hear her whisper in that soft, sweet voice that she was going to check on Jack, anticipate her coming back to him.

Something right and complete, and not just spur of the moment. That's what was missing. He felt it keenly enough to know he was going to wake up in the morning and realize this had been a mistake.

*****

Yeah. He was right. This had been an interlude, pleasant enough. Liz must have sensed his withdrawal, because when he woke the next morning, she was gone, sparing them the awkward goodbyes. But she'd left a note, written on a piece of the Monteleone's complimentary stationery.

Hey, Keithie baby, don't feel bad, I wanted last night as much as you did. I could tell toward the end, though, that your heart wasn't in it. I'll be watching you on the field, and available any time if you ever want to play. Thanks for the memories... Liz.

She'd made it easy on him, and that made him feel bad. He had the world's worst headache. *Your own fault, you should have laid off the champagne before your brain started swimming in it.* He didn't know if it would have been better if he'd been so drunk he couldn't remember he'd had Liz give him head in the middle of the postgame celebration or that they'd fucked at least three times before he started to sober up and came to his senses.

This wasn't the kind of life Keith wanted for the rest of his career. Partying hard might do it for a lot of pro athletes. Fellow Hedgecock County star Dave Delaney had turned postgame carousing into an art form, if half the rumors around the league were true. But Keith had been domesticated early. He'd do without sex before fucking any willing female that walked just so he could blow off steam and maybe hurt some woman who should have been looking for a lover, not a one-night stand.

He lay alone in the big bed, his eyes closed. The playboy image wasn't for him. He wanted a woman to want him because he was Keith Connors the man, not Keith Connors the Super Bowl MVP. He wanted a woman, not a trophy wife to make all his teammates drool with envy. A woman who could make him feel again, who could be a mom to Jack and love him as if he were her own child. The way Tina did.

Unexpectedly, he recalled Bobby and Marly's wedding, a brief flash of how Tina had looked. At the reception, she'd sat holding Jack, nuzzling his curls. She'd worn a wistful expression, seemed sad as she watched Bobby and Marly take their first dance as man and wife. He'd been fighting off the maid of honor's determined passes, but he remembered it now, clearly enough. No doubt about it. Tina was the sort of woman a man could take home. She was no sex bomb, but she fired his blood. Every time they were together, if he was going to be completely honest about it.

There was that kiss on Christmas Eve. And the warm feelings that flowed between them when they came home from the team's turkey giveaway and he brushed his lips across her soft cheek.

The warmth had stayed with him for a long time after he kissed her and Jack goodbye before coming here a week ago today. The sweet, minty taste of her mouth suddenly came to the forefront of his mind, along with the feeling of rightness that had swept over him when he held her, his son laughing between them.

She's too young. Too tender. Unless you're in love with her — unless you want her not just now but for the rest of your lives — you mustn't hurt her. Lying back against the pillows in a room that smelled obscenely of fresh sex and stale perfume, Keith closed his eyes and waited for the pounding in his head to go away.

Chapter Four
Memphis, eight days later

☙

Keith tossed back a shot of single-malt Scotch, hoping it would shut down the fast-forward mode in his brain. It didn't. Neither did staring at the flames in the fireplace or reviewing a tape from a game he'd missed during the season that just ended. Jack was fast asleep upstairs, and Tina had turned in for the night. The housekeeper, Mrs. Gardner, had long since retired to her apartment over the garage.

A fierce wind whipped through the trees outside, pushing water from the lake up onto the dock and patio where it immediately froze into a treacherous glaze of ice. Limbs crackled, the sounds ominous. The girl on The Weather Channel had predicted several inches of snow tonight, a relative rarity in Memphis, and if she was right they'd be pretty much confined in the house until the mess melted off. Memphis didn't have enough snow plows to get that much of it off already icy streets.

Normally Keith played golf nearly every day during the off-season, but this wasn't exactly golfing weather. Staring out the bank of windows and French doors, he watched snow come down. Shit, he probably wouldn't even be able to drive to the Maulers' training facility to do his daily workout, and talking with the trainers and a few fellow players who lived in Memphis year-round was about the only pleasurable human contact he looked forward to these next few weeks, outside of playing with Jack and Tina.

He paced around in the game room, finally picking a pool cue from the rack on the wall and listening a moment later to balls breaking on the table with a satisfying splat. It was okay that he'd dumped the cue ball. It wasn't as if he'd thrown a pick-six, or even an incompletion. Playing quarterback for the Maulers was his job. Playing pool was supposed to be fun.

Fun, hell. He guessed he was cranky because, in the aftermath, he realized that even winning this Super Bowl hadn't brought the lasting emotional high it had the first time he and the Maulers did it together three years ago. He guessed the celebration and his drunken interlude with Liz had been an aberration.

Tell the truth, this win had left Keith with an empty feeling, as if he'd hit the pinnacle and had nowhere further to go. It didn't help that he'd missed six games during the regular season or that he felt that Bobby Anthony had done as much as he'd accomplished to secure the divisional championship. Lucky bastard, he was enjoying a belated honeymoon with Marly on some tropical Caribbean island.

For a moment Keith imagined himself and Tina sipping frozen margaritas in a place like that, listening to waves breaking across a white-sand beach. The fantasy beat the reality of a stormy night in Memphis all to hell.

He missed an easy shot on the two ball. After missing and digging the pool cue into the felt, he set the cue down. No need to rip the table top in a fit of emptiness. He had to get a grip. Tomorrow was the anniversary of Jackie's death. Worse, her parents would be descending on him, commemorating her death by doling out their guilt and condemnation in person under the guise of visiting their grandson on his birthday.

The impending anniversary explained a good part of his moodiness tonight. Despite the bad times, he and Jackie had some good years, made good memories together. He'd had a partner, somebody to listen to and share things with other than when he needed to talk about his career. This house was too damn big and cold not to have somebody to share it with. It was time for him to move ahead.

He wanted Tina.

There, he'd said it if only to himself. He just wished he believed they were right for each other. He was certain she was right for him, but that wasn't enough, knowing he'd been a lousy husband once and might let history repeat itself. Keith threw back the rest of the shot, savored the burning sensation in his throat.

The wind was blowing so hard outside that the floor-to-ceiling windows seemed to shake. Somewhere near the lake a limb shattered and slammed to the ground, helpless against the strain of ice and wind. Keith looked through the window but couldn't see the fallen limb. Only darkness, bittersweet memories and an uncertain future.

A tortured cry cut through the sounds of the storm. His imagination? He thought so at first then listened harder. "No. Please no. Get away from me." The terrified pleas were coming from upstairs. It had to be Tina, and she sounded as though someone were there, frightening her to death. Threatening her.

Taking the steps two at the time, Keith barreled to her room and flung open the unlocked door. She was sitting up in bed, her arms wrapped around her body, horror reflected in blue eyes that seemed almost black. They glistened with unshed tears.

"Tina?" He had to do something. But what?

Over these months, from her initial wary reserve around him, to her reaction to Willis' anger, to Bobby's vague references to problems with her stepfather in Hedgecock, a picture had been building. Keith hadn't wanted to look at it too closely, hadn't intended to get so involved.

But he was going to get involved now. Somebody had hurt Tina once, and he wasn't about to let that happen again. Not even in her nightmares.

He didn't hesitate. He moved to the bed, sat on the edge and wrapped his arms around her. His touch seemed to bring her back from her own private hell and loosen the taut muscles that had her practically immobile. He laid his cheek against hers, spoke just above a whisper so as not to spook her. "It's okay. Cry it out. I've got a good shoulder for leaning on."

She was shaking like a leaf, and her skin was clammy. "I—I'm sorry. Didn't mean to disturb you. It just seemed so…so real." As though she needed reassurance that he was there and real, she clutched him, fisted her hands in the fabric of his sweatshirt. "Please don't go."

"I'm here, and I'm not going anywhere. Why don't you tell me about it? Sometimes it helps to get whatever's scaring you out so you can see it can't hurt you in the light of day." When she just shook harder he brought her head onto his chest and stroked her back to try to soothe her. "I won't let anybody hurt you."

He'd never felt so helpless, so angry at whoever the bastard was who'd caused this sweet, caring girl to quake with fear. He also felt himself starting to react to her feminine softness but willed his body to behave. "Come on, let's go downstairs by the fireplace and have a drink while you tell me about this bogeyman that has you scared to death."

She only burrowed deeper, clasped him as if he were an anchor in the storm that had engulfed her. "Hold me. Please hold me."

"All right." Though he'd already made a decision to move forward with exploring a relationship with her, he knew this wasn't the time, so he used all those earlier rationalizations as he worked to calm down his libido. How she was ten years his junior, not long away from her teens. That she'd been a pesky tomboy he recalled from his childhood.

That she was wearing a fairly sexless sleep shirt, one that was thin and soft and let him feel her body beneath it… This wasn't working…

Not working at all. His damn twitching cock would just have to suffer. But there was something about being in her bedroom, the feminine smell of fresh linens and flowers on a bedside table that had him thinking about loving her fears away. He drew a mental picture of himself, stretching her out on top of these crisp, white sheets and covering her not with the comforter but with his own aching body. If he didn't get them to someplace neutral, he'd be seducing her while her thoughts were still on the terror she'd just faced in her mind. That wouldn't be right for either of them.

Keith scooped her up, surprised at how light she felt as he carried her downstairs and set her on the one end of the sectional sofa in front of the fireplace. He noticed a fire was still smoldering. Needing to put a little distance between himself and Tina, he laid another log on the grate then strode to the bar and filled two brandy snifters with Louis XIII Fine Champagne Cognac from a bottle one of the team owners had given him for Christmas.

"Here, you'll feel better if you drink this." He joined her but sat at a safe distance on the opposite end of the sofa and sipped his drink. "Tell me about why you left Hedgecock so abruptly."

"After Mom died, h-he came after me."

"Who? Your stepfather?" Keith tamped down on the fury he felt when she nodded, saying nothing, hands trembling so the amber liquor in the snifter quivered. "He left me alone until after Mom died. But then…then he started touching me, cornering me. Pushing me against the wall and grinding himself against me. Saying filthy words about what he intended to do." She paused. "His breath stank of cheap whiskey and rotten teeth, and he wouldn't stop, not even after I moved out of the house where I thought he couldn't get to me."

She lowered her gaze, stared at her drink. "He caught me in a storeroom at the school cafeteria where I was working. He raped me. And he still comes back at night in my dreams. I'm so afraid." Her tone was flat, almost as if she were talking about somebody else's nightmare and not her own. But tears streamed down her cheeks, denying any lack of emotion on her part.

Apparently she'd counted on Bobby to chase away her demons when she followed him to Memphis, only to find him engaged to Marly Ragusa. But since Bobby had never mentioned the actual events that had driven Tina away from Hedgecock, Keith doubted that she'd ever told him exactly what had gone down. Keith sensed she'd kept the memory buried deep inside, and that this was the first time she'd told anybody the complete story. Hearing how her stepfather had raped her had Keith's blood boiling, his fists aching to choke the life out of the fucking pervert who'd hurt this lovable young woman.

Tina sat in the glow of the fireplace, seemingly calm now that she'd explained what had her waking, terrified, even now when she was safe and seemed happy to be taking care of Jack. Keith felt flattered that she'd trusted him enough to tell him…and that she could be sitting less than four feet away from him and not be trembling in fear.

He imagined most women who'd gone through what she had would have wanted to keep a safe distance from all adult men. But Tina often joined in when he played with his son, and she'd never given Keith any indication that he or any of his friends who'd come over to the house had frightened her. "I'm surprised you don't seem to be afraid of all men, me included."

"I trust you." She looked up, met his gaze. "You're a good man, nothing at all like *him*. I've never thought that all men were like him. Edgar Garcia is a monster. He's not any part of a human being."

In the time she'd been living there and taking care of Jack, Keith had thought of Tina as that kid she used to be, the tomboy he vaguely remembered from his own teenage years. Holding on to that picture of her had kept him from acting on the vague arousal he'd experienced when she was near. But it changed for good a few minutes earlier when he'd held her, felt her ripe breasts pressing against his chest, her warm breath making sensual patterns on his throat.

While he listened to her confess what she saw as her shame, his blood pounded in his head. Fuck, having been raped by her pervert stepfather wasn't anything for her to be ashamed of, no matter what she thought. Keith found himself not only wanting to find Garcia and beat the life out of him, but needing to reinforce to Tina that sex didn't have to be brutal or scary. That not all men were evil.

"Come here, little one." He had to hold her again, absorb her fears. "Don't be afraid of me."

She met his gaze, her eyes shining with unshed tears. "I'm not. I know you'd never hurt me." Setting her snifter on the cocktail table in front of her, she slid over and let him arrange her so they were half sitting, half lying together. They were close enough that he could smell the slight aroma of fine cognac on her lips, see the outline of her panties and her firm, full breasts beneath that simple sleep shirt that shouldn't have been turning him on.

He shouldn't have been doing this. He risked hurting her, only not in the way she apparently was certain he wouldn't. Despite his resolve that he was ready to move forward with Tina, that was before he'd heard this story, about how badly a man had let her down—a man she should have been able to trust. As a result, the same demons ripped at his heels, making him doubt himself. He was too raw, too hung up in his own mixed feelings about Jackie and the way she'd died. Too leery about opening himself up to more emotional pain. When he desperately needed sex, there were plenty of willing women who wanted nothing more than a roll in the hay with an all-pro quarterback.

With every stroke of his fingers over Tina's soft, pale arm his conscience screamed at him to stop. She wasn't a groupie hot for a piece of him, but the woman who'd stepped into his home and given his son a mother figure. And him a friend.

But Keith couldn't stop. Some emotion stronger than he was had him in its grip. Desire, yes. He was a normal male, and normal males didn't go without regular sex as long as he had without reacting to a woman whose nipples hardened at his touch the way Tina's were doing now. When the tension in her body gave way to pure, female softness he was lost.

"That feels good," she murmured, turning her face up to his. "I should be apologizing for keeping you up."

"Hush. I couldn't sleep anyway. When I heard you crying, I wanted to help. You know, you've helped me more than I can say, being here for Jack. For me, too, although you probably didn't know it." Keith shifted, brought their bodies in closer contact. "You feel damn good."

"So do you." Tina couldn't help the heat that began as a little twinge in her belly and spread like molten lava through her veins. It was a good feeling, being in Keith Connors' arms, knowing that anything that happened between them would be mutual, friends giving comfort to each other. Nothing permanent but something good, satisfying an attraction she'd felt toward him during the first few days they'd shared this big house and his little boy. "If you want…"

"I want, believe me. But I'm not much of a prize. I like you, I appreciate all you've done for Jack and me. I've got a feeling you need more than liking and appreciation to wipe out the bad memories that had you screaming and in a cold sweat not too long ago. You need more than I've got in me to give."

She didn't care. She knew he must still be hurting for Jack's mom, the beautiful woman who smiled down from a portrait above the living room mantel every time Tina walked by the room. Keith had to cope with having lost her while taking care of the baby they'd made and keeping up with his demanding job. She imagined he might be living with misplaced guilt as well, since his wife had died giving birth to Jack. His fast pulse and the growing tension on his handsome face let her know he was aroused. And she wanted to give him release. "All I want is now. I think you want that, too."

"You're sure?" He traced her lips with his thumb, looked at her with hungry eyes that burned right through her, made her pulse race and her skin grow hot.

"I'm sure."

He moved smoothly, his arms taut as he lifted her onto his lap then found and captured her lips. Small, sweet kisses that felt of affection as much as lust calmed her worries, gave her a sense of rightness, a security that meant worlds to her even if it was just for now. His kisses reminded her of ones he pressed on his baby son's chubby cheeks, only these were different. More intense.

Thunder rolled outside and a bolt of lightning lit the sky. It wasn't just the storm raging over the lake. It was the one brewing inside her, making her clasp Keith's broad shoulders, press closer to his long, muscular body. His erection branded her with its heat and hardness, made her shudder for just a moment.

She knew he wouldn't hurt her the way her stepfather had. Keith would make her feel good in a way nobody had for a long time. He reminded her of Bobby a little. Their bodies were similar, both tall, lanky and powerfully athletic. But the way Keith was kissing and caressing her now made bells ring. They'd never rung like this when she and Bobby had experimented with sex under the bleachers when they were in high school. Bobby had been a boy back then. Keith was a man, a successful man who'd had years to develop the technique that had her wet between her legs and panting for more. He was making her feel cherished, even if the feeling would only last a little while.

Tina guessed she was still the same insecure girl she'd always been, needing sexual fulfillment but wanting a white knight to come swoop her up, deliver her from her own difficult life and take her to the place she'd always dreamed of.

Only now she'd settle for the promise of an hour in fantasyland with Keith.

She threaded her fingers through his longish, light brown hair, loved the way the silky strands contrasted with the shorter, crisp hairs at the back of his neck. When she stroked him there he deepened the kiss, ran his tongue over her lips and thrust inside when she opened to him. For a long time he kissed her, his tongue making a lazy exploration in her mouth as if he wanted to memorize her taste, the textures of smooth flesh and teeth she'd always wished were a little straighter. He aroused her slowly, his big hands caressing her neck, her spine, seeming to avoid the places she'd learned as a teenager that boys liked to zero in on. He hadn't even gotten rid of her sleep shirt yet.

He didn't need to. His sensual touch through the light fabric had her squirming against him, clutching his muscular arms like a lifeline when she was about to melt in erotic sensation. "Easy there, I've been starving for this a long time. I'd like to make it last." He sounded breathless, as if he was as affected as she by the contact, the promise of fulfillment he seemed determined to hold at arms' length.

Tina didn't doubt at all that he wanted her now. That was evident in his touch, in the taut expression on his handsome face. In the way he whispered her name. Hers. Nobody else's.

Not once did he make her believe, while he slowly built up the need in both of them, that he was seeing his wife's ghost. She wouldn't have believed that even if he hadn't often called her by name, whispered how much he needed this, how badly he wanted her. By the time he raised her sleep shirt, ripped off his sweatshirt and lowered his head to her aching breasts, she was nearly crazy, craving more.

She wanted it all. Wanted him to rip off his pants and her damp cotton panties and fill the emptiness inside her with his hot, rigid shaft that now throbbed against her swollen sex. "Take off your panties and lie back on the couch. Open up for me so I can taste your sweet honey."

"But—" She'd heard a lot about oral sex but never experienced it. "You don't have to."

"But I want to. Unless you're afraid?"

"I'm not afraid of you, Keith." Everything else he'd done to her felt delicious. The idea of him burying his face between her legs and stimulating her with his mouth somehow seemed more intimate than the prospect of him plunging into her core. Too intimate, almost, for this interlude she was sure wouldn't blossom into a lasting relationship. Yet not intimate enough, not unless... "I'd like to taste you, too."

"Me first." When he stretched out between her legs and spread her outer lips, she shuddered. His hot breath on her damp flesh sent little tremors along her nerves, made her hold her breath with anticipation. Then he found her clit and took it between his teeth. When he licked along the tip of her sensitive flesh she tensed. It was like when she satisfied herself, only better. His tongue felt like wet velvet, his touch sensual and sure. "You taste so damn good," he muttered, lifting his head for a second before diving back in, this time licking along the length of her swollen, wet slit.

She felt pressure building, making her muscles tighten, her body gush hot lubrication. The musky smells of sex and pungent smoke from the fireplace filled her nostrils, surrounded her with an almost desperate need for release. Could she come this way? Would Keith want her to?

He zeroed in on her sex, plunged his tongue deep inside her. His lips put delicious pressure on her clit. She wanted to give back the pleasure, take his long, thick sex in her mouth. "Please. I want to taste you, too."

"Not until you come for me."

A dam of sensation broke inside her, spread through her veins. "Omigod, I'm coming now. Don't...don't stop." She wanted more, wanted him to claim her fully. "Please. I want you. All of you."

He muttered something then resumed fucking her with his tongue.

It wasn't enough. "You're not going to…"

"Do what I'm aching with the need to do? Not tonight. I don't have a single condom in the house." He resumed sucking her clit, making her squirm against his mouth, splay her fingers over his shoulders.

Her good sense warred with the need to have him inside her, feel his heat and hardness. She wanted him to take her fully even as she appreciated him being considerate and not willing to risk making her pregnant. "That doesn't seem fair to you."

He backed off, blew on flesh already sensitized by the rasp of his evening beard, the smooth slide of his tongue. "Don't worry about me. I'm getting more pleasure than I've had for a long time. Besides, you can help me come, too, if you really want to."

"Oh yes, I do." She'd touched Bobby once or twice but never when she was starving for fulfillment. When her high-school friends had talked about going down on their boyfriends, she'd had mixed feelings about trying it. Now, with Keith, she wanted to touch him, taste him, do for him what he was doing for her.

Oh God. His long fingers and agile tongue worked magic on her, made her shatter again like an overfilled balloon into what seemed like a thousand pieces of pure pleasure. He kept it up, and the sensations intensified. She wouldn't have believed that possible. "Please don't…don't stop." She threaded her fingers through his hair, pressed him closer. "Omigod."

"Keith!" She called out his name as shock waves kept going through her.

Chapter Five

He lifted his head but kept his fingers inside her, hard and hot for her inner muscles to clench around. Her juices glistened on his mouth, his cheeks. His eyes expressed hunger. Hunger she longed to satisfy, however he wanted. "Tina, baby, you have no idea how much I want to…"

He was about to explode, holding on by a thread to keep from ripping off his pants and burying his cock to the hilt in her wet, welcoming pussy. "Feel your hands and mouth on me."

Keith felt her tremble, sensed her hesitation. More than that, he recognized her need. "Come for me again, little one." He drew her clit into his mouth, sucked greedily while he slid two fingers inside her warm, wet pussy and scissored them. She tasted so damn good, clean and soft and so arousing it was all he could do to hold back his climax. Her soft cries excited him more as she came again. He'd never experienced such a powerful response from a woman, as if her entire being centered on him. Soon she'd be climaxing while he buried his cock deep inside her. He'd be absorbing her cries of satisfaction in his mouth.

He shifted away from her spasming pussy and licked her juices from his lips as he met her stunned yet contented gaze. How could he ever have thought she was plain? "You're so damn beautiful when you come."

He rested his head on her belly, tried to concentrate on the storm that was raging outside. On anything but the one inside him that was sweeping him up in its fury, robbing him of the self-control he had to maintain.

"May I?"

Yeah. God yeah. His cock ached with anticipation. He sat up then lifted himself enough to pull his pants off. "Please touch me." Last week's debauchery had taught him he liked oral, too. A lot. His cock swelled with anticipation when she first touched him. She was no expert, he could tell by her tentative touch, but he liked her slow exploration of his shaft and he loved the way she bent and put her tongue to the lubrication on the tip of his cockhead. "That's the way."

She slid off the sofa and knelt between his legs. Her hungry gaze, the warmth of her breath as she leaned closer, fired his libido, made him clench his fists to keep from grabbing her head, guiding her mouth to his throbbing cock. *Let her do it in her own time. You can wait.*

Slowly she sucked the tip of his cock into her mouth, her tongue exploring as though she'd never done this before. She cradled his balls in one hand, her touch all the more arousing because it was so obviously unpracticed. Keith drew in a deep breath of air, let it out slowly when she sank deeper onto him and began to suck, first gently then harder, as though she wanted him to come in her mouth the way she'd just come in his.

He'd never wanted anything more than to drag her off his cock, slide down on the floor with her and fuck her until neither of them could see straight. But he couldn't. He held on, not wanting to come in her mouth just yet. Keith gritted his teeth, tasted her on his lips, in his mouth, smelled the heady musk that surrounded them.

He threaded his fingers through her silky hair, tried not to force her to take him deeper. Until his lust took over, stole his desire to protect her, left him in a white-hot fire of mindless need to come, to take the release that called every pore in his body. "I'm coming. Can't help it. Let go."

But she didn't. Instead she held on to him, took him deeper as she squeezed his balls. His climax built. His cock convulsed against her throat. The first hot bursts filled her mouth, escaped her lips. Slick ejaculate tickled his balls as she kept caressing them. He barely heard his own scream of completion as he fell backward onto the sofa.

"Thank you."

She looked up at him, her hair disheveled, her mouth and chin translucent with the remnants of his climax. Her pretty blue eyes shone brightly. Wanting to hold her, he drew her up his body, settled her against his chest. He loved the way her soft hair tickled him, the slight weight of her body warming his. Their hearts beat in synch, strong and slow.

Then she looked up at him, tears in her eyes. "Thank you. For everything. For listening, but most of all for showing me sex can be good. Very good."

Keith had seen more beautiful women. He'd fucked women who'd been more skilled. But he'd never made love with a woman before who made him feel invincible. At that moment Tina was his world. "It will get better, I promise, just as soon as the weather lifts enough that I can make a trip to the drugstore. I've got the feeling this was just a little practice session for the real thing."

"You mean..."

"I mean I'm looking for a hell of a lot more than a one-night stand, and I hope you are, too." The way he hadn't with Liz, the way he hadn't with Jackie for a long time before she died, he felt content. Emotionally engaged. The feeling he had when he stretched out on the carpet and drew Tina into his arms felt almost like love.

* * * * *

When Keith woke the next morning in front of the fireplace he reached for Tina, but she was gone. He vaguely recalled her having stirred in his arms earlier, saying something about needing to go take care of Jack. When he blinked he saw Mrs. Gardner, her expression as icy as the winter scene outside.

He figured now was as good a time as any to have it out with her. "Good morning to you, too."

Even if he didn't suspect she'd been spying on him for his mother-in-law, Keith had never liked Mrs. Gardner all that well. The woman acted as though she could barely stand him, always had. Well, this morning he guessed she had reason for her evil-looking scowl.

Bare to the waist, sweatpants untied, one foot bare and the other in an athletic sock, he definitely looked disheveled. Though he didn't have a mirror, he could guess his chin was bristly and his hair looked like it had been combed through by human hands, not a brush. He couldn't help grinning when he followed the woman's gaze to the empty brandy snifters and a bunch of sofa pillows someone had tossed in front of the fireplace.

Mrs. Gardner eyed the pillows then looked back at him, disgust in her expression. "It seems like somebody had a good time in here last night."

That was pretty obvious, and even more obviously it was none of the snooty housekeeper's business. After all, it was his house. Keith shot her the fake smile that had sold millions of bottles of pricey cologne. "Actually, we did. Is there any reason you need to be cleaning up in here this early in the morning, or are you just getting information to pass along to Georgia?"

"Mrs. Bern? What do you mean?"

"I think you know. Either you're talking to her or she's scary psychic about what goes on here."

She seemed to miss his sarcasm. "I—I'm going to visit my daughter later today. I thought I told you I'd be gone a day or so."

"You probably did." Keith didn't care, he just wished the housekeeper would leave him alone so he could ruminate on what had almost happened last night. "Are the roads around here safe enough to drive on?"

"My daughter said they would be. She's going to use her husband's four-wheel-drive truck."

Keith didn't own a four-wheeler, but he figured he could probably make a half-mile round trip to the nearest drugstore in his Lexus or the new Escalade SUV. "I'm going out for a little while, so you won't have to clean around me."

"It's not a problem." The woman pursed her lips as though looking at him turned her stomach. "Don't forget, Mr. and Mrs. Bern will be here tomorrow to see the baby."

God, Keith hoped not. Surely they wouldn't be coming if the Memphis airport was shut down, and he imagined it was. He had no desire to listen to his in-laws cry about Jackie and coddle his son. "I won't forget. They may be snowbound, though."

After all, Jack was only a year old. He wouldn't know whether or not his grandparents came to see him on his birthday. Keith tied his sweatpants, grabbed the hoodie off the floor and pulled it over his head before escaping the room. He tried not to let the prospect of that birthday visit get him down as he showered, dressed and sought out Tina and Jack in the nursery.

* * * * *

"Morning, guys." He couldn't help seeing Tina differently. The grown-up tomboy seemed to have disappeared, replaced by a woman he was suddenly finding incredibly sexy even while she was wearing shapeless sweats and feeding Jack his breakfast. "That stuff taste good?"

"Da-da-da." The baby held out hands smeared with the peaches and cereal Tina was trying to get down his throat.

"Eat your food, Bruiser, don't wear it. If you don't you'll never grow up big and strong." Keith spared a look for Tina, who looked at him, questions clearly in her eyes. "You look like you've got this little piggy under control. I'm going to the drugstore." He paused, his cock already hardening as those doubts in her eyes were swallowed by desire before she ducked her head, busying herself with Jack's bib. "Do you need anything? Juice, formula, more of this stuff for Jack to smear all over everything?"

"We're fine. You be careful. It's awfully icy out there for you to be going out."

Keith met her gaze, warmed by the emotion he saw there. "There's one thing I don't plan on waiting to get. I'll take it easy and be back before you know I'm gone."

* * * * *

Had he meant that million-dollar smile for Jack or her, or maybe for both of them? Tina tried to concentrate on cleaning up after the baby's breakfast but her mind kept going back, not to the nightmare that had brought Keith charging into her room last night but to what had happened later. Her confession, him showing her he didn't find her tarnished from what that bastard had done to her, all resonated in her head. But not as much as the memory of how generously he'd held her through the storm outside as well as the one that had raged in her mind.

She didn't expect forever or even long-term. Keith was her employer. He was also one of the best-known and best-loved athletes in the country. Not only had his late wife been a gorgeous socialite, but he had women accosting him on the street and constantly trying to bribe their way past the gates to this luxurious community—not to mention the groupies who lined up outside the stadium after every game, hoping to get a piece of him.

Tina sighed as she wiped the last of the peaches off Jack's chin and picked him up. "You've got a wonderful daddy, do you know that?"

"Da-da-da." That was Jack's favorite word, his only word so far, except that Tina thought she'd heard him try to say her name the other day. Wishful thinking, she told herself.

She set him on the floor and watched him take three or four halting steps before toppling onto his diapered bottom.

"Tina?"

She looked up to see Mrs. Gardner standing in the doorway. "Good morning." It was unusual for the housekeeper to seek her out. As a matter of fact the woman normally seemed determined to avoid unnecessary contact with her or Jack.

"I'll be leaving now. I thought I should remind you the baby's grandparents will be arriving tomorrow for his birthday. I may not be able to get back before they get here, what with the weather."

"All right. Keith mentioned the other day that they were coming. Is there anything in particular I should do?" The woman usually didn't want any interference in the kitchen, or anywhere else in the house, for that matter.

"No. I've already made a birthday cake. Food's ready for lunch and dinner for the next two days. All you'll need to do is heat it. Mrs. Jackie's parents don't usually stay more than a few hours at a time, now that she's gone."

Jack's maternal grandparents hadn't visited Jack at all since Tina came to stay, but she'd definitely caught undercurrents that there was some sort of rift there. Since their daughter had died giving birth, she wondered if that was it, but she found it hard to believe they wouldn't want to spend time with the baby their daughter had been willing to give her life to have. It wasn't her business, of course. Nothing had changed in the last day to make it so, and she'd do well to keep that in mind. "I'll make sure Jack is spit-shined for Grandma and Grandpa," she said, trying to coax a smile from Mrs. Gardner.

She sniffed. "You might want to make sure his father is, as well. And that he doesn't have another one of his floozies messing up the game room again before they arrive."

Tina turned away. No need for Mrs. Gardner to see her cheeks that she was sure were turning beet-red. "Have a nice visit with your daughter."

"I will. Thank you." With that she turned and walked away. "There she is now. I hear her truck outside."

When Tina picked Jack up and took him downstairs to play, the phone rang. It was Jack's grandmother, who sounded irritated that Keith wasn't home but even more put out because the housekeeper had left. "We won't be flying down tomorrow because of the weather. I'm hoping Keith will postpone the baby's birthday celebration until the weekend. Surely the storm will have passed by then."

Tina didn't want to commit him or hand over his cell phone number in case Mrs. Bern didn't already have it. "I'll have Keith call you when he gets home. He shouldn't be gone long."

Unlike Keith's own mother, who called often and wanted to "talk" with baby Jack, Mrs. Bern didn't express much interest in her grandchild. She sounded annoyed about them having to delay their visit to celebrate his birthday. When the woman hung up, Tina sighed. Jackie's parents must have been what her mom used to call "occasion people" who set great store by milestones but not a lot by the actual people involved.

She couldn't help stopping in the foyer, looking at the portrait above the living room mantel. "That's your mommy, Jack. She'd be so proud of you."

"Yeah, she would." Keith came through the front door, bringing some swirling snow along with him. "Did Mrs. Gardner already leave?"

"Yes. About ten minutes ago. Right after she left, Jack's grandmother called. They won't be coming until the weekend because of the weather. I told her you'd call her back."

"Thanks, I will. I wouldn't have put it past them to have found some way to get here in spite of the weather. What say we all go in the kitchen and see what we can find to eat? One thing I can say for Mrs. Gardner, she's a damn good cook."

* * * * *

"Mrs. Gardner mentioned you had some woman in the house last night," Keith's former mother-in-law said without so much as greeting him when he called during Jack's afternoon nap. "I hope you're not exposing Jackie's little boy to your debauchery."

Keith clenched his fists, wondered how much severance pay would be in order because the housekeeper was history, no matter if she made the best beef stew he'd ever eaten. "Jack is just fine," he said tightly. "I called to tell you this weekend's not good for you to visit."

"Why not? I'm sure the airport will be open by then."

"I have other plans." Keith didn't know yet what those plans might be, but he had no intention of entertaining Georgia and Tim, not until he got his temper under control. "I'm sure that if you check later with Mrs. Gardner, she'll tell you what they are."

The conversation went from bad to worse, quickly. Georgia wasn't used to being questioned, especially from Keith. She tolerated him only because her daughter had wanted him, much like she'd taken in Jackie's chocolate lab after her death because Jackie had loved him. Keith had loved Rufus, too, not that Georgia had cared when she'd commandeered the big dog and dragged him back to Chicago.

After he hung up, Keith felt another albatross sliding off his shoulders. He'd had it. Jackie's parents didn't like him, and they'd regrettably never shown much interest in Jack except as the line to keep giving him shit about Jackie's death. Well, Jack didn't need that, and neither did he. They could never visit again and that would be fucking A-okay.

It was past time for him to look at everything clearly.

For a long time after getting off the phone, he sat in his room thinking about what he needed besides to ease the desire that had come to life last night. He wanted Tina, needed her. Jack needed her, too. Keith told himself he should go slowly, let the relationship they began last night grow and develop at its own pace.

But Keith didn't do slow. Although he'd made a mistake, thinking Jackie would always go along with what he wanted, he hadn't been too discontent with the decision to marry her — a decision he'd made practically the moment he first laid eyes on her. After all, they'd stayed together twelve years. They probably would have been together now if she hadn't died.

But Jackie was gone. Thinking back, he recalled as many good memories as bad ones. In many ways they'd hidden their deepest desires and aspirations from each other. Still, the bloom of first love, the star quarterback and the most beautiful debutante on campus, had stuck around in spite of them having harbored entirely different pictures of the life they'd share. Even near the end, Jackie had still wanted to show off her jock to her snooty friends — and he'd held on to a certain amount of pride that he'd corralled a beauty who knew exactly how to run his charity, how to help him mingle as easily with the team owner as with his teammates.

In time he figured the good memories would stick around while most of the bad ones would fade. He'd hold onto them, pass them along to Jack when he got older.

He wanted Tina now, not only as a bed partner but as the woman who'd hopefully share the rest of his life. Although they both had roots in the same small west Texas town, they hadn't really shared a past as neighbors might be expected to have done. Not that they were strangers. Far from it. In just a few months they'd become good friends, spending time together with Jack while trying to ignore the inexorable pull toward intimacy by skirting the difficult stuff, avoiding topics either of them might have found painful. Last night Tina had opened up to him. But in many ways, he was still a stranger to her.

Keith wanted to correct that. He wanted to dig deeper, learn all about Tina's hopes and dreams so he could make them come true. And he needed for her to really get to know him—not just the football star who had lost his wife, not as Jack's dad, but the man inside, complete with a lot of faults he tried to hide from most of the world.

He went downstairs, started a fire in the fireplace and nuked a pot of Mrs. Gardner's homemade cocoa, thinking as he tasted the incredibly smooth stuff that he'd miss it when she was gone. The woman was a damn good cook.

He took the pot to the game room and set it on the table. Then he went looking for Tina.

* * * * *

He found her in the nursery, her feet tucked underneath her on a platform rocker as she stared out at a sheet of ice that had formed along the outer edges of the lake.

For a minute he stood in the doorway, just looking at her, imagining things he might do to her. Like picking her up and hauling her across the hall to the bedroom where he'd slept since Jackie's death. He'd strip her slowly, touch every inch of the body that suddenly seemed sexier than any other woman's, even the buxom groupies who kept stepping into his path at every turn.

No, he wanted to watch her in here, hold her. Warmed by the picture she made here in the nursery, he stepped inside, scooped her up then sat in the chair with her on his lap. This felt good, holding her while they both watched Jack sleep. "How long will he sleep?" he asked, amazed at the total look of relaxation on his son's baby face.

"A couple of hours. Maybe more. He played pretty hard this morning."

Keith recalled the playing, Jack's delight at walking around downstairs, one plump hand clutching his leg while Tina held the other one. The kid had his old man's strength, for sure. And he was stubborn. Every time he toppled over he pulled himself back up, laughing as though he'd intended to lose it in the first place. "Pretty soon he's gonna get to be a handful." *The little bruiser's gonna need us both to keep him out of trouble.*

"You're right there. But he's a happy little guy. Who could fail to love him?" Tina turned, nuzzled his scratchy cheek. "Except for his blond curls, he looks just like you."

Keith turned, tasted Tina's tempting lips. "Good for him. His mom was beautiful all right, but I don't know if those delicate features of hers would look too good on a boy."

He liked the way Tina laughed, a soft, tinkling sound that tickled the spot on his neck where she'd buried her face. He hugged her, thinking he'd like staying here forever, enjoying the sense of them being a family — him, her and the baby.

But they needed to talk. Somewhere he wasn't bombarded by the emotions he needed to explain. Abruptly he stood, setting Tina on her feet and striding across the room.

She looked confused when he picked up the baby monitor and put it in his pocket. "Let's go down to the game room. I started a fire and nuked us a pot of hot cocoa."

"Is this about last night?" she asked as they went downstairs. "If it is, you don't need to worry. What happened, happened. There's no need for us to talk about it."

"Yes, there is. Unless you'd like to pretend last night never happened." He took a seat at the game table and motioned for her to join him. "I hope you don't feel that way."

"No. Of course I don't." When she looked across the table at him, he thought he saw love in her eyes. Hoped he wasn't seeing emotion that wasn't there.

"Then I think you need to know a bit more about what you'll be getting yourself into with me." He motioned toward the insulated pot in the middle of the table. "Would you mind pouring us some cocoa? It makes me cold, just looking at the weather outside." He figured his extreme reaction toward the unusual winter chill was a holdover from having been practically frozen during that playoff game a few weeks earlier. "I don't think my body's gotten completely thawed out since Pittsburgh. You and Jack were lucky, all cozied up in that heated suite."

She smiled. "That was nice of you, making sure we stayed warm."

Keith noticed her hand was steady when she handed him his cocoa. He was glad. He never wanted her to be nervous around him. When she poured a mug for herself and took a tentative sip, her expression was blissful. "I wish I knew how Mrs. Gardner makes this. It's delicious, and just right for such a gloomy day." As though she didn't know exactly what to say, she licked her lips and looked over at him, her expression expectant as though waiting for him to respond.

"I'll ask her before I send her on her way." At Tina's odd look, Keith explained that the housekeeper's days were numbered and why. "I think it's reasonable for me to expect that she not be a pipeline to my former in-laws about everything that goes on in this house."

"Oh. I'm not surprised, but still I'm sorry you're going to have to let her go. She shouldn't have been gossiping, and she certainly ought not to have spied on you." Tina paused then continued. "But maybe she felt justified. Your wife was the one who hired her. She probably feels a sense of loyalty to her, even though she's not here anymore."

Tina was too kind, although Keith found he loved her for it. "It doesn't matter. I value my privacy. Our privacy." What he wanted was to pull Tina onto his lap, warm her with his own body heat. But they needed to talk first. He needed to tell her where he was coming from, make sure she saw the pitfalls as well as the potential benefits of being Mrs. Keith Connors.

He took her hand, massaged her palm with his thumb. "I grew up in Hedgecock like you did, but I left fourteen years ago. Since then I've lived a lot differently from the way I was brought up. The only tie I have to Hedgecock now is the invitation I got from Bobby's mom to come back this spring for a reunion." He paused, considering how much Tina might have wanted to escape from her own painful memories there. "And my sister Diane. She still lives there, and I've been trying lately to rebuild some kind of relationship. Her son will be starting high school next fall. I'm not proud of myself, but I pretty much turned my back on my roots when I went to college and got married my sophomore year.

"You see, my mom remarried right after I finished high school and moved to Denver. She likes it there and has never wanted to go back to a town where she was never happy." If Tina never wanted to go back there after what her stepfather had done, he'd understand, and he could rebuild his burned bridges with Diane and his nephew Dylan via long-distance.

Tina cocked her head, studying him with those beautiful blue eyes. "I wondered. It was like you were there and then you were gone. Everybody in town talked after Diane's husband left her, about whether or when she'd pick up and go stay with you or your mom, but it never happened."

The local folks had probably thought he was a class A jerk when he never came to Diane's rescue after she finally came to her senses and threw her husband out. Come to think of it, Keith had spent a good many hours thinking that about himself, but he hadn't wanted to ruffle Jackie's feathers when the blow-up had happened so soon after they found out she had a bad heart. "Diane always loved that rickety old ranch where we grew up. She and Mom never got along—she was Dad's girl. She was never close with me, either. I guess the age difference was too much for us to have been pals. Besides, I took a real dislike to Frank Granger after they got married and he moved in. But I was wrong. I should have kept up with her and her son. Dylan's going to be in ninth grade next year."

Tina reached over, took his hand, a gesture of comfort, understanding. "I'm sure you've been busy with your own family and career."

"You don't have to make excuses for me. I've made plenty for myself, that one included. But I could have made time for my own kin." Another flaw to lay at Jackie's feet. She'd wanted the college football hero, figuring he'd grow up and become her father's lackey. But she'd made it clear almost from the beginning of their marriage that she hadn't wanted any part of Hedgecock, Texas, or his "countrified" relatives.

That was wrong, laying blame on his dead wife when most of it belonged to him. He could have made time to keep in contact with his sister and ignored Jackie's feelings about that, just as he'd managed to flout her distaste for him playing football. Who knew? She might have taken to his relatives, understood him better if he'd shown her where he'd come from. But he'd been afraid she'd laugh at his humble beginnings, comparing the rundown ranch where he'd grown up with her parents' Skokie mansion. Now he'd never know. He took Tina's hand, hoped she'd understand and cut him the slack he probably didn't deserve. "I'm ashamed of myself."

"You shouldn't be. From all I read online and in the papers, you do all sorts of good things for kids here in Memphis."

Keith couldn't help laughing. "I write checks to the foundation Jackie set up in my name. And I do a football camp every summer for underprivileged teenagers. I could have made it a point to send some of the goodness home but I didn't. Jackie wanted us to live year-round in this house, and she liked choosing the charities the foundation supported. I haven't even checked up on what's been going on there since she died." It was past time he looked into the charity that bore his name, maybe diverted some funds to help folks back in Hedgecock. Keith sighed.

When Tina met his gaze with tears glistening in her eyes, he realized how generous she was, worrying about how he felt. "She was so beautiful. You must miss her terribly."

"Not as much as I probably should." He traced his thumb along the smooth skin on the backside of her wrist. "I can't help wondering if you're thinking of her as an angel, a dutiful wife who gave her life to provide her selfish husband with a son."

"I could never think of you as selfish, Keith."

"I am in lots of ways. I want to continue playing ball as long as it's fun and profitable. I want Jack to grow up happy and healthy. I want to live life my way, with a partner who's everything Jackie wasn't."

Tina was confused. "What wasn't she?"

Keith leaned his elbows on the table, propped his head on his hands. "Jackie was the most self-centered woman I ever knew. She hated me playing pro ball and did everything she could to make me act civilized enough to move in what she called decent society." He paused, met her gaze. "That's not to say I didn't love her, because I did. At first I was dazzled by her looks, by the fact she seemed crazy about me—and probably a little bit by the fact she had a shiny black Porsche convertible that was the envy of the entire Northwestern football team. Our first years together when we were in college were damn good. Then, when I refused to go into business with her dad, she was furious. We fought about that for months until we finally agreed to disagree about my career.

"The only thing she wanted from me besides to run my foundation was a baby, and I was willing to cooperate. For several years we tried, but nothing happened. Finally a fertility specialist suggested in vitro fertilization, and she got pregnant only to lose the baby in her fifth month. That was five years ago, when we found out she had the serious heart condition that nearly killed her. The doctors told us that if she got pregnant again she'd be risking her life."

"Oh no. I'm so sorry."

"So am I. Even though I was against it, she insisted on trying again. Wouldn't even consider adoption. Almost two years ago she found a specialist who thought that with some new drug, she might be able to have her baby after all. She talked me into trying IVF one more time, against my better judgment."

"And…"

"She got pregnant with Jack. Everything went pretty well until about the seventh month. Jack was getting bigger and putting a lot of pressure on her heart, so the doctor put her to bed and came to check on her every day. She went almost to term, insisting she wasn't taking any unnecessary risks."

"What happened?"

Keith sighed. "I came home from working out a year ago today. She was gasping for breath and white as the sheet on the bed. She'd gone into labor, and I found out later she'd also been having a massive heart attack. An hour after they took Jack by C-section, she died."

Tina lifted her hand, brushed away a tear he hadn't realized was making its way down his cheek. "You must have been devastated."

"At that moment I hated her for insisting on killing herself and leaving me with a helpless baby I didn't know how I'd take care of and keep on earning a living playing football. I hated her for killing the feelings that we'd had for each other when we were college kids. And fuck it, I hated myself for not being as sorry as I should have been that she was dead."

"So you felt you let Jackie down?" Tina's heart was breaking for Keith, who stared down at his hands, seemed to expect her to reject him for what he apparently believed was an unforgivable sin.

"I know I did. Somehow I ought to have been able to persuade her all we needed was each other. Or that an adopted baby would be as much ours as one we'd created. I should have quit football and been the kind of husband she wanted. And I shouldn't have hated her for dying and leaving me with Jack."

"She died having the baby she wanted so much. That has to count for something."

He looked up, met her gaze with eyes that were as sad as any she'd ever seen. "I love my son more than I ever dreamed I would. I want him to have the best life any kid could have, but I also want a life for myself. I don't want to sleep alone every night. I don't want to have a woman only when the team has a big win and I let some groupie take care of my sexual needs in a haze of booze and euphoria." When he paused and met her gaze, she saw the shame there. "I did that last week, you know. I fucked a woman I hardly know and don't have any desire to get to know better."

"You d-did?" She tried to tell herself she didn't have the right to feel like something had speared her heart. That there were no promises between them. Plus, when she'd been staying with Bobby and he'd told her what it was like being a player, it made perfect sense. How difficult it would be for players, particularly stars like Keith, to resist all they were offered after a big win when the alcohol flowed hard and fast and willing women were neck deep. Keith was human. It still hurt to hear him say it, though she tried to hold in those feelings.

Apparently she wasn't entirely successful, because this time it was Keith who reached out and carefully closed his hand over hers, drawing her gaze up to his face. "I told you that because I wanted to tell you this, too. That night I played the MVP superstud and didn't much like myself for it. What happened between us last night seemed…a lot more right."

What did he mean? "It seemed right to me, too, but you don't need to feel obligated."

"I don't feel obligated," he said, a tone of exasperation in his voice as though it irritated him that he wasn't getting through to her. "I'm honored that you trusted me to comfort you, and that you knew I would never hurt you the way your stepfather did. And I want to keep you in my house, my bed and in Jack's and my lives. We're both crazy about you. He loves you, and that's a big part of why I'm asking you to marry me."

Marry him? Tina looked into his eyes, found his expression deadly serious. "I—I..." Was he actually asking her to marry him because Jack loved her?

He gave a nervous sounding laugh. "Is us getting married such a lousy idea that you're speechless?"

"N-no. I don't know..."

"I do. We'll be good together. You won't have to worry that I'll be unfaithful. I never was to Jackie. We'll build a good life for Jack. I'll play a few more years and then we'll live wherever we decide will be best to raise him. Maybe I'll coach high school or something once I quit playing. I can't imagine giving up football entirely, and I don't think I'd make a very good sports commentator."

Tina was speechless. Should she marry him? She didn't know. He'd promised her a good life, but he hadn't said a word about loving her. Was liking her and enjoying her company enough for either of them?

She wished she could believe Keith loved her, the way she'd always dreamed her man would. But before she could think of what she wanted to say, his jaw had tightened.

"One thing, though, you need to know upfront. If you want kids, it's going to take me time to get there. Maybe later, when the memories aren't so fresh, we could try for a pregnancy, but only the old-fashioned way."

"That's fair." Tina understood how Keith might feel Jackie didn't get pregnant naturally because her body knew she shouldn't, and how he could feel at fault because he'd agreed to the in vitro procedures. "I'd really like for Jack to have a brother or sister. Not right away, of course. Could we?

That is, could we get a baby the old-fashioned way, as you put it?"

Keith looked over at her. "I don't know. My sperm count's not the greatest but I'm not sterile. Chances are you don't have the sort of problem that kept Jackie from conceiving naturally."

"You don't need to explain. It's just...I'm an only child, and it got pretty lonely for me sometimes."

"I imagine it must have. I wasn't an only kid, but Diane was too much older than me for us to be very close. What do you say now? Will you marry me?"

Chapter Six

From Keith's expression, Tina gathered her hesitation had caught him off guard. "Come on. I'm not all that bad a match. I've got a good job, money, all the things most women want." He paused, grinned. "Hey, I may be ten years older than you, but I've still got all my hair." Getting up, he stood behind her chair, laid his hands on her shoulders. When she tilted her head back he stroked her throat, sent shivers down her spine. Her nerves hummed not from fear but from a desire so strong it almost squashed her doubts.

He must have sensed her weakening resolve, because when he spoke again, his voice rang of honey and persuasion, made her think of their hot bodies tangled, slick with sweat and a desperate need for completion. "The sex will be damn good between us. Want me to show you now?"

God yes. She wanted to feel his weight and strength. She wanted to feel him buried deep inside her, the way she hadn't last night. But she wasn't sure she wanted to marry him. "You don't have to marry me for us to have sex. It's not as if I was a virgin or anything like that. Even before..."

"Before you were raped? I wouldn't expect you'd have been. I wasn't, either, since a good while before I met Jackie. You forget I grew up in Hedgecock, too. Experimenting with sex was just about all there was to do other than go to high-school games and eat burgers at that place across the road from the school. My desire to marry you has everything to do with wanting a good mom for Jack and a friend to help me raise him, less to do with me wanting to have a handy bed partner." He glanced out the window at the frozen scene outside then turned back and met her gaze. "Not that I won't enjoy going to sleep every night with you in my arms. And waking up to the sight of your pretty face."

She loved the way Keith was looking at her now, as though she were every bit as attractive as the beauty captured in the painting above the marble mantel in that cold, formal living room. As though he really did have feelings for her, Tina. If he hadn't been watching her she'd have pinched herself.

He put one big hand on her cheek, turned her until she was looking into his greenish-blue eyes. She wanted to trust him completely, fall hopelessly in love with this man half the females in the country would kill to get this close to. But she was afraid that if she did, she'd get terribly hurt if he walked away. While she knew now that she'd leaned on Bobby much more than she'd loved him, it still had hurt when Bobby broke it off, telling her before leaving for college that he wanted her as his friend, not his lover. Who was she to even consider that she might be able to hold on to Keith Connors, even if they were married?

"Come on, now. You're gonna give me a complex. Don't you want to be my wife, be Jack's mom?"

"Yes. But..." How could she tell Keith she didn't trust him not to find somebody else better and dump her? "Nobody's going to think you've got any trophy wife in me. I'm just a country girl, not a very smart one at that. You're...you're a huge hero. You're the league's best quarterback."

He laughed. "Brett Favre and both of the Manning brothers might disagree there. Come to think of it, so would a few others. Drew Brees..."

"You know what I mean, Keith. You don't need to recite the name of every other quarterback in the NFL. Your face is splashed on billboards all over town, not to mention that you show up in ads on TV every few hours. You're famous. Damn it, Keith, you're every woman's dream. You can have anybody you want. Why on earth would you want me?"

"I want you because you make me happy. Comfortable, both on the field and off it. No matter what you may think, I'm not exactly every woman's fantasy, and even if I were it wouldn't matter. I won't be chasing skirts. Once I make my bed, I lie in it. I have a feeling you'll be a lot more pleasant to live with than Jackie sometimes was."

When he moved, his motion was swift. Smooth. Like the skilled athlete he was. Before she could protest he'd lifted her in his arms. "You want this. Quit fighting it."

Yes, she wanted him more than she craved her next breath. But she couldn't talk, not with his lips hovering above hers, coaxing...coercing her to toss caution to the winds and take everything he offered. When he kissed her and traced his tongue along the seam of her lips, she couldn't deny him. But when she opened to surrender her mouth, he pulled back. "This will feel so much better when we're sitting."

When he sat on the couch, he cuddled her on his lap and shot her a grin that melted her heart and banished her second thoughts. "I bet you'll even let me buy us a house where I can feel comfortable in more than just one room. And that you and Jack will come watch all my games."

"Of course I'll let you pick out a house for us. After all, you're the one who'll be earning the money to pay for it. You should be able to enjoy living in more than just one room." She paused, laid her head on his broad, muscular shoulder. "I've got a feeling I'll be more comfortable, too, in this house that you pick out."

Keith held her close, traced along her throat, over the curve of her breasts. "I think you will be, too, because I'll be thinking about us both when *we're* doing the dream home search. How about it? Will you be happy living with a football player, watching him play and tending his bruises on days when his linemen haven't done too good a job protecting his tender hide?"

"I love watching you play. How could I not? I can't remember a time I didn't look forward to watching football every fall. It's even more fun watching when I've got a special player I've got reason to look for. I'm sure Jack will love the games, too, as soon as he's a little older." Keith's nearness, the woodsy smell of his cologne and the comforting heat of his muscular body made his proposal seem more feasible. The mere thought of massaging his beautiful, sore muscles was making her wet with anticipation.

The only thing was, he hadn't said he loved her. She was fairly sure he didn't, not the way she wanted, needed, to be loved. Still, she believed he'd take good care of her, and that he'd be faithful physically, no matter how much he might want to stray.

Maybe friendship and sex would be enough after all. "Still…"

"Hush. I'm going to take you upstairs to my room and show you how good we can be together. Grab the monitor." He picked her up again and lifted her over his shoulder.

Tina knew this couldn't be good for the shoulder Keith had needed to baby most of last season. "I can walk. I bet your coach wouldn't like it if you hurt yourself carrying a grown woman around."

He laughed. "There you go, sounding like a wife already. I like it. If you insist, you can walk. But it wouldn't hurt me at all to carry you — you're light as a feather."

Too light. Last night he hadn't seen her naked. Now, as she watched him toss his parka off the bed and set a huge box of condoms on the nightstand, she figured that would be the next step. Undressing. She knew this wasn't the room where he'd slept with his wife, so Tina had no reason to feel any more uncomfortable than she would having sex with him anywhere else in the same house where he'd lived with Jackie. The same house where they'd lived together platonically for the past five months.

"You'll think I'm too thin," she said, recalling his "light as a feather" comment and Bobby's apparent concern when he'd first seen her again about the weight she'd lost. "It's awfully bright in here."

Keith paused, his belt hanging loose, jeans unzipped. "Baby, I won't think anything of the sort. I want you exactly the way you are. So maybe you're a little skinny. You felt damn good to me last night. Come on, now, don't get shy on me."

He obviously had no doubts about his own buff, muscular body, because he dropped his jeans and boxers in one efficient motion before shedding his sweatshirt. "Come on, I bet you've got a lot less scars than I do."

Even in the bright light, she couldn't discern any flaws anywhere on Keith's well-toned, gorgeous body, all six feet four inches of it. "Quit teasing me. You're perfect and you know it." Trembling as she did it, Tina peeled off the rest of her clothes, praying he wouldn't be turned off by her prominent ribs, by boobs that had to seem almost nonexistent compared with the silicone-enhanced assets of some of the groupies she'd seen .

Was it her imagination or had the room suddenly gotten cooler?

Keith's gaze on her body scorched her in spite of the breeze that had her pores puckering. His long, thick sex registered appreciation too, curving upward against those rigid, well-delineated abs. Its tip glistened with lubrication, as though it was eager to get inside her.

"You're wrong, honey. You're exactly what I want." He moved a step closer, cupped the breasts she'd always wished were larger. He bent and drew a nipple into his mouth then stood and looked at her, his expression serious. "And I won't have you thinking like a gaping groupie, not looking past the Photoshopped images on billboards and ads, and all the media hype that goes along with my job."

He paused, skimmed his hands over her torso then drew her face to his chest. "Believe me, I've got scars you can see and ones you can't. You'll be getting a guy who's close to passing his prime in his profession. A guy who had to have help from doctors to get his wife pregnant. Then there are a collection of interesting cleat marks and surgical scars you haven't looked at very closely yet. They're anything but pretty. To me you're the perfect one."

She couldn't believe him, but oh, how she wanted to. "If you really think that, then take me to bed now. Show me."

In one smooth motion he picked her up, placed her in the middle of the king-size bed and came down over her, a hot look in his eyes. "See how perfect I think you are?" He guided her hand to his hot, swollen sex. "I don't get hard-ons like this for every woman I see."

He was huge, hot and throbbing against her fingers. She wanted him inside her. He was using his free hand to skim over her body, as though he wanted to learn every inch of her, as if he found her desirable—as desirable as his beautiful dead wife, as sexy as the faceless groupie he said he'd celebrated with after the Super Bowl a week ago. His hot breath scalded her when he bent and found a sensitive spot above her prominent collarbone.

Her nipples tightened at the touch of his calloused palm. Her pussy clenched. Her heart beat faster when he laid one leg over her belly, and his erection branded her mound with its throbbing intensity. She wanted him to take her now. Claim her. But he only explored her with his hands while he claimed her mouth, holding her still beneath him so she couldn't spread her legs, invite him in.

Firm yet velvety soft, his lips caressed hers, coaxed them open. He sampled her mouth with his tongue. It felt wonderful but she wanted more. She wanted him to slide his long, thick cock inside her pussy, pound into her with reckless abandon.

Squirming beneath him, she tried to get closer. "Easy, little one, we've got an hour or so before Jack wakes up. Let's make the most of it."

"I need you inside me. Please." She wanted Keith now. Not just his mouth and hands. While she loved him touching her, caressing her all over with his big but ever-so-gentle fingers, she needed it all. She wanted him to brand her with his hard, muscular body, fill her aching sex with his throbbing heat. The foreplay, sweet as it was, could wait for later, after he satisfied this gnawing need in her belly. "Make love to me. Please."

"I am. God but you have the sweetest mouth, the softest skin." He kissed her again, long and deep, as he found her core with one hand and plunged two fingers inside her wet, swollen flesh. "Tell me you want my cock in your hot, wet pussy."

Sex talk that usually put her off now made her even hotter. "Oh yes. I want it. I want it badly. Now." When she spread her legs wide apart, he slid down, found her, pressed barely inside her outer lips then plunged in all the way.

"Is this the way you want my cock?"

"God, yesss." She loved the feel of him throbbing inside her, stretching her tender flesh. His heart beat solidly against her breasts. "Don't stop."

"I won't. Not ever. Your pussy's just right. A perfect fit. Hot and wet and so tight I want to come right now but I want to keep fucking you all night. Does this feel as good to you as it does to me?"

His breath felt warm and damp against her ear. "Oh yeah. I love it." *Love you more than I've ever loved anybody in my whole life.* His hot flesh throbbed inside her, stretching her almost painfully. Yet it felt incredible. Better than anything she remembered or could have imagined. Heat spread through her veins and her body tensed, as though a bubble inside her was about to burst. "Omigod."

"I'm not wearing a condom. Want me to pull out and put one on?" He slid halfway out then hesitated.

"You'd better." She didn't want him to leave her, even for the few seconds it would take him to sheathe himself. But she didn't want to take a chance, either. If they married, and if they decided to try for a pregnancy, that would be okay. "It wouldn't be okay for us to risk having a shotgun wedding."

"Okay. Only we're not waiting to get married long enough for us to know if a shotgun might be in order." Getting up, leaving Tina feeling empty for a moment, he moved off her and tore open a condom. "I'd forgotten how much I hate wearing these things," he muttered, settling back between her legs and sliding slowly back inside her warm, welcoming channel.

"You don't have to."

"Yeah, I do. Wrap your legs around my waist. We can pretend we're kids again, celebrating a win by fucking under the bleachers at the high-school football field."

Then Keith realized what he just said. "Oh hell, I didn't mean that..."

Tina locked her smooth, slender legs around his waist. "You didn't?" she asked, her tone making the question sound ridiculously innocent.

He couldn't hold back the laugh that bubbled from his belly, and that sort of negated the horror of what he'd just said. "No, baby. For a minute there, I forgot there's half a generation between us. Honest, I'm not really a dirty old man."

"No, you're not. Think about those bleachers if you want. Imagine us doing this there, now, only we're both seventeen. That's the nice thing about fantasies. They can be whatever you want them to be." Tina touched his cheek, shot him an impish grin.

"By the way, I love the way your cock feels inside me."

Damn but she knew how to get his mind away from the gaffe he'd made and back on fucking. "Did I remember to bring a blanket?" he asked, rubbing his hand between her smooth skin and the smoother surface of the fine Egyptian cotton sheet. "Or is your cute backside getting scratched by all the blades of cold, dead grass?"

"You're a considerate lover. You brought along a nice, soft blanket. Even a pillow. And you didn't forget the condoms. After all, you're the team's star quarterback. You know how to make a forward pass and do it right."

"Yeah, I do. So do you, baby." He dipped his head, drew a pink, pebbled nipple between his teeth and sucked it while sliding in and out of her wet, hot cunt. Her clit felt hard as a rock when his cock rubbed against it. Moving to her other breast, he bit the nipple lightly then flailed it with his tongue.

She bucked against him, took him in all the way to his balls. "Omigod! Don't stop. I'm—I'm coming. Feels so good. I've never come like this before."

He felt her contracting around him, the welcoming wet glove that made him forget he was wearing that condom. Her nails dug into his shoulders, hard, but he didn't care. His balls tightened. He wasn't gonna hold out much longer. Keith hadn't felt so hot in years. "Baby, I'm gonna love being married to you." His muscles tightened as he tried to hold back, but he couldn't. Not now, when she was milking his cock, digging her nails into his chest and screaming out her pleasure. "God, yesss, I'm coming."

When they quit shaking and he rolled her on top of him, Keith shot Tina a shamefaced grin. "Baby, I'm sorry this went so fast. Next time maybe my cock won't decide to pretend it's seventeen and almost-virgin. Honest, I've been able to hold out a lot longer."

"You did fine. All I need to do is look at your gorgeous body, and I'm ready to come."

He drew her down on him, took her sweet, sexy mouth. "We're getting married next week. Hey, isn't that Jack making noise like he wants some attention?"

"It sounds like he's awake and tossing around his toys. We'd better get up now and take care of him."

"Not until you say you'll marry me." He pulled her down hard, clasped both hands around her slender waist. "Say it. Please."

She looked down at him, silent for a long, scary minute. "All right. I'll marry you. But there's Jack, starting to cry. If you'll let me up we can go see what Jack wants."

So that was why she was hesitant, he thought as he rolled over and got up, extending his hand to her. He saw it in her eyes, and he didn't blame her. Most women wanted a declaration of love along with the proposal, and Tina deserved one. "You know I love you, baby. Maybe I just want to tell you the right way, the right time." Even though she wouldn't expect all the hoopla of diamond rings and engagement parties, he wanted more than anything to watch her eyes light up with surprised delight.

And he wanted to set his family, Jackie's parents, his teammates and the whole goddamn world straight. Tina was his woman, his life, his love, and nobody better dare say otherwise. "I'm gonna spend the rest of my life showing you how much you mean to me."

Chapter Seven

Tina's head was spinning. She could hardly believe all that had gone on in the two days since she'd agreed to marry Keith.

First thing when Mrs. Gardner returned, Keith gave her notice. She'd stay until they moved or until she found a new job, whichever might come first. Meanwhile Tina would look for a housekeeper or housekeeping service both she and Keith could trust fully.

He put his house on the market, furnished, because he said he wanted them to have everything brand-new. They sat in the game room with the realtor while Keith described the sort of place he wanted for them. "Something big enough that we can entertain our friends. But I don't want anyplace that's so grand it will intimidate anybody, including me."

He went on to insist on tight security, which she approved of heartily. While she had no doubt Keith could and would protect her and Jack, she didn't want groupies climbing down the chimney, or would-be kidnappers maybe getting close enough to grab Jack.

The next morning Keith left for a while. Movers arrived and took down Jackie's portrait. They were carrying it out when he came back in and looked wistfully at the blank, slightly darker spot on the pale cream colored wall where the painting had hung. "I've got more pictures of Jackie. I'll save some for Jack to have when he's older. But it was past time for that one to go."

Tina agreed. It would be hard enough for her to keep from worrying about gorgeous groupies who were very much alive and lusting after Keith. She refused to be jealous of a ghost, and not having that portrait around would make it much easier to keep that little green monster inside her from rearing its head.

"Come with me. Jack's napping, and Mrs. Gardner will watch him for a little while. We've got a few errands to take care of."

* * * * *

They made a quick visit to his lawyer. Afterward they stopped at the training center where they spoke with Coach Lyle and Keith picked up the ring he'd asked the coach to collect this morning from Memphis' best-known jeweler. He wanted to have everything ready for the surprise he had in mind for later.

Oh no. When they pulled into the driveway back home he saw a black limo parked at the front door, he knew. Mrs. Gardner apparently had done her last spy job for Georgia and Ted because he was pretty sure they were here and all hell was about to break loose.

"You're the woman I intend to spend the rest of my life with. Keep that in mind," he said, squeezing Tina's hand as they walked inside through the garage door. "I'm afraid we're in for some unpleasantness."

She tightened her arm around his waist when they moved through the kitchen toward the front of the house. "It'll be okay. I love you."

The empty spot where Jackie's portrait had been stared at him as he stepped inside the living room. He tried to maintain his composure, but it wasn't easy when Jackie's parents were standing stiffly, staring him down with as much malice in their expressions as a pair of linebackers eager to overrun his protection and smash him into the ground. "Georgia, Ted, this is Tina Black. My fiancée. You should have let us know you were coming today."

Silence reverberated against all four walls of the huge room. Georgia's sky-blue eyes, so much like her daughter's, welled up with tears. Grief? The woman obviously was still feeling the pain of losing Jackie, but beyond that Keith sensed her fury behind a barely there screen of civility. Ted just looked miserable, as though he didn't like the awkward scene but couldn't figure how to escape it.

Keith couldn't stand the silence any longer. "Since you're here, would you like a drink? Some coffee? We might as well sit down. There's no need for us to stand here staring at each other."

"How could you?" Georgia took a step toward Keith. "It's only been a year since you killed my little girl and here you are, selling her house and planning to marry her baby's nanny."

When he felt Tina start to tremble, he tightened his arm around her waist, a silent message that everything would be okay. Then he met Georgia's icy gaze. "I love Tina. So does Jack. I won't have you saying anything against her. If it makes you feel better, blame me for not dying along with Jackie."

Ted shot a miserable look toward Keith and Tina. "I'm sorry, Keith. I know you didn't cause Jackie to die. But Georgia…she misses her so much. And it's so soon…too soon for you to forget her."

"I'll never forget Jackie. We had twelve years together, and I see her every day in our little boy." Keith paused, looked down at Tina, hated that he could still feel her trembling in his loose embrace. He'd have given anything to have managed for her to avoid this scene. He looked back at Ted. "But life has to go on. Jack needs a mom, not a nanny. And I need Tina."

Georgia stepped a little closer, as though she intended to slam a bejeweled hand into him or Tina. "Stop right there, Georgia, before you do something you'll regret." Keith ground the words out, hoping he sounded as menacing as he felt.

She stopped but shot him a disgusted look. "You—you animal. What you need is a woman to warm your bed. You always did. Jackie said so. It's a pity nobody ever told you that you don't have to marry every woman you dip your—"

"Georgia, that's enough." Ted put his hands on his wife's shoulders, drew an evil look from her. "Your hate's got to go or it will kill you, and I don't want that. Our daughter picked a good man in Keith. And he didn't kill her. She did that to herself because she wanted a baby the doctors said she mustn't have. If her dying was anybody's fault, it was ours, because we spoiled her rotten all her life. Come on, let's go home."

Keith looked at Jackie's father with new respect. He'd never have believed the mild-mannered gentleman would stand up to Georgia—but he had. "If you'd like to see Jack while you're here, we'll go upstairs and see if he's up from his nap."

"Next time," Ted said. "I think what Georgia needs now is to think about some things she's said." When he stepped up and held out his hand, Tina extended hers when Keith hesitated. "Be happy, both of you, and take good care of Jack. When you think he's old enough, let us know and we'll send him one of Rufus' pups when it's weaned. If Tina doesn't mind, that is."

"Tina doesn't mind at all," she said, smiling at Ted and then at Keith. "I think a pup would be wonderful for all of us."

Keith hadn't asked her, but somehow he'd known any woman who took to a baby the way she'd fallen for Jack would love animals, too. "This one will grow up to weigh about sixty pounds," he warned her after they'd walked Georgia and Ted to their limousine.

"What kind is he?"

"A chocolate lab. At least I guess he'll be chocolate, although he could be black, I suppose. Rufus is brown, with light golden brown eyes. Jackie got him the first year we were married."

"They took him?" Tina sounded surprised.

"Georgia insisted he'd be too rambunctious, that he might hurt Jack. I miss him. It will be nice to have one of his pups—after we get back from our honeymoon."

"Mmmm. I can hardly wait."

An idea crossed Keith's mind, one he hoped would take the last of the sting from this unexpected encounter. "Come on back to the car. Jack will be okay with Mrs. Gardner for another hour or two. I have a surprise, and I know the perfect spot to give it to you."

* * * * *

A few minutes later Keith was opening the passenger door of the Escalade, helping her inside before moving around to the Lexus and retrieving some remote controls. "Why aren't we going in your other car? It's already warmed up." She turned to him after he slid behind the wheel and started the powerful vehicle that, so far as she knew, he'd never used since the local Cadillac dealer had brought it to the house.

"You'll see." He reached over, took her hand and placed it on his thigh. "We're going someplace that belongs to us. Just us. And the SUV has more room inside."

Had the realtor found them a house already? Tina didn't think so. In the first place, he'd turned out of the gated community where they lived, in the direction of downtown rather than toward the area where the realtor thought they might find the home they wanted.

Then she saw the stadium and realized Keith was bringing her here, to the place where they'd spent their first hours together away from home, where she'd watched him throw passes for the first time at a home game in early December. Tears came to her eyes.

He pressed a remote control device, and a gate opened. The big SUV barely made it through a narrower gate that led onto the narrow ring of concrete around the playing field.

"Come out here with me," he said, shutting off the car and grabbing a blanket off the backseat before stepping outside.

She followed him, wondering what he had in mind. It was about thirty degrees outside, not exactly ideal weather for outdoor lovemaking, but...

Keith had shown her in the past few days that he could keep her warm anyplace, anytime. She stepped out of the cozy vehicle and walked over to the blanket he'd just spread on the cold artificial turf. She stared at the blanket for a minute then grinned up at him. "You know, honey, the back of that SUV is plenty big for what you have in mind."

He laughed. "How do you know that? Maybe what I want is just to hold you, tell you how happy you've made me." He sat and drew her down beside him. "Maybe I want to do things right this time."

Shivering a little, Tina cuddled up next to Keith, used his big body to shelter her from the cold wind. "What things?"

"Will you marry me, let me spend the rest of my life trying to make you happy?"

She'd already said she would, so she shot him a questioning look. "I said I would. In every way I could think of." She'd told him with every kiss, each embrace, and there had been so many in such a short time.

He pulled out a small box from one of the pockets in his black parka and flipped open the lid. "Then I want you to wear this. It's got a matching band I'll give you next week." Fumbling to take off his gloves, he lifted a huge, sparkling diamond solitaire from the box. "Baby, you need to take off a glove so I can put this on your finger."

Her hands shook so, she could barely peel her glove off her left hand, but he steadied them as she trusted he'd steady her when she started to doubt herself—and him. Then he took all her doubts away.

This was Keith Connors, all-pro Maulers quarterback, seller of razors and TV sets, incomparable groupie magnet—

and the only man Tina wanted. His expression serious, he met her gaze. As she watched him, he let those gorgeous eyes fill with something she realized had already been there for some time. Only she hadn't had the confidence to give that something a name until now, as he gave voice to it.

"I wanted to make sure to do this right, so I haven't said much about being in love with you before. But I'm telling you now. I love you, really deep down love you, as much as I love playing football, as much as I've ever loved another person in all my life." Very gently he pushed the ring onto her finger then brought it to his lips.

While tears filled her eyes and her heart ached, he continued with a smile. "If we were kids I'd let you wear my letter jacket to cover up with while we made love back behind the high-school bleachers. Since we're both grownups and I just won that rolling bed over there, I think I'll see if the back of it's big enough for a guy as tall as me to make it with his lady." He grinned then lowered his voice. "No one's in the stadium but us, just in case you care."

She didn't. Keith loved her and she wouldn't mind shouting it to the whole world. "I'm glad you love me. Because I love you, too. I want you now, and I wouldn't care if all seventy thousand or so seats in this place were full." Tina had never been happier. Never felt more cared for, protected. Or desired. Keith lifted her, retrieved the blanket and set her down inside the warm car.

Echoes of cheering crowds rang in her ears, though the stadium was quiet. As Keith bent over her, taking her mouth as he splayed one big hand over her belly beneath the zipper of her jeans, Tina explored the rugged planes of his face. The face that smiled at millions but looked at only her with love. Already a hint of stubble scraped sensuously against her fingers when she caressed his cheeks, the sinewy column of his throat.

She felt her hero unzip her jeans and slide them down her legs, heard him unzip his own. The sound of silk tearing when he tore away her panties, a burst of cool air on her naked flesh made her whimper against his insistent mouth. The heat of his long, thick cock seared her channel when he flexed his hips and joined their bodies. The slick abrasion of flesh on flesh made her clench her inner muscles, welcome him inside.

Nothing wild. He took her missionary style, as though they were new lovers, kids experimenting under the bleachers for the first time. Though he lay over her, the heat of his big body pressing her, controlling her, this wasn't a raw kid but a full-grown man, a skilled lover coaxing her climax with patience, with love. She lifted her hips, answered his silent demand for all she had to give.

His jeans abraded the tender skin of her thighs with each hard plunge into her core. She loved it. Loved him, more than she'd ever thought she loved her childhood friend. When he sank deep inside her and shouted out his pleasure, she knew. This was the man she'd been born to love.

"Hold me. Don't stop loving me."

"I'll never stop loving you, as long as there's a breath in me."

Epilogue
Hedgecock, Texas, the following Saturday
ಬ

Melanie Tate looked over the small crowd then turned to her husband Cal. She'd done a great job putting together Tina and Keith's wedding in such a short time, even if she said so herself. Of course Keith's mom had been helping since she and her husband got in town two days ago.

Mel looked on with satisfaction as the newest newlyweds stood in the living room at the Tate house, holding hands and chatting with her son Bobby and his wife. Cal's twin sons were home from college for the occasion, laughing and playing pranks and, if she didn't miss her guess, plotting a *ménage a trois* with the pretty brunette they'd brought home with them for the wedding.

Good thing Cal's grandpa had built a house big enough to put up half the Texas cavalry, because every room was full with laughing, happy football players and their significant others. Mel had commandeered the hotel and even put up some overflow guests with Keith's sister in her own small house and at Tina's empty place.

One face thankfully wasn't anywhere to be seen. Something or someone apparently had made that bastard, Edgar Garcia, take off last weekend for parts unknown. "Cal, did you have something to do with Tina's stepfather leaving town?"

"Not me. I wouldn't put it past Keith to have issued a warning, though. I've never seen a man more protective of his woman." He bent, dropped a quick kiss on Melanie's lips. "Unless it would be me, taking care of you."

Dave Delaney, who'd just arrived in town a few days ago, watched the festivities from a distance, a hard look on his darkly handsome face. If it weren't for the obvious way the man adored that silly, shaggy-looking poodle he said was his daughter's, Mel would have thought he had it in for everybody on Earth. Hopefully coming home, getting away from the playboy life Keith mentioned had pretty much destroyed his NFL career, would be good for him.

She figured it was pretty much time he retired anyway. Dave was pushing forty-two, a year older than Mel herself. From the research she'd done while planning for the upcoming quarterback reunion, she knew his talent had been as mercurial as his taste for the playboy lifestyle. "Let's go over and say hello to Dave," she told Cal. "He looks like he feels out of place."

Seeing Keith and Tina so happy together warmed Mel's heart. Not that she didn't feel the same about Bobby and his effervescent bride, but they were so young. So untouched by the tragedies that had tempered Tina's youthful exuberance, left Keith to put his life together after his first wife's untimely death.

When Tina had left last October, Mel hadn't thought she'd ever come back to Hedgecock. She was glad for them all that she'd been wrong. For years Diane Granger had insisted she didn't miss her mother or Keith after they left, but today a weight seemed to have lifted from her shoulders.

"I'm glad they decided to come home to get married," Mel said as she greeted Keith's sister on the way toward the corner Dave had staked out for himself.

"So am I. Who'd have thought my baby brother and my best friend's daughter would have found each other, in Memphis of all places." Diane's eyes were bright, her smile sincere. "I'm glad Mom and Zach came for the wedding. You know, I never realized how much I missed her, or Keith..."

"Sometimes we don't realize how much people mean to us until it's almost too late." Mel glanced at Keith's mom, saw she was heading for Diane with Keith's son in tow. "We'll talk later. Right now I need to go cheer up Dave Delaney. He looks a little bit lost among all the happy faces."

* * * * *

Keith could hardly wait to get Tina to himself. His mom had Jack for two whole weeks, and tickets to Honolulu were practically burning a hole in the pocket of his suit jacket. They'd get to their suite at a five-star hotel on Waikiki, crawl into bed and stay there until exhaustion and hunger took over and sent them out in search of sustenance. When he'd mentioned Hawaii, Tina's eyes had sparkled with excitement. He wanted to see sights through her eyes, feel her enthusiasm. Her love.

He'd been right about having their wedding here, though. Tina needed to feel the love of everyone who'd been part of her life since she was born. What the hell. He'd needed that, too, to mend fences and renew old acquaintances. Today he felt that love he'd turned his back on for so long.

He took Tina in his arms, kissed her soft, sweet lips. Life was good. Better than he deserved, but he wouldn't dwell on that.

Coach Williams, fifteen years older and even more grizzled than Keith remembered, tapped him on the shoulder. "I've been awful proud of you since you went away to college. Still am. You know, I'm retiring. I'm hoping to leave it to Dave over there to carry on the Hedgecock tradition."

Keith followed the old man's gaze to the Hedgecock star he'd followed, felt bad in a way for Dave Delaney. Dave had always been a bad-boy player, but he'd been hot in the clutch last season, so hot he'd taken a battered and bruised Savannah team all the way to the Super Bowl. And almost won. If it hadn't been for that last hail-Mary touchdown, it would have been Dave, not him, hoisting the Lombardi trophy.

"I heard he might be moving back here. You know, the guy used to be my idol." Like Bobby had tagged along behind Keith, Keith had pestered Dave. He guessed Dave must have idolized Colin Zanardi, the first of the Hedgecock quarterbacks.

"I know. I'm happy for you and your bride, even though I used to think it would be Bobby taking her down the aisle someday. He sure found himself a pretty one." Coach Williams' watery gaze shifted to Marly, who was holding Bobby's hand and captivating Carl and Eddie, guys who'd protected Keith's blind side back in the day. "You know, Keith, she's a hot one, all right, but I think you may have gotten the best of that deal."

He pulled Tina close. "I know I did. We're going to go now, enjoy being newlyweds."

"Don't blame you, son. Just don't forget us anymore. We all like seeing you once in a while other than on TV."

Keith motioned for his mom to join them then gave his old coach a quick bear hug. "We'll be coming back here next month. I'm hoping you'll help me set up a football camp for high-school players."

"Sure thing."

* * * * *

They'd gone home, where neither of them had intended to go. And it was good. They'd go back again for the reunion. And more.

Later. Now, in a suite overlooking the beach at Waikiki, Keith and Tina sealed the promises they'd made. With love.

The End

Also by Ann Jacobs

eBooks:

A Gift of Gold
A Mutual Favor
Another Love
Awakenings
Bittersweet Homecoming
Coach Me
Colors of Love
Colors of Magic
Commitment
Dallas Heat
Dark Side of the Moon
Entrapped
Eternal Surrender
Eternal Triangle
Eternal Victory
Eternally His
Eye of the Storm
Firestorm
Forever Enslaved
Forward Pass
Gates of Hell
Gettin' It On
Haunted

He Calls Her Jasmine
Her Very Special Robot
Hitched
Hot for the Reunion
Hot in the Clutch
Illusions
In His Own Defense
Lassoed
Learining Control
Love Slave
Loving Control
Mastered
Naked Bootleg
Out of Bounds
Roped
Switching Control
Tip of the Iceberg
Topaz Dream
Unexpected Control
Vampire Justice
Wrong Place, Wrong Time?
Zayed's Gift

Print Books:
A Mutual Favor
A Shining Future
Another Love
Bound by Love
Controlled by Love
Dallas Heat
Enchained
Eternally His
Firestorm
Forbidden Fantasies
Full Circle
Haunted
Heart of the West
Lords of Pleasure
Out of Bounds
Sandstorms
The Defenders
The Prosecutors

About the Author

෨

Ann Jacobs is a sucker for lusty Alpha heroes and happy endings, which makes Ellora's Cave an ideal publisher for her work. Romantica®, to her, is the perfect combination of sex, sensuality, deep emotional involvement and lifelong commitment—the elusive fantasy women often dream about but seldom achieve.

First published in 1996, Jacobs has sold over forty books and novellas, some of which have earned awards including the Passionate Plume (best novella, 2006), the Desert Rose (best hot and spicy romance, 2004) and More Than Magic (best erotic romance, 2004). She has been a double finalist in separate categories of the EPPIES and From the Heart RWA Chapter's contest. Three of her books have been translated and sold in several European countries.

A CPA and former hospital financial manager, Jacobs now writes full-time, with the help of Mr. Blue, the family cat who sometimes likes to perch on the back of her desk chair and lend his sage advice. He sometimes even contributes a few random letters when he decides he wants to try out the keyboard. She loves to hear from readers, and to put faces with names at signings and conventions.

Ann Jacobs welcomes comments from readers. You can find her website and email address on her author bio page at www.ellorascave.com.

Tell Us What You Think

We appreciate hearing reader opinions about our books. You can email us at Comments@EllorasCave.com.

Why an electronic book?

We live in the Information Age — an exciting time in the history of human civilization, in which technology rules supreme and continues to progress in leaps and bounds every minute of every day. For a multitude of reasons, more and more avid literary fans are opting to purchase e-books instead of paper books. The question from those not yet initiated into the world of electronic reading is simply: *Why?*

1. *Price.* An electronic title at Ellora's Cave Publishing and Cerridwen Press runs anywhere from 40% to 75% less than the cover price of the exact same title in paperback format. Why? Basic mathematics and cost. It is less expensive to publish an e-book (no paper and printing, no warehousing and shipping) than it is to publish a paperback, so the savings are passed along to the consumer.
2. *Space.* Running out of room in your house for your books? That is one worry you will never have with electronic books. For a low one-time cost, you can purchase a handheld device specifically designed for e-reading. Many e-readers have large, convenient screens for viewing. Better yet, hundreds of titles can be stored within your new library — on a single microchip. There are a variety of e-readers from different manufacturers. You can also read e-books on your PC or laptop computer. (Please note that Ellora's Cave does not endorse any specific brands.

You can check our websites at www.ellorascave.com or www.cerridwenpress.com for information we make available to new consumers.)
3. *Mobility.* Because your new e-library consists of only a microchip within a small, easily transportable e-reader, your entire cache of books can be taken with you wherever you go.
4. *Personal Viewing Preferences.* Are the words you are currently reading too small? Too large? Too… ANNOYING? Paperback books cannot be modified according to personal preferences, but e-books can.
5. *Instant Gratification.* Is it the middle of the night and all the bookstores near you are closed? Are you tired of waiting days, sometimes weeks, for bookstores to ship the novels you bought? Ellora's Cave Publishing sells instantaneous downloads twenty-four hours a day, seven days a week, every day of the year. Our webstore is never closed. Our e-book delivery system is 100% automated, meaning your order is filled as soon as you pay for it.

Those are a few of the top reasons why electronic books are replacing paperbacks for many avid readers.

As always, Ellora's Cave and Cerridwen Press welcome your questions and comments. We invite you to email us at Comments@ellorascave.com or write to us directly at Ellora's Cave Publishing Inc., 1056 Home Avenue, Akron, OH 44310-3502.

COMING TO A BOOKSTORE NEAR YOU!

ELLORA'S CAVE

Bestselling Authors Tour

UPDATES AVAILABLE AT
WWW.ELLORASCAVE.COM

Discover for yourself why readers can't get enough of the multiple award-winning publisher Ellora's Cave.

Whether you prefer e-books or paperbacks, be sure to visit EC on the web at www.ellorascave.com

for an erotic reading experience that will leave you breathless.

Made in the USA
Lexington, KY
29 November 2010